An Ink So Dark

Martin Davey

This is a work of fiction. Names, characters, places and incidents are either the product of the author's imagination or are used fictitiously. Any resemblance to actual persons, living or dead, events, or locales is entirely coincidental.

Copyright © 2023 by Martin Davey

All rights reserved.

No part of this book may be reproduced in any form or by any electronic or mechanical means, including information storage and retrieval systems, without written permission from the author, except for the use of brief quotations in a book review.

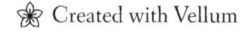

❦ Created with Vellum

For my Natalie

Contents

Prologue	1
Chapter 1 *The Truth and the Needle*	9
Chapter 2 *A Distant Rumble*	18
Chapter 3 *A Knife in the Night*	20
Chapter 4 *Gibbet and Hench*	23
Chapter 5 *Century*	28
Chapter 6 *The Transfer of the Tattoo*	33
Chapter 7 *The Forlorn Hope*	41
Chapter 8 *The Knife Dies*	50
Chapter 9 *Black Maria*	57
Chapter 10 *Mary Blood Red Maroon*	72
Chapter 11 *The Fear of the Fae*	82
Chapter 12 *Nora Knows*	97
Chapter 13 *The Dog and Bone*	102
Chapter 14 *Festie-Bestie*	105
Chapter 15 *A Place of Beginnings*	107
Chapter 16 *Legionnaire*	128

Chapter 17 *Gone to the Dogs*	138
Chapter 18 *Blood and Skulls*	147
Chapter 19 *The Pen That Was a Mountain*	154
Chapter 20 *A Change in Course*	164
Chapter 21 *A Dark Dream*	173
Chapter 22 *To Arms*	183
Chapter 23 *Rough Repton*	186
Chapter 24 *What the Dark Brings*	200
Chapter 25 *Shooting Fish*	210
Chapter 26 *It Fades*	215
Chapter 27 *Angel in the Middle*	220
Chapter 28 *Bulls-Eye and the Bottles*	226
Chapter 29 *Overdosed*	230
Chapter 30 *Dark Days*	232
Chapter 31 *Blood Red Rust*	234
Chapter 32 *Rough*	241
Chapter 33 *Escalation*	246
Chapter 34 *Lace*	251
Chapter 35 *The Saint From the Sea*	257

Chapter 36 *Hanging*	263
Chapter 37 *The Drop and then the Stop*	279
Chapter 38 *The Long Walk*	283
Chapter 39 *The Fast Maria*	285
Chapter 40 *The Drawing Out*	287
Chapter 41 *The Courtesy of Crows*	295
Chapter 42 *Threads*	301
Chapter 43 *She Wanders*	303
Chapter 44 *The Bridge*	306
Afterword	309
Also by Martin Davey	311
About the Author	313

Prologue

Jarlath's Monastery. Connacht. Eire. AD 510.

The flame that danced atop the candle could best be described as being a bit on the *thin side*, nevertheless, it was doing its job and allowing the boy carrying the candle to navigate the dark corridors of the monastery without tripping over, or falling down any of the steep stone stairs and breaking his neck. The youth was slightly taller than average, had very dark brown eyes, almost black when caught in a certain light, and a pale complexion. His darling mother, who had not warmed to the child at first, now doted on the boy and had remarked to any that had not already heard the story a hundred times that year, that her son had never suffered a moment's illness, that all the usual ailments present in childhood had passed him by – and for some strange reason, of which she was justly proud – the boy never felt the cold. Or at least he never complained of it, or of an empty stomach – which all other young boys seemed to suffer from all of the time.

The boy's name was *Odhran*, meaning dark-haired, and he was walking down a narrow hallway with one hand cupped protectively around the thin flame, shielding it from the legions of draughts that whistled through the gaps between the bricks and under the doors, intent on the annihilation of any naked flame. As he padded along in his threadbare slippers and flimsy cassock, he smiled, then chuckled to himself, because something had occurred to him: the little flame was like everything else inside this monastery. The food the monks ate was … *thin*. The menu each day was much the same – soups with less flavour than the average contents of a puddle of rainwater and bread that could have been passed under a closed door. The fires in the hearths were almost transparent (one could get more warmth from cradling a recently used privy pot) and the flagstones underfoot were colder than the layer of ice found on the horse troughs at first light.

The monastery was a place of prayer and self-reflection and was as damp as a trout's pocket, and Odhran could not wait to get back to the wild pathways, the clean air and the open skies, with his master. They had set out from the west coast of the country and were making their way inland, visiting as many places of worship as they could. His master referred to their jaunt as a long walk with a pilgrimage thrown in for good measure, and he had enjoyed every step of it. Odhran was on his way to wake his master, and tell him that the horses had been fed, a bowl of something hot – *and thin* – was waiting for him in the refectory, that his master's belongings were packed, and his favourite travelling cloak was aired and ready.

As he drew near to the door of his master's cell, he was

half expecting to find him asleep. He spent long hours in prayer and in discussion with his close friend the Abbot, and was often to be found snoring loudly or emitting sudden snuffles that would startle him awake, at least for a second or two. This morning, however, was different.

Odhran heard raised voices from inside his master's room and he stopped abruptly. He should have coughed to announce his arrival, or knocked, but Odhran was fond of listening at keyholes. He loved to hear and to spread gossip, saw no harm in lying if required, and always made a note of what he had seen or heard in his *book* so that he might use the knowledge at some point in the future if he needed to get his own way – to secure a promise from someone, or their silence if he had been caught doing something wrong. The book also contained some of his 'other' thoughts, snippets of phrases and sketches of shapes that came to life as he drew them on the page.

He knew deep down the images he created were not entirely decent. They always felt wrong at first but somehow, after a while, they became strangely right. At first, he had been petrified that someone would see them and he would get into trouble, but then a thought occurred to him. If the words were written in a secret code then whatever he thought would be disguised and kept safe. So he devised a secret language to hide their meaning from prying eyes. How he had learnt this new language was a mystery but he cared not. He loved his secret words and the comfort they gave him.

Odhran took a deep breath, then crept up to the door and pressed his ear against it. The first voice he did not recognise. It wasn't the Abbot. It could have been the Abbot's second in command, the Prior perhaps? The second voice, however, belonged to his master, and their conversation chilled him to the bone.

"The child has to die! You know this to be true, my friend. It is quite clear that he is Fae, or something even worse. He is without doubt a mirror child. He stands in the light of day but all he reflects is darkness. Many have sensed it and recoiled. It is the real reason you have come on this supposed pilgrimage, to seek out friends and allies in other holy places that have an understanding of the twilight world, is it not? Does the boy know what he is? And the words he scribbles in that infernal book of his ... you know as well as I do what they mean."

"Yes, my friend," his master replied. "I persuaded his mother to let me take him on this journey, citing that he was by far the best and the brightest that I had met and that he should broaden his horizons and drink in the culture and the history of this island. She was happy and not a little proud to allow him to leave. He is the greenest apple of her eye and it took some flexing of the truth to convince her that his talents should be shared. The boy has been observed and studied and it is clear to everyone that I have spoken to that he is indeed what we have feared for so long. I cannot like the child or come to feel any warmth for him, but he is still only a child. Is there nothing we can do for him?"

Odhran's master sounded genuinely sad but the other voice in the room had no such misgivings.

"He must die! There is no other way! How he came to know the dark verses is beyond me. To my knowledge the Lost Songs are all accounted for and hidden away, yet he writes them down as if he has known them all his life! How can that be? Some knowledge has been gifted to him, but by whom? And when? And where?"

Odhran's master sighed and said, "I discovered the boy

so it must be me that ends his life. I shall not shy away from my task. The boy will die by my hand, and I shall leave the body by a standing stone if I can, so his true people can perform whatever ceremony they choose if they find him. It's the least I can do."

Odhran stepped away from the door quickly, stung by the words he had heard and the tone of his dear master's voice. He needed to act, and quickly, so he blew gently on the candle before stepping away into the arms and comfort of darkness. His first instinct was to cry out and plead with his master to save him, but something inside the boy, a voice that had been developing over time, had a better idea.

"Why not kill the old man instead?" it said.

"Why not push him into the bog and then hold him under the brown water? You are younger than he is, you could outrun him, and just think what fun it will be to draw his bloated white corpse on a fresh page in our book."

The voice was familiar to him. It comforted him, and he whispered his reply.

"I'll steal his soul and keep it inside my book so that I can look at it and scratch away at it when I feel low. Yes, I'll draw him dead, surrounded by my symbols, and then I can keep him alive and torture him."

When the door to his master's chamber opened moments later and the boy's name was called out to come and collect his master's belongings, there was no answer. He was called for again and again, and when he could not be summoned, the monks searched the monastery for him. Even the stables and the hen coops were investigated, but the boy was gone.

It was nearly mid-morning when one of the field hands returned to the monastery to arrange transport of the recently harvested turnips and cabbages and heard the monks wittering about the dark child. Had the boy stepped through a doorway into the underworld and disappeared? Or had he swapped clothes with a big black crow and flown away into the morning mist? All of this speculation was laid to rest by the farmhand who had seen the boy stalking away that very morning, wrapped in his cloak with a pack on his back and a box under one arm. Once this story had been told to the Prior and then communicated to the Abbot, the search was called off and the monks returned to their tasks. The boy would not be missed or mourned. In fact, the mood amongst the remaining monks and novices lifted when news of his disappearance was made known.

Odhran's master did not participate in the search. Instead, he turned the boy's cell upside down looking for the book, and when he could not find it, he retired to the refectory where he sat down with the Abbot and they spoke in hushed tones until the cooks started to slap the monks' wooden bowls down in preparation for the next meal.

"Where do you think he will go?" asked the Abbot.

"If I had seen the direction he was heading in when he left this morning, then maybe I could suggest a destination, but he could be going anywhere."

The Abbot looked uncomfortable, and when one of the kitchen boys tried to edge a stone jar full of cold water between them, he shouted at the boy and sent him scampering back to the kitchen. He rubbed his thumb against the index finger on his other hand, a sure sign that he was perplexed.

"Why do you think he fled?" asked the Abbot.

"I have asked myself that question many times since he disappeared. My only conclusion is that he must have been coming to wake me and heard the conversation between myself and the Prior."

"What do you think he will do?"

The Abbot was getting worried now.

"If we just stand back and let him go, he might come to harm in the wilds. He might find others that feel as he does, and if he is one of the mirror children, he'll have power over them and we could have more than one problem to deal with. And there is something else. The evil that created the boy could come looking for him or have some form of a plan for him."

The Abbot reached out for the stone jug at his elbow and poured himself some water. His mouth had suddenly become very dry.

"But it will all come to nought because I will find him first and deal with him. If it takes me a day, a month or a year, I will prevail, have no fear of that, my dear Abbot."

And with that, Odhran's master stood up, said goodbye to his old friend, mounted his horse and rode out into the waking world under a sky so blue that the birds did not fly for fear they might spoil its brilliance. A light dusting of snow had fallen during the night and turned the fields to silver. It was a beautiful sight, and would normally have brought him great joy, but he had a heavy heart because he knew what must be done.

As his horse trotted down the path and away from the abbey, he started to entertain some very dark thoughts indeed.

What if the lad was hiding on the road up ahead, behind some vast oak tree or hidden in the reeds by the water's edge, just waiting to step out and destroy any who followed him?

The thoughts chilled him, but the boy must be stopped before he came into his powers. It did not matter how long it took to find him or where he went. Odhran could travel to the far ends of the earth, it mattered not. The man patted his horse's neck and clamped his heels into its flanks. The horse responded. If it had known how many shoes it would wear down over the course of that year, it might have thrown its rider and bolted instead.

Chapter One

The Truth and the Needle

Herne Hill, June 2022
Cross the Tracks Festival

Maureen – or Mo – or Major Mo – or even Dictator Mo, as she was known by the rest of the festival organisers – flicked the pages on her clipboard backwards and forwards. She was perturbed, nonplussed and a little bit put out because there was a large fly in her ointment. Something was here that shouldn't be. She ran the tip of her index finger down each page of the list but could not find a booking for a rickety old wooden caravan on her 'master form'. Mo always knew who was coming, and when and what they were going to be supplying but she looked left and right, scratching at her dreads.

Plot 16 was reserved for The Harlem Trotters Pork BBQ and was right where it should be, and in Plot 17 was the Death Chilli Deli, again, right where it should be; but there was no record of a wooden caravan. Plot 18 had not been taken by anyone, not as far as she was aware, and she was just about to march up to the rear of the caravan, bang on its door and ask the owner to move on when she checked again to find that Plot 18 had in fact been taken by *The Black of Beyond – Magical Tattoos*.

Mo could have sworn that it had not been there five minutes ago, but if its name was on the list, then the caravan was getting in. She closed her folder and snapped the elastic band around it, just to keep everything in its place. Then she went in search of a drink and some good music. This was the last time she would volunteer to help organise Cross the Tracks.

"Well, until next year," she chuckled to herself.

She walked away, and night fell.

Charlie Watson was the 'plus one' for his mate Nathan. He hadn't really wanted to go to a festival. The images of enlightened and spiritually liberated numpties surfing through mud and whatever it was that the chemical toilets leaked out had never really piqued his interest but Nathan, his best mate from school had begged him and promised him any number of banker benefits to do the right thing and man up. Charlie, who could have easily played the Covid card, decided to help a friend out and agreed to join. He had played the *wingman* before and hated himself for doing so afterwards. This weekend had been different. Nathan's girlfriend's friend was called Emily. She was remarkable in every way. She had that Emilia Clarke thing going on. She was blonde, feisty, clever, sensitive, and far more intelligent than he was, about everything. She'd sussed him straight away. He'd been trying to work out how to put up the tent and she'd just grabbed the fabric, given it a shake and then staked the fully formed shelter to the ground with plastic pegs before he'd had a chance to show his hunter-gatherer skills.

"Now that's out of the way why don't we find a drink and you can tell me how you got roped into coming to the festival as well," she said.

"I wanted to come," said Charlie.

"Really? Who's headlining tonight and who's on the main stage tomorrow?" said Emily with a look on her face that suggested she already knew the answer to that question or any other.

"The Charlatans are on the main stage tonight, and tomorrow it's The Killers."

Emily laughed and said, "that was last year. At the Virgin Festival. In Peterborough."

Charlie was embarrassed at his stupidity. He liked this girl. He couldn't put his finger on why, but he just did, there was something natural about her. He didn't need to big himself up or create a false narrative. She would see right through it anyway.

"Okay, smart arse, who is headlining tonight then?" he said.

"I haven't got a clue," Emily replied, giggling.

"You're a bit of a berk, you know that?" said Charlie.

"It's just like looking in a mirror, isn't it," she smirked.

And after that short exchange, Charlie and Emily became soul mates, lovers and partners in crime – all in the space of an afternoon. They listened to music, queued for hot dogs that were more dog than hot, made love under the trees, and then as a mark of their true and undying love for each other, decided on a temporary tattoo.

. . .

The gypsy caravan was wearing its Sunday best. Garlands of wildflowers had been wound around the wooden spokes of its wheels and lanterns of all shapes and colours swung gently from the roof, as if pushed by invisible hands. The caravan's engine was giving the grass under the tree a trim and Emily, who had once upon a time harboured desires to become a jockey, wandered up to the nag and patted it on the neck.

"She won't pay you any attention when she has a mind to feed," said a voice from within the caravan.

"Now, if you had an apple or a handful of wild oats, then she might look up for a second or two if you were lucky."

The owner of the voice appeared in the doorway at the rear of the wagon and Emily stepped away from the horse. She couldn't work out from the tone of the man's voice whether or not she had taken a liberty with it so she erred on the side of caution. Charlie pointed at the sign hanging from one of the branches of the nearby tree.

"Are you open?" he asked.

"Always," said the man.

He pushed the bottom of the caravan door open with his foot and beckoned them inside with a theatrical wave of his hand. Charlie stepped up first and Emily followed.

"Tardis!" they both said simultaneously.

"You are not the first to call my humble home that. It is the skill of the carpenter to make it appear so roomy, but there is no science to it. A little magic, perhaps?" The man's voice was pleasant, there was an Irish lilt to it. He wore old-fashioned clothes, a homespun shirt and hard-wearing corduroy trousers that were buckled at the knee. His boots could have doubled for a pirate captain's in a Christmas panto, and he had tied a burgundy cotton neckerchief around his neck. His face was brown. Hours of sitting outside had given it a rustic tan, and his hands appeared strong and steady. A good sign for a tattooist or someone who handles the reins each day.

The walls of the caravan were decorated with the designs of the tattoos that he offered. All of them were incredibly intricate, and the needlework was incredible. Emily thought she saw one of the designs flicker but when she looked more closely, she realised it was just a trick of the light. At the far end of the caravan there was a wooden stool, a comfy-looking bunk strewn with pillows and racks of different coloured inks, arranged in straight lines along the walls. When the light caught the small glass jars it created a rainbow effect, albeit a rainbow that was straight. There was also a small desk with a neat row of brushes, and pens with golden nibs.

"Please take a seat and tell me what you want. You can have anything on the walls and if you cannot see what you desire there, you only have to tell me, and I shall draft you a sketch in no time at all," said the tattooist.

"How long do they last?" Emily asked.

"Only a short time, a couple of days at best, and then it will be as it is now, gone forever." The man sat down on his stool and took up a piece of paper and one of his pens.

"I'll go first," said Emily. She already knew what she wanted.

"Can I have a symbol that means 'truth', please, here on my forearm?" She pointed to the inside of her left arm.

"Truth? Why of course, young lady. Sit yourself down, and tell me ... what colour would you like?"

Emily sat down on the bunk and looked up at the rows of bottles and jars. Each of them wore a beautiful hand-drawn label in copperplate script. One of them was called

Mary Blood Red, another was *Sad Prussian Peter*. *Brave Brown the Bard*, read another.

"They have interesting names," she said.

"All things have names, colours too. It gives them power, and if you know them, you can understand them better," said the man.

"Oh," said Emily. It was the best reaction she could come up with on the spot.

"Now then, shall we begin?" he said, taking her arm in his strong hands.

"Why not?"

Emily sat back on the bunk and watched as the man drew on her skin in a deep green colour that she didn't remember choosing, but didn't mind either. He was very good. The quality of his penmanship was remarkable and his linework was beautiful. He hummed as he worked and never looked up. Before she knew it he was wiping her arm with a smooth, scented cloth.

"All done! What do you think?" he asked.

Emily loved her new ink, and the colour, only temporary of course, was so vivid that it looked like a real tattoo.

"It's amazing!" she exclaimed and sprung up from the bunk to show Charlie.

In the natural sunlight it was even better and Emily squealed with delight.

"Your turn now," she said to Charlie.

He chose the image of two crossed daggers, observed in the nautical style, with a moon and stars above.

"A fine choice for a strong young man," said the tattooist.

Later, after they had shown all their friends and bored them to death with how skilled with his pen the tattooist was and how quaint his little caravan, like something out of

An Ink So Dark

a fairy-tale, they laid out on the grass beside their tent, held hands and looked up at the night sky. This was the last night of the festival. Tomorrow was Sunday, and the day after that was a work day. Neither had been in their current jobs for long enough to consider taking a sickie, so they made love under canvas and fell asleep, both feeling happier than they had done in a very long time.

They woke to the sounds of stirring and movement outside their tent. Zips flew up and down and lighters flickered below cigarettes. A dog barked, and someone nearby farted, making Emily giggle. Lots of the other festivalgoers were on the move already, trying to avoid the inevitable crush at the gates and the exhausting squeeze of the Tube.

Charlie and Emily waited until it was relatively quiet and then stuck their heads out of the tent, not quite ready yet to leave its warmth. The delicious aroma of fresh coffee and bacon sandwiches wafted across the park towards them. If someone hadn't flushed the nearby Portaloo and sent a mushroom cloud of gas their way, it would have been the perfect start to the day.

Later that morning, after a mighty hot dog and a banger sanger, they packed their tents away, collected the empty cans and packets of used wipes and said their farewells to each other. Emily kissed Charlie hard on the mouth and they promised to call each other later, for a chat.

The caravan was locked up, the lanterns were gone, and the sign that hung from the branch of the tree was no more – but the horse was still munching on the grass nearby. Inside the caravan, the man was awake and busy. He was sitting on his bunk, fully dressed. He was taking the small tissue squares he had used to wipe the arms, legs and backs of his customers from a small drawer under the rack of ink bottles and smoothing them flat.

He had quite a collection but there were only two that he could use properly, so he discarded the rest, putting them all into a bowl on his wash stand and setting light to them with the flame from an oil lamp. Then he took two empty bottles from the drawer and carefully attached a label to each one, and after he was satisfied that they looked suitably neat and tidy, he inserted one tissue square into each bottle.

"I shall name this one 'Emerald Truth', and this one, 'Black as Night'," he said softly.

Then he started to hum. It was a mournful tune and the oil lamp flickered and nearly went out as if it were retreating from the sound. The tune wandered on and on and after a spell, the Irishman picked up the bottle marked Emerald Truth and began to gently tap on the glass with the golden tip of one of his pencils. A faint glow appeared inside it and soon the bottle was full of light, and the symbol that the man had drawn on Emily's skin formed. At first it looked beautiful and intricate, but soon it began to twist and turn in on itself. It stretched and tore and started to disintegrate. Bits of the design wilted and decayed until there was nothing left of it. The light flared then disappeared. All that was left was an inch of green liquid at the bottom.

The man looked very happy with himself and placed the bottle in his rack. Then he picked up the remaining bottle and began to hum once again.

The following morning, Charlie awoke to the dulcet tones of Nick Ferrari on LBC, and Emily to the bang and crash of Absolute Radio. Both went about their morning rituals, feeling energised and ready to face the week ahead. But something wasn't quite right and neither could put a finger on what it was.

Each of them was pretty sure they had enjoyed a fantastic weekend. The music had been off the scale and the people had been friendly, but neither Emily nor Charlie could remember who they had met or what they had done after pitching their respective tents. It was all a bit of a blur. Emily could not have picked Charlie out in a police line-up and Charlie, who was a serial gossip when it came to his lovemaking prowess had nothing to say for a change. The only thing that they remembered about the festival was having an amazing temporary tattoo.

Mo, whose job it was to help clean up after the hordes had dispersed and make sure that the vendors and food wagons hadn't left any of their equipment in the park, weaved from one plot to the next, making notes about the conditions of each. There would be no space or place for them next year if they had blotted their copybook. When she got to the plot where the old rickety caravan had been, there was no sign that it had ever been used. It was immaculate. She couldn't even find a single cigarette butt or a squashed tin foil container in the grass. If anything, the plot looked lovely, green and fresh. And when Mo looked for the festival booking for the temporary tattoo artist known as The Black of Beyond, there was just an empty panel where his details should have been.

Chapter Two

A Distant Rumble

Judas was sitting in his favourite armchair nursing a large vodka tonic and thinking about the night that Angel Dave had died. He could still see his friend clearly, cradling that horrific bomb in his arms and using those powerful wings to take the infernal device as far away as possible from the hundreds of innocent Under Folk who had been trapped inside the White Tower. It was the night that the giants Gogmagog and Corenius had been due to fight. Judas remembered the look on his face. Angel Dave had been excited and determined, and it hurt Judas to think that he would never see that face again.

Judas had not seen him die, but had been told by shocked onlookers that Angel Dave had exploded in the night sky. But there was no new star to remember him by. Judas felt angry and impotent and had not wanted to return to the Yard and to the Underworld, but knew what would happen if he didn't. God would send one of his servants to escort him back to the Black Museum and persuade him to fulfil his obligation and continue to fight the good fight.

He had only been back home for a few hours and the

tasks of unpacking his suitcase, performing some household chores and freshening the stale air in the apartment had occupied him to the point that he had not noticed the feather. It was on the bookshelf opposite. It was about a metre long, white with grey tips, and when he picked it up, weighed as much as a large kettlebell. Judas had seen feathers like this before. The Archangel Michael had come to pay a call it would seem, and Judas didn't need to think too hard about what he wanted to talk about. The death of an angel was uncommon, and the circumstances in which it had happened would need some explaining and Michael, the Lord's muscle and weapon of choice, was not a particularly good listener.

"Well, big boy, you're going to have to wait until I'm ready," said Judas.

There wasn't a cloud in the sky but suddenly, Judas heard thunder. It rumbled across the city and when it found him it made the windows of his apartment rattle.

"Okay, I hear you! And just so you know, breaking and entering is a crime down here, I could have you nicked!" said Judas.

Nothing happened for a moment but then there was a second boom, and Judas decided it was probably best not to threaten the Archangel Michael again, so he closed the plantation shutters on his window and went back to his vodka and tonic, which was mostly ice and the slice now, and needed reinforcing.

Chapter Three

A Knife in the Night

Gassiot Road in Tooting SW17 was quiet and perfectly still. The glow from the streetlights was moth-free and the foxes had already completed their nocturnal sweep of the neighbourhood so there was no yapping, screeching or the tumbling of bins.

Suddenly, there was movement and a shape appeared at the end of the road where the chip shop was situated. It advanced down the pavement for a hundred metres and then transformed into the silhouette of a young man. He stopped midway down the road, then hopped over the nearest hedge and into the paved garden of Number 26. He approached the front door and bent down as if to look through the letterbox. He was not delivering anything tonight though, at least not anything good. Instead, he whispered something into the keyhole and the door opened, softly. The man stepped inside and closed it behind him.

He climbed the stairs quietly. The carpet was new and the pile was deep, so his footsteps were reduced to soft huffs. The silence made him feel powerful and confident.

He could move around the house with ease, just like a ghost, observing yet unseen. The man entered the first bedroom.

There were two mounds of equal size under the duvet. He heard a snuffle and froze, but the moment passed, and he drew the knife from the inside pocket of his jacket. It was a recent purchase from a survivalist website, long and dark with a saw on one edge and a cruel blade on the other. He didn't know he'd bought it until it arrived in the post and he'd been a bit uneasy about having it but something told him *it was a nice knife, nothing to worry about, just put it at the bottom of your wardrobe, and then forget about it.*

Now, here he was, with the knife, and the man and his wife, whom he'd never met. He walked over to the far side of the bed and drove the sharp point into the sleeping woman. He heard a soft groan. The man next to her woke up so he stabbed him too. There was a little bit of noise and a lot of blood. He stood there looking down at them both for a while. The house creaked and from downstairs, he heard the tick and tock of an angry clock, but no alarm was sounding, so he left the two bloody mounds on the bed and visited the other three bedrooms, killing anyone he found there too.

Afterwards, he washed his hands, called the police on his mobile phone, told them what he had done and where he was, and then settled down to wait for them in the front garden. When the squad car from the local station arrived, accompanied by an ambulance from nearby St George's Hospital, they found a young man standing in the garden. He had removed his clothes and folded them into a neat and tidy pile. The knife was back in its sheath and placed on the floor at his feet. A pool of dark blood had formed around it. The murderer did not speak or answer the police officer's questions. He just stood there, mute and unblinking, like a white statue in the half-light.

The senior officer ordered his men to cordon the area off and make sure that any neighbours who had been awakened by the sirens did not spill out onto the street or start filming the crime scene with their phones. Then he donned a pair of white gloves and made a sweep of the house, returning quickly, ashen faced, to confirm that the family were all dead from multiple stab wounds, and that the ambulance could be released. They dressed the young man in a white paper forensics suit and cuffed him. A search of his clothing revealed that he wasn't carrying any identification. He didn't have a wallet and his mobile device was what is commonly known in the trade as a 'burner', so they could not identify him using that.

The only thing the officers noticed before he was clothed in white was what looked like a freshly inked tattoo on his back. Two crossed daggers, with a moon and stars above them, styled in the nautical fashion. The officers took a couple of snapshots of the design before escorting him to the waiting police car. They were driving towards Wandsworth when the young man spoke for the first time.

"Where am I?" he asked.

The policeman in the passenger seat called his superior officer and reported what the young man had said.

"Now what?" asked the driver.

"We're taking him to Scotland Yard instead, mate. Take the next right."

Chapter Four

Gibbet and Hench

The grave had not been tended. Thick brambles and stinging nettles covered it, and discarded cans and the ripped and yellowing pages from read-and-throw newspapers were its only decoration. Foxes and badgers navigating the burial ground via their secret pathways avoided this plot because they could sense that there was something not quite right about it. The earth was sick and the ground was cold all year round.

Henry Haverstroke, a man of business and a right bastard to boot, had been buried here in the year of our Lord 1745. At the time of his death, he was a wealthy man. His house was vast, and his business concerns in the city and in the Americas and beyond turned him a pretty penny. He was a ruthless operator though, happy to be hated by all that had the discomfort to come into contact with him, and quick to pounce and then profit from a fellow businessman's shortcomings. It was possible that his essence had seeped into the soil beneath him over the years, and that his decay may have been the poison that killed the ground. Whatever it was, Gibbet and Hench liked what they smelt.

They had marked it for liberation on one of their nocturnal fact-finding missions. Grave robbers by profession and ghouls by design, they liked cold graves because they liked to work without distraction. Well-kept graves were always being visited and laid with fresh flowers. There was no chance of getting a body out of the ground undetected. No. They liked a quiet, cold, off-the-beaten-track grave, and if it felt a bit nasty, all the better. Nevertheless, they were having a tough old time lifting this corpse out of its grave and getting it onto their barrow.

Gibbet had the head end of the body, which as every grave robber will tell you is the heavy end, while Hench was lollygagging again and pretending to puff and pant as he grappled with the feet.

"Any more of that wheezing and huffing is going to wake the rest of those sleeping hereabouts! Be quick now, or the moonlight will swap to daylight and we'll be forced to camp out here," said Gibbet.

"I am trying, but these feet are cumbersome and ill-weighted! No sooner does I have one in the crook of my arm than t'other spills out and lands on my poor foot, which it has done at least twice now," Hench remarked with a squeal.

"Oh, Hench, you are becoming a bit of a bore. Now swing him up and let's get him on the wheelbarrow, and we can be off. We don't want anyone getting involved in our affairs now, do we?"

The grave robbers dragged Henry Haverstroke – or what was left of him – away from his old home and across the path, towards the place where they had hidden their body conveyancing device. Once free of the brambles and the gnarled old roots they made good time and both breathed a sigh of relief when they removed the branches they'd used to camouflage it. But someone was sitting there, and they were very much alive.

"Evening gents," said Sergeant Lace.

Gibbet dropped Henry's head, which hit the turf with a muffled thud. Hench, who wasn't that quick on the draw at the best of times, let go of the feet he was carrying and they landed on his toes.

"Owwwwwww!" he squealed.

"It's Gibber and Hunch, isn't it?" said Lace.

Gibbet frowned.

"You know exactly who we are, so play nice. What can we do for the Black Museum and its fair lady?" he asked, with a little sneer thrown in for good measure.

"You can cut that out for a start, Gibbet. You two have been warned about this on more than one occasion. The last time we had cause to chat you promised me that you'd leave this cemetery alone. It isn't safe, and you know why."

Hench was hopping on one foot. He had removed his boot and the ripe fragrance in the air was already causing Lace to take a step back.

"What does she mean, Gibbet?" asked Hench.

"I told your good friend that the Black Museum has business here. Something has been crossing over into the mundane world and distressing the normal folk. It's already killed one of them, and that's one too many. Now, please put your sock back on, Hench, my eyes are bleeding." Lace motioned towards his boot on the ground.

Hench hopped over to it and slipped it back on again.

"Thank you," said Lace.

"My pleasure," said the little ghoul.

Sergeant Lace pulled the remaining branches away from the wheelbarrow and turned it towards them.

"Come on you two, let's get that body back where it belongs," she said.

Gibbet stuck his bottom lip out like a chastened child.

"We only just got that one up, we've got a buyer and everything! Please, Sergeant Lace, give a grave robber a break, we're destitute!" Gibbet grumbled.

"And we're really poor right now," Hench added.

Gibbet and Hench had been together since birth but Hench still had the power to stun Gibbet with his stupidity. If they hadn't been standing in the middle of a cemetery in the dead of night with a decaying body and the Black Museum's second in command, it would have been funny, but as things stood right now, they were in trouble. They needed a way out and Gibbet was thinking really hard about pretending that he had just seen a shape in the darkness behind them and alerting Sergeant Lace to the fact when they were reprieved – unexpectedly.

"Look, I need to track this beast, or whatever it is, down. But I can't be here all night every night. So, how about I forget that I have seen you with Mr Smelly-and-nearly-falling-apart here, and you put in a couple of shifts for me?" said Sergeant Lace in her official tone.

"And we get to keep the body?" Gibbet asked, hopefully.

"You're pushing it now, Gibbet," said Lace.

"We normally pull it, Sergeant, it's much easier that way," said Hench.

"The sergeant doesn't mean pushing or pulling the wheelbarrow, Hench, you duffer!" said Gibbet.

"You want me to let you off and let you keep your spoils, am I hearing that right? asked Lace.

"Call it an advance payment if you will," said Gibbet.

"As I said, gentlemen, you are pushing it, but it seems

fair to me. Take the body and get moving but I want you here tomorrow night, same place, same time. I will be here so if you don't show up, you know who will be coming to find you and he doesn't like Under Folk who break their promises. Okay?" said Lace as she was zipping up her jacket and putting her ASP back inside her pocket.

"We shall be here as requested, my lady, have no fear," said Gibbet.

"Make sure you are. Now, if you see anything you let me know straightaway. You don't get involved and you don't interfere. Those are the rules and if you cross the line you go inside the Museum, right?" Lace's tone was serious, and the ghouls nodded.

"Right then, get this contraption and that festering lump out of here before I change my mind!"

"Yes, Sergeant Lace, directly," said Gibbet.

"And we shall do it right away too," said Hench.

Chapter Five

Century

She remembered looking up into the eyes of Eros and feeling the shoulders of tourists and theatregoers jostling for position to capture his statue in Piccadilly in all its glory. Love and arrows and digital cameras and camera phones, and the waft of steam from the illegal fast food trolleys, she could picture all of that too. What she did not remember was ever having a membership at Century, the private club and restaurant halfway up Shaftesbury Avenue. The receptionist, a flighty, silly girl from Watford, recalled hearing the intercom buzzing and looking into the security camera and seeing a person she knew to be a member, and unlocking the door, remotely. The footage from the security camera later showed that the young woman who was admitted was not a member at all, just a random stranger with a new tattoo on her arm.

Emily walked up to the bar and surveyed the clientele. It was your random bunch of London luvvies, all dressed up with nowhere to go, or waiting for their friend from South London to land with their 'Barley'. Good looking, well dressed, and financially mobile, that was what they all were, and proud of it by the smarmy looks they were giving each other. The barman, an affable, approachable black man with dreads, bleached blond, made a fuss of her and rustled up a G&T that looked like half an iceberg mixed with the rare orchid collection at Kew. It was a ridiculous beverage and weighed a tonne. She paid with a swipe and retired to a table on the far side of the bar overlooking the lawn in front of the nearby church on Wardour Street. Then she turned her attention to the other people in the bar.

The first person that she was drawn to was a very pretty lady wearing half of Dover Street Market's latest, and this season's must-haves. Her trainers alone would have cost more than Emily's entire wardrobe, and possibly the wardrobe itself. She was gazing into the eyes of her partner, another very well-dressed lady, more Selfridges than Dover Street. She was doing most of the talking, well, talking might not be the best way to describe what was happening. She was talking *at* the other lady; there was no exchange of thoughts and ideas happening, she was broadcasting and not receiving.

Emily sipped her drink and her interest was piqued by a young man who had just returned from the men's room. He had forgotten to wipe a small white smudge away from underneath his nose. As he drew closer to the table he was sharing with his mates, one of them quickly pointed this out to him. It was farcical to watch. The young man pretended to run his fingers through his hair, and then to quickly adjust his spectacles until the wasted cocaine was removed. The sudden movement drew the rest of the bar's attention to the group and he had to sit down very swiftly. There was an embarrassed silence, but soon the effect of the marching powder kicked in and the social faux-pas was forgotten.

Emily signalled to the barman and received another

avalanche in a glass, with a twist of lime. He was very attentive but soon realised that Emily was not impressed with his newly whitened teeth and bulging gym-bod. She sat back instead and returned to her game. On the table nearby was a couple, middle-aged perhaps, possibly from out of town, very much in love. They were holding hands and beaming at one another. The very picture of satisfaction and contentment. But Emily knew different and she decided that the rest of the room deserved to know what they really thought of each other, and what they did when the curtains were drawn and the lights were off.

"It's David, and Michelle isn't it?" said Emily.

She had placed her G&T on the table and walked over to the soon-to-be very unhappy couple.

"Yes, yes it is," said Michelle.

"I thought so. Do your neighbours know about the fetish parties in your garage?"

David sat up straight and a little nervous smile appeared on his face. Michelle gripped his hand tightly.

"Who are you?" said David.

"Oh, no one important. I'm not a friend, but I do have a Jewish friend. I presume that he would not be welcome at one of your dressing-up soirees?" she continued.

"I don't know who you are..." David tried to speak but Emily had decided to turn things up a notch.

"Nazi! Nazi! Nazi! You love to dress up in Nazi clothing, authentic Nazi clothing that you've acquired over the Dark Web, the real stuff, worn by the guards at Belsen. And then you and your mates all get drunk on Schnapps and sing songs about death and ashes. I bet the cost of housing in your area would drop through the floor if people knew about you."

David tried to stand up but Michelle was paralysed

with fear and kept him anchored to the table. Emily smiled and moved on to the next table.

"Oh hello, Babs, this is Rose your significant other, isn't it? Does she know that you're not gay at all? In fact, when she goes off to Zurich for one of her work thingies, you ring up your old boyfriend, the rugby player, and you let some steam off with him, and sometimes with a couple of his friends. That's right, isn't it?" Emily was on a roll.

Babs turned as white as her new Comme des Garçons t-shirt and her mouth opened ever so slowly. Emily moved on to another table and then another. She went from couple to couple, and group to group and then the solitary drinker, telling the world in general about the secrets they hid from everyone else. Emily was telling the truth about them, all the dirty little lies, the deceits, the broken promises, their desires and debauchery. She told the truth about anyone that came near her. She was nearly done with the bar and something inside her was telling her to go up to the restaurant. Surely there were more people up there that would appreciate seeing their dirty laundry aired in public?

Emily nearly made it to the door, but Rose had other ideas and she punched Emily in the side of the head, snapping four of her acrylic nail extensions in one go. Then David waded in. He was not wearing his German Army issue jackboots tonight but he did have a good pair of shoes on and he wasted no time in introducing Emily's legs to their leather. The barman hit the panic button under the counter but he was too late. Emily was on the floor by now and all of the individuals she had 'outed' were getting their revenge. Emily was down and she was not getting up again. Boots, fists, chairs, ashtrays, glasses, and even a coat stand were being used to smash her into tiny pieces. When the doormen stormed into the bar all they saw was an out-of-control mass brawl. They licked their lips and steamed in. It was the highlight of their evening.

When the police arrived the bar was quiet, apart from the moaning of the punters who had resisted the security, and the barman who was sweeping up the broken glass. Every single person was taken down to the waiting police vans and secured inside. The officer in charge took the security cameras and the guest book from reception with him when he left. Emily was taken to the hospital; she had been beaten into jelly and the paramedics feared that she would not make the journey. Every inch of her was beaten black and blue, all apart from her forearm and her new tattoo, which was unmarked and undamaged.

On the way, one of the paramedics said to the other:

"That's the Gaelic symbol for Truth, isn't it?"

Chapter Six

The Transfer of the Tattoo

Acklam Market in W10 was alive and growing, stretching itself out, hungry and actively consuming more and more of the empty spaces under the Westway. Gone were the needle swallowers and the rough sleepers, swept up by the new brooms of ever-eager councils, London's unfortunates brushed aside to make room for yet more trendification and at some later date, hopefully, *gentrification*. Even now the estate agents in their colour-coded electric vehicles were sniffing the winds of change and hoping that a microbrewery or a search engine campus might take root and help to push up the property prices.

The market was full of the bright young things, drinking and swiping on their mobile phones for the next love of their lives. The music was loud but not too loud so as to stir the residents of nearby Cambridge Gardens. There were formidable opponents to the market living there, and they had the Noise Abatement Society's number on speed dial. At the northeast of the market was a driveway that led to an emergency exit. On one side of this passageway was a collection of portable toilets, blue in colour and rancid by odour. No amount of industrial cleaner could dampen their aroma. On the other was a mural that started well but finished badly and had been scrawled over by the local gangs with postcode tags.

Then there was the emergency exit, a wire fence with a barbed wire hair-do and wearing last year's carnival posters. The gate opened out onto Acklam Road, a stunted bit of tarmac that went nowhere important. Parked in this small space was a medley of vehicles, the vans and estate cars used by the market's stall holders, the owners of Bay 68, and sometimes the emergency services. On occasion, private cars were parked here too because there was a roadside burger van. Not a Burger King. This was the one and only *Burger Queenie*.

The smell of the fried onions and the grease floated down the road like a sentient mist. It wrapped itself around every bollard and post, clung to the branches of the soot-stained bushes, and stuck to the wheels of the cars. There was always a demand for a double-dog with extra onions and fried eggs from the hot plate of Burger Queenie's road-side eatery. Especially tonight.

One of Queenie's regulars, a sanitation software salesman called Sonny was steaming up the windows inside his Ford Mondeo with his favourite burger, the *Chilli-Death* with jalapenos and tabasco, when he noticed the caravan. He wiped the condensation from the driver's side window with a well-used serviette, smearing more than wiping, to get a clearer look at it. Sitting on a small ledge at the back of the caravan was a young man. He was framed within a rectangle of soft light that emanated from inside and smoking a small clay pipe. The only things missing from this scene were a dog on a string, a crystal ball and a red neckerchief.

"Bloody pikeys," said Sonny, turning his attention back to his hotter-than-hell burger.

If Sonny had continued to stare at the caravan he would have seen the young man throw his head back and laugh, just as though he had heard what Sonny had said – which he had. After he had finished his burger, Sonny burped a loud, satisfied burp, wiped the last remaining ooze of red sauce from his chin and then turned on Talk Sport radio. The presenters were practically shouting at each other about a comment that some football player had made about another. It was hard to discern what the argument was about and after a while, Sonny grew bored of the chatter and decided to answer the call of nature instead.

When he stepped out of the car he was relieved to see that the gypsy had gone inside his hut on wheels. Sonny would not have to make any small talk. He slipped behind the caravan, unzipped his fly and produced an arc of silver steam onto the wall behind it. As he was nearing the end of his ablutions something occurred to him and for no reason other than spite he decided to turn about and wee over one of the caravan wheels. It was a petty act, a weak show of defiance, but he couldn't help himself. It was as if he was being goaded by an invisible mate.

Once he had finished, Sonny put his midget-hood away and returned to his car, but he froze a few feet away. Something was wrong. The door was open and the light was on inside his prized Mondeo. He checked his pocket for his key; there it was, safe and sound, and he was sure that he had locked it just now. Sonny approached cautiously. He pulled the driver's side door fully open and saw it. Someone had urinated on the driver's seat. A big, smelly puddle that steamed and stank of porridge and apples. No man or woman could have produced it.

Sonny was confused and appalled all at the same time. It was disgusting, but he had only been gone a minute, possibly even less. Who could have done something like this, and so quickly? Sonny slammed the door closed. He looked at the caravan first. There was a wisp of smoke coming from the small chimney stack on the roof and there was a sliver of golden light under the door at the rear. The young man was inside, but he'd have had to move like a ghost on roller skates in order to leave the caravan, do the deed, and then return without Sonny seeing him. No. It must have been one of the other drivers hanging around outside Queenie's.

So, Sonny drew himself up to his full height of 5 feet 7 inches and marched into battle.

"Right you lot!" he shouted.

One of the other men who was sampling Queenie's wares dropped a Styrofoam cup full of scalding hot coffee onto his own foot and yelped, another dropped his bacon sandwich and Queenie, a 6 feet 4 inch cross-dressing ex-Matelot, dropped a tray of eggs.

"Which one of you joker's used my car as a toilet?"

Sonny was fuming and balled his fists, tilting his head to one side because he'd seen it in a Kung-Fu movie and it was supposed to make you look like you knew the ancient art.

Queenie looked puzzled.

"What the hell are you going on about?" she said.

"One of you hilarious berks has drenched my driver's seat in piss, and I'm not having it! Whichever one of you it was better get over there and give my upholstery a big shampoo and set, or I'm going to unleash merry hell on you all!"

An Ink So Dark

Sonny raised his hands. One was in a fist and the other was open, palm upturned. He was trying to channel his inner Bruce Lee but was coming off more like a short Bruce Forsythe.

"Why would any of us take a leak in your car? There's a Portaloo over there and a toilet in the bar," said Queenie.

"That's what I thought! But then, who did it? Which one of you sick gits hosed down my Mondeo? You and your sort like that sort of stuff don't you? Water sports and splashing each other?" Sonny looked up at Queenie.

"My sort? Can you expand on that?" said Queenie.

Sonny realised too late that his mouth had earned him yet another beating and he tried, in vain to retract his previous statement.

"Forget about it, I'll go and stand over there and whichever one of you did it can go and clean it up. I won't look, just as long as it's gone by the time it takes to count to 300."

The rest of the group were stunned and stood there in silence, apart from the man who had spilt his coffee. He was still wincing and waggling his foot.

"My sort?" said Queenie.

Queenie had been a member of the navy provost due to his height, build and ferocity. He was not a man to be trifled with and once the red mist descended it tended to go very dark for anyone nearby. He had been struggling with his true identity; he had known deep down that he wanted to be a woman, the times that he had nearly been caught dressing up in his mother's dresses and make-up were legion. He had pretended to be the alpha male for so long in order to disguise his true self and when he did finally 'come out' and reveal himself, he vowed from that point on that he would not regret the decision, or feel ashamed of it. Ever.

Sonny sensed the change in the mood of the group and

decided that quick flight would be better than a one-sided fight, and edged away, but it was too late. Queenie was on her way, and she didn't look happy. The man in the caravan smiled. He could feel the tension in the air. It was palpable, like static before a storm. He opened a cupboard and took out a shiny green apple. It would be payment for the horse. He slid the latch on the door and stepped down from the caravan. The fight between the man who had urinated on his caravan and the tall woman was in full flight. The painted lady was rag-dolling the shorter man, and shouting something about wigs and make-up. It was hilarious and the man felt a warm glow begin to grow in the pit of his stomach.

He walked away from the beating, chuckling to himself, and made his way towards a small piece of grass in front of one of the terraced houses nearby. He had paid the owner of the house £50 to let his horse graze there. And graze it had done. It was calmly munching on the city grass and the man patted its neck, ruffled its mane, and then offered up the apple which disappeared into the horse's mouth so quickly that it looked as though the man had performed some sort of sleight of hand magic trick.

"Well done, Bessie," the man said.

The horse snuffled and stamped one hoof into the grass.

"Even if they'd seen me lead you to the car and pissing into it, they wouldn't believe it. That's the problem with *them*, they want to believe in magic, but when it happens right in front of them, they go blind."

A scream followed by a thud came from the burger van, and the man decided to go and catch up with the carnage.

When he returned to his caravan, he found that the man who had made his toilet against his home was laying on the bonnet of his car, beaten, bloodied and battered.

"Serves you right, little man. One bad deed deserves another," he said.

Then he climbed the steps up to the door at the rear of his caravan and went back to organising the colours of his inks. He sat down on his bunk and scanned the shelves. One of the bottles was pulsing with light. It was the glass bottle with the label that read *Emerald Truth*. The inch of green liquid at the bottom was moving. It had become thicker, like green treacle. The man smiled and let out a little yelp of pleasure. The liquid was reacting fantastically, bubbling and popping and slithering around as if alive. The man lifted it from the rack, removed the cork stopper, then drank the liquid down in one gulp.

As the ink passed into him he let out a purr of pleasure and licked his lips like a warm lizard behind the glass in a tropical zoo. Then he replaced the stopper and eased the small glass bottle back into the rack. Gently, very gently. He stroked the side of the bottle and sighed as it was returned to its place on the shelf. Once it was secured he reclined onto the pillows of his bunk and closed his eyes. The lantern hanging from the ceiling sputtered twice and went out, plunging the interior into darkness. The silence grew and filled the small space to the point that the thrum of the cars passing by on the elevated section of the road above was muted and could not be heard. The man stopped breathing, but he did not die. His eyelids flickered and when they opened fully, his eyes had completely disappeared – only black empty sockets remained, and from their dark depths the sounds of wailing and sobbing came.

In the emergency room at the hospital, Emily shuddered, and the machine that was keeping her alive started to scream at the top of its electronic voice. When the crash team entered the room seconds later, Emily's mouth was wide open and from inside her throat, a sickly light flickered. It disappeared immediately and the nurses and the doctors swarmed over her, fighting valiantly to keep her alive but to no avail. Her soul was already being consumed by a wicked man that lived in a rickety caravan, and he was enjoying the taste of her death very much.

Chapter Seven

The Forlorn Hope

Judas opened the fridge door in the small galley kitchen in the office. The light inside was broken again. For some reason – as yet unknown to science – light bulbs did not do well in the presence of spirits and the undead. The Fae lived charmed lives; bayonet or screw fix bulbs lived short ones. The milk, a two-pint bottle rescued from the office behind the front desk only a day ago, was nearly empty.

I'll have to do a run for some more, he thought.

He made a cup of coffee using his own personal coffee maker, and coffee beans from his man down in Bermondsey. The merchant purported to be from the village next to the one where Judas had been born long ago. Regardless of his origins, false or otherwise, Judas liked the man and his shop. It smelt of memory and history. The beans that were for sale came in packages. Paper packages. And sometimes, when Judas hefted one in his hands he felt a pulling sensation and wondered if maybe his people wanted him back? Not likely. Not even remotely.

For a second he felt that awful longing and despair that

had haunted him for hundreds of years, but the aroma of the freshly ground coffee saved him from sinking any further into the darkness he had created for himself. Judas took a spoon from the drawer underneath the sink and gave it the necessary three wipes with the end of his blue woollen tie. Once he was satisfied that it was moderately clean and free from harmful contagions, he stirred his coffee with it and returned to his desk.

I wonder if I could pay one of the inmates to clean the office? he thought.

Judas took another sip of his beverage and then got down to work. He moved the brown manilla folders around his desk, first this way, then that. To an observer, it might appear that he was hiding a pea under one, or a shiny coin, like a streetwise hustler trying to mesmerise some poor sap and relieve him of his hard-earned cash. The folders contained the reports that the normal rank and file had made prior to calling the 7th floor. Sometimes there were clues hidden inside those card covers. Judas had learnt long ago that where the occult, the Fae, and the rest of the monsters were concerned, the Devil was most certainly in the details, and if you did not look for him, then more often than not you got hurt.

After a couple of hours of reading reports from young PCs and WPCs about strange shapes departing from crime scenes and that uneasy feeling of dread that you only got when playing Zombie Death on the X–Station or some other gaming platform, Judas couldn't read any more. He knew straightaway what they had seen, and he was glad that they had documented the event, but he just wished that there were more of him. He needed more officers. London Under was growing restless and it appeared to him that the evil elements were getting braver, and that must not be allowed to happen. The Chief Superintendent had already sent him six emails in the last month.

If only he'd send me some more operational funds instead! he thought.

"JUDAS!"

Judas fell off his chair and reacted as fast as he could. He rolled to one side and then jumped up, both fists and anger at suitable levels. He saw something in the corner like an inverted shark fin and launched himself at the shape. The blow he received threw him across the office and he landed in a crumpled heap below the map of London with its blue pins. He groaned. The blow had been savage and he knew that his rib cage was not intact. He stood up quickly and readied himself.

"Do not raise your hand to me again! Do not even raise an eyebrow, or you will be in pain for much longer than the last time!"

The Archangel Michael was in the house and the look on his face was terrifying.

"What the Hell was that all about?" shouted Judas.

The next blow was even harder than the first and Judas bounced off at least two walls.

"Do not mention that place, its regent or its followers in my presence, Judas!" screamed Michael.

Judas had a broken arm to go with his broken ribs. There was blood in his mouth and when he coughed there was enough to cover a whole floor tile. His head was throbbing and the world and the galaxy it resided in were spinning. He stepped backwards, but not because he wanted to. Gravity was calling the shots now. He tripped over his own feet and fell over, landing on his bottom with his head smashing into one of the metal filing cabinets. He groaned. His own body was attacking him now.

The light in the room, daylight, not the neon variety, flickered and went out and he felt something encircling his neck. It was like a hoop of cold iron, the width of a car tyre. When it began to tighten he realised it was not an object, but Michaels's great big hand and it was crushing his neck like a dandelion stalk. The pain was intense and darkness behind his eyes was falling fast but then something happened, and things took a turn for the worse.

There was a blinding flash, as though a lightning storm had chosen to target a space the size of a snooker table and unload the skies upon it. But there was no sound. Judas tried to blink but it felt as though his eyelids were being held open and a channel of hot light was being forced into his brain. The room turned into a negative version of itself; silver windows became black rectangular voids, the patterns of the tiles on the floor turned into white holes in space and the filing cabinets and desk were mere x-rays.

Then there was a silence. A silence that frightened him more than the Archangel, and more than Lucifer the Morningstar. Their Master had come.

Judas saw the Archangel then, assuming a position that he'd never seen before. He was kneeling, head bowed, and his arms raised above him as if waiting to be handed something. Michaels's body was steady, his muscles taut, and there was something of the child about him, a desire to please, a wish to be rewarded even. Judas was paralysed. But then he heard something, low and deep, and he recognised it. There were words in that noise, sounds the size of continents, vowels that could crush and consonants that could boil. Such were their intensity and potency that Judas wet himself. And then he passed out.

In the void, the space between the planes of reality and substance, Judas was cast adrift. His mind was nearby but he could not feel it, there was some sort of delay in his thinking. He wondered where he was and then his own words, repeated, found him in the darkness. Then he saw a light. And seconds later his thoughts confirmed it. The light grew vast and it was travelling at speed. The darkness around it was burnt to grey and then the shape formed and grew wings and arms and it came for him.

Judas woke in the office. Night had fallen. He saw London's skyline through the window. She had her frock on, and she was going out to party. He wanted to go with her but he was unable. His body was stiff and it hurt. It hurt everywhere. He was angry and he was feeling something that he had not felt for some time. He felt *innocent*. It was odd. Judas opened his eyes to a view he had never seen before. He had journeyed into the depths of Hell, across the Time Fields, mirror images of the most evil locations in human history, and seen executions and the stoning of women and innocents, but he had yet to see an Archangel weeping at his feet.

"It seems that we are both out of favour, Judas," said Michael.

"For ... Angel Dave?" Judas found it difficult to say his friend's name.

"I have overstepped my boundaries. My heart has ruled my sword, and I am found wanting. Please, accept my apologies for striking you. I was not myself, it seems."

Michael lifted his huge head. There had been tears, Judas could see the dry lines on the skin of the marble colossus in front of him. Pain left its mark on all, the high and the low. Michael had lost a step. He was still Michael, but he had been pulled to heel, the master of the heavens had been hammered and there was no pain here, only shame, and Michael, for all his glory and savagery, was more dangerous at that moment than he had ever been. Judas shuddered.

"I lost Angel Dave, Michael. I am truly sorry. He flew away so quickly that night and I did not act swiftly enough. He was working for me, helping me, trying to repay a debt that he had already repaid in full, more than once. His blood is on my hands."

Judas was healing fast, and his words were coming more easily now.

"Can angels really die, Michael?

The archangel stood up, unbuckled his sword and laid the scabbard on top of the table. It had to be ten-feet long and at least two-feet wide, and it crackled like a roaring fire. The blade was in constant use and Judas imagined that if it were kept enclosed, wrapped up inside the scabbard for too long, it might eventually start to weep and whine like a half-starved dog.

Michael sat on the floor near the window. It was the only place in the office where he could stretch out properly. Judas had thought of requesting some additional funding so that he could raise the ceiling in the office but then if that occurred, Michael might decide to check in on him more often, and Judas preferred to keep his visits to a minimum.

The archangel spoke then, and Judas took a seat at his desk.

"Angels can die, Judas, but some of us, like me and the Morningstar, cannot. We are bound to Heaven and to the *other place,* and it is impossible for us. When one of the Host falls in battle, they return but not in the same form; they have no physical body or wings to speak of. They become beings of light, like a silver vapour, and they speak in echoes. They are not sad, Judas, they are still joined to *HIM,* and *HE* speaks with them often."

Judas sat back in his chair, and it creaked.

"There's going to be a big 'But' now isn't there, Michael? I can feel it."

The archangel smiled. It was an unusual sight and it caught Judas off guard for a second.

"Always interrupting, Judas, you can never listen for long, can you? Yes. You are right. There is something else. Sometimes an angel can be stranded, caught between worlds, unable to pass over and take up their place in the City of the Heavens."

A helicopter passed overhead and Michael watched as the blinking red light on its undercarriage faded away into the night sky. It was heading for the heliport at Battersea, another oligarch heading home, or possibly a footballer. Michael turned back to Judas and continued to talk.

"Have you heard of the Winghurn Bridge, Judas? The mortals have assigned many names to it already. Some call it the Bifrost, others call it the Chinvat Bridge. Angels call it the Winghurn because one side of it is made from the wings of dead angels, and the other side is constructed using the horns and scales of demons who have been dispatched. If an angel is caught between places then he or she is confined to the bridge. Demons taunt and toy with the stranded angels and the angels repay the demons in kind. It is a monstrous place, Judas."

"Why are you giving me the geography lesson, Michael? What am I supposed to do with this knowledge?"

The Archangel shifted his weight and the window rattled.

"Because, you sneaky little bastard, that is where Angel Dave is right now. Standing on Winghurn Bridge, darkness is all around him, cold unlike any that you have experienced chill his bones and he is always at the mercy of the demons who try to persuade him to walk across the bridge and into Hell."

Judas stood up quickly.

"Angel Dave is alive?" he asked.

"In a manner of speaking, Judas," said Michael.

"Can he be saved?"

"He *could* be, Judas, but not by me. I am forbidden to walk on that bridge. But you are not," said Michael.

Judas started to pace around the office, and instinctively he reached into his trouser pocket and removed his silver coin and started to rub its face with his thumb. Michael, smiled.

"Is that one of the thirty pieces that you were paid with, Judas?" said the archangel.

"You know it is. Stop messing around. How do I get there, and what will I need to rescue him with? A sword like that one, a magic book, or is it something else?" Judas asked.

"You will need a weapon, that much is true, but I do not know which one. I will have to return to the City in the Heavens to find out. And, Judas, there is something else. You will have to come to terms with the demon guarding their side of the bridge. And it will cost you dearly. I will try to advise you as best I can, but once you set foot on the bridge, you will be alone, I cannot help you."

Michael stood up – well, he stooped up – took his sword and its scabbard from the table and strapped it to his waist. The blade growled and Judas took a step backwards. Then Michael flicked the catch on the window sill. The frame around the glass had been specially built so that it could open fully to let angels in or out; the lifts were far too small for them. He turned back to Judas. All his strength had returned and he was imposing despite being bent over double. He nodded at Judas and then eased himself out of the window and disappeared. When he wanted to be, Michael was fast.

Judas closed the window after him and returned to his seat. He still had his coin in his hand and he rubbed at it and thought about Angel Dave and the demons he was facing. Judas owed Angel Dave, it was as simple as that.

Chapter Eight

The Knife Dies

Sergeant Lace was not in the best of moods. Her relationship with her boyfriend was not going well. *He* was a member of the secretive Mudlark clan and spent a great deal of time sailing up and down the Thames getting up to no good. *She*, on the other hand, was a police officer and responsible for stopping any of the Under Folk from getting up to no good. It was a delicate balance of turning a blind eye and pretending to go deaf at times but he was worth it, or at least she hoped he was. At the moment, they were ships in the night and she felt as though they were drifting apart.

Lace waved at Sergeant Henshaw, the desk sergeant and recognised font of all knowledge and wisdom when it came to the Force and the Yard, but he was knee-deep in the general public and did not see her as she passed through the foyer, stepped inside the lift and pressed the button for the 7th floor. There were a couple of other coppers in the lift but they chose to ignore her and she was relieved when the doors opened and she was able to escape without being scarred with small talk.

When she entered the office, Judas was already there.

"It's carnage down there, Guv! Why are Thursdays always ridiculous?" she said.

"Guv?" Judas replied, looking up at her.

"Sorry. *Sir*," Lace replied sheepishly.

"We're not the Sweeney, Lace. Sir is fine, or Lord, I'd even stretch to Emperor at a pinch," Judas said, with just a hint of his usual sarcasm.

"Can I offer the Emperor a cup of coffee or tea?" said Lace.

"One would like a cup of coffee from the machine, and make it snappy or it's the noose for you!" Judas smiled as he said it and brandished his special mug at her.

Lace made the coffee and they sat down to discuss the Highgate Cemetery situation.

"I stumbled across two shifty little grave robbers whilst I was staking out the area," she began.

"Gibbet and Hench?" said Judas.

"The very same, your *Emperorship*," said Lace with a small bow.

"Those two are mostly harmless. I say mostly, they can be cruel and are devious when it comes to negotiations, best watch them, Lace," Judas replied.

"I will do, Sir."

Judas sipped at his coffee and waited for Lace to continue with her report.

"The sightings of this menacing creature that smells of acrid smoke have continued. We're getting a few reports coming in from Under Folk now too. Gibbet and Hench don't appear to have seen anything but the Gate Keeper says he's not venturing out to walk the cemetery's boundaries as much."

"Who is the Gate Keeper?" asked Judas.

"It's …" she flicked open her police issue notebook, thumbed a couple of pages and then said, "… Caracticus Ironpeg the Third, Sir."

"That's fortunate, the Ironpegs are good people, brave and responsible. I knew his father, he was one of the first characters I met when I joined the Museum. I did a tour of London's cemeteries, met the Gate Keepers and learnt about the places of the dead. He was a good man, ready and willing to spend time on a wet behind the ears *cozzer*. He helped me track down a Hell Hound that was frightening the locals at the time." Judas nodded to Lace indicating that she should carry on.

"Ironpeg says that some of the corpses that he looks after have taken to going quiet in the early hours. He thought it odd because that's the time when they all get up and go for a wander, catch up with the other corpses, chew the fat, that sort of thing. He says that it's unusual for the cemetery to go as silent as the grave, Sir."

Lace had obviously been waiting to use that line.

Judas did not look up from his coffee, and after a beat, he said quietly.

"Boom, boom, Lace. Very funny, do go on."

Lace let out a small but satisfied giggle.

"Yes, Sir. The beast, or whatever it is, tends to stay in the Western Cemetery. It never goes far but it has been seen crossing Swan Lane and going into Waterloo Place. The dryads that live there are frightened and say that at least two of their kind are missing, feared dead." Lace finished reading from her notebook, then flipped it shut and returned it to her pocket.

Judas placed his empty cup on the table, removed his silver coin and started to make the customary small rotations across it with his thumb. It was Lace's turn to sit and listen now.

"If this thing is killing dryads it's either desperate or has a death wish. The dryads might not look ferocious but they can protect themselves when pushed. I'd be more inclined to think that this beast is desperate. Something might have moved into its territory or frightened it, and if that's the case then we have a bigger problem, Lace. What's your next move?"

"Well, Sir, because I caught Messrs Gibbet and Hench red-handed, I threatened them with a spell in the Black Museum, which I would waive if they acted as my eyes and ears for the next few nights."

"Good. That will keep them out of trouble for a bit and might just keep them safe. Let's check in on them tomorrow and see if we can grab five minutes with Ironpeg. Now, what else are we supposed to be looking into, Lace?" Judas asked.

Lace was just about to speak when the desk phone sounded. It was Sergeant Henshaw, and he was requesting their presence in the cells – there was something that he wanted Judas to take a look at. Henshaw was not given to flights of fancy and he was as steady as a rock with the handbrake applied so Judas slipped on his jacket, and he and Sergeant Lace descended into the bowels of Scotland Yard.

When they arrived, Henshaw was standing in front of one of the cells, the metal flap in the heavy steel door was down and he was staring through it. When Judas approached he straightened, smiled, and then motioned to the peephole.

"This is Mr. Charlie Watson. He was arrested in Tooting

– murdered a family as they slept, and then called us. He has no priors, a good job, his employer speaks highly of him and he has absolutely no connection whatsoever to the family he killed. He used a big hunting knife that he got online, as you do. The ferocity of the attacks was unusual and when we arrived he had no idea what he was doing there, couldn't tell us anything. Funny thing is, Sir, it seems he'd recently had a large temporary tattoo drawn on his back, *a big knife,* as it happens. The tattoo was photographed at the scene but now there is no sign of it. Usually there is a mark or a smudge and these henna things last for a week, maybe two. But it's gone, completely."

Judas looked in on the young man. He was sitting on the edge of the hard bench on the far side of the cell. He was wearing a white paper suit, his hair was unruly and his eyes had dark circles beneath them. There was a faint glow just above his suprasternal notch, but that was all the life left in the man. Judas could sense something and he felt as though he should know what it was. There was a familiarity and it prickled at his senses.

"There is something not quite right here, Sergeant Henshaw. Do you have the report?"

Henshaw handed him a blue clipboard with a small file attached. Inside the file were the images that the officers on duty had recorded with their police issue phones. Judas handed the photographs to Lace and then skimmed the report.

"The tattooist was very good. Sir, the knife was well drawn, really good detailing for a temporary tattoo," said Lace.

"There is something else, Sir," said Henshaw.

Judas looked up from the report.

"We've got a body at the morgue, a young lady. She wandered into one of the clubs on Shaftesbury Avenue a

An Ink So Dark

few nights ago and proceeded to tell the rest of the patrons what their deepest and darkest secrets were, whereupon they attacked her and beat her to death. None of the witnesses knew her or had ever set eyes on her. How she knew what she did is a mystery. There is no research or evidence on her laptop, and she's not connected on social media either. Oddly enough, she also had a temporary tattoo done recently, a Gaelic symbol of truth, I'm told. Most of the young officers have tattoos these days and one of them pointed it out to me. The tattoo is still visible. Most of her skin is either black or blue but the area around the tattoo is untouched. Very strange, Sir. I'd value your opinion. Feels like one of yours, to be honest. We've got all of the security tapes from the club if you're interested?"

Henshaw cleared his throat and then closed the metal flap on the cell door.

Judas liked Henshaw. He was one of the more open-minded coppers, more interested in protecting the innocent and less bothered with the latest mandate sent down from the mandarins at Whitehall. Henshaw had graduated top of his class and made a name for himself as a pretty decent thief-taker in the East End, a good honest policeman with a family and the desire to see a safe neighbourhood for his children, and their children.

"I think you're right, Sergeant Henshaw, there are too many similarities here and I don't believe in coincidences. Have the witnesses from the incident at the club been released? It would be good to get a statement from them."

"We can't release them, Inspector. They are on camera committing murder. They are in the other cells, and I'm coming under a lot of pressure from the Chief to move them on."

Judas looked at Lace and said, "Bloody Nora?"

Lace smiled.

"I was thinking the same thing, Guv – I mean 'Sir'. Sorry, Sir. I think Bloody Nora would be perfect."

Henshaw cleared his throat for the second time in under a minute.

"I'm afraid the good doctor is not at home at the moment, Sir. Her department and its facilities are locked up, and we're not allowed to force an entrance. Something to do with the Black Museum, Sir."

Judas turned away from Lace and Henshaw. The corridor was empty and anaemic. A neon light tube flickered to its own pointless beat, and the Yard hummed with the cries of insults and the sobs of the incarcerated. Judas closed his eyes and listened. Somewhere, not that far from where they were standing he sensed a hollow space, ages-old, and full of anger and enmity. He turned back.

"Sergeant Henshaw, thanks for calling me. We will take these unfortunates off your hands. They are, as you suspected, a matter for the Black Museum, and, seeing as you have no room at the inn for them, and Bloody Nora is still away, we shall have to transport them to another safe location. Leave it with me, I have an idea."

Chapter Nine

Black Maria

Judas and Sergeant Lace returned to the 7th floor. Sergeant Henshaw had allowed them to keep the blue file and the photographs. The images were strange. They seemed to be changing; the layers of colour were softening and they appeared to be losing their sharpness. Lace noticed it first and when she showed them to Judas he nodded and asked her to lay them out on the desk and try to take a shot of them all. Lace fiddled with her smartphone, adjusting the settings of the camera before taking as many shots as she could and sharing them to her laptop.

"How many people do we need to transport, Lace?" said Judas.

"Well, Sir, we have twelve people from the bar, the young man in the cell, and one dead body. Thirteen living and one dead," she replied.

Judas scribbled a note on a piece of A4 paper and handed it over to Lace.

"The address of the person I would like you to visit is on this note. Let her read it and then get back here as soon as you can. She talks fairly directly, and whatever you do, don't let her break the speed limit in that contraption of hers."

Sergeant Lace turned the paper over in her hand and read the address.

"Shepherd's Bush? What's over there?" she asked.

"You'll see when you get there," said Judas, smiling a smile that Lace thought was far too broad for its own good.

Once she had departed, Judas moved over to the window and looked out over his favourite city. Barcelona had been his favourite at one point. He missed its verve and the heat, and the people that were laid back yet with passion to burn. But there was something about London that had hooked him. He watched as two angels flew past the building. They were carrying a huge blue bag with yellow handles between them, full to the brim with cardboard boxes. Someone had obviously just moved into a new property and needed all the fittings and a lot of self-assembly furniture.

He thought about the White Witch and the Ley Line Express. Subconsciously, images of making a home, settling down and growing old together had slipped into his mind.

How long do witches live for? he thought to himself.

Then his mobile rang. Sergeant Lace had encountered yet another problem. Their car had been taken for a routine check and tune, but she had been able to cadge a ride with an old friend from her college days, so all was well.

WPC Claire Evans was a demon behind the wheel, and she made up for any time lost at Scotland Yard by taking a few *police turns* (or blatant flouting of the Highway Code in modern parlance) to shorten the distance between the Yard and the address that Lace had given her, a red-bricked building sandwiched between the White City Bus Stop and the Westfield Centre.

"Here we are then, Lace, hope I haven't made you late!" said Evans.

"I don't think anyone has ever been late with your driving. No, we made good time, I just hope you don't get an earful from traffic control about that U-turn you made." Lace flicked the catch on her safety belt.

"Before you go," said Evans, conspiratorially, "what are you up to the weekend after next? Fancy coming to a festival? No Wellington boots, tents or bulk-buy packets of wet wipes required. The festival I have tickets for is in London – more or less."

Lace turned to face her friend.

"You know what, Claire, I think I will. It might make my other half buck his ideas up, plus, it will be good to let my hair down a bit. Drop me a line a little closer to the day. Thanks for the lift, Claire!"

"No problem, Lace, see you in a week or so."

Lace stepped out and onto the pavement. A lady of advanced years scowled at her from the bus stop, clearly unhappy that a police car had stopped in the bay reserved for the number 21B. Lace gave the woman her best police officer smile and walked away. She thought that she had got away with the parking situation but just then, Evans decided to put her foot down and the police car performed a disgraceful doughnut, wheels spinning, rubber-burning, and then she put the blues and twos on for good measure. Lace did not look back.

. . .

The red-bricked building was once the power station for the Central Line, or so it said on the plaque on the wall. Then it had gone up in the world and become the home of Dimco Tools. Lace considered this and thought that being a power station was much better than being a tool company. She retrieved the note that Judas had given her and re-read it.

There should be a large metal door down here somewhere she thought to herself.

Lace finally found the door by accident. She was walking down the side of the building, inspecting each brick for a secret hatch or door handle when the wall opened up right in front of her and a couple of fairies flew out. Calling it 'flying' might have been a bit generous – the two fairies were struggling to escape and had their heads down and wings flapping. One of the little chaps, who was wearing a Clash t-shirt and a pair of Bathing Ape trainers looked as though some huge monster was after him. It turned out that what was chasing him was far worse.

Lace took a step backwards and instinctively reached for her extendable baton. The fairies must have thought that they'd won their freedom, until, that is, a huge arm shot out of the opening in the brick wall and the hand at the end of it plucked not just one, but both of the two escapees cleanly from the air. Both yelped and started to swear in the language of the Fae. Lace had worked with a couple of fairy pickpockets in one of her first cases so she knew what they were saying – and unfortunately for them, so did the owner of the huge arm.

"Since when did my name mean so little then, Fae? How did it come to pass that the Under Folk thought I could be trifled with? Get back in here, you little worms! Pay what you owe or I shall take those pretty wings of yours and turn them into a pair of knickers!"

An Ink So Dark

The two fairies went into reverse and were pulled back into the opening. Lace took the opportunity to announce herself and stepped forward with her warrant card held high.

"Stop right there! My name is Sergeant Lace and I am here on Black Museum business!" she shouted.

There was a sudden silence – even the fairies' wings stopped buzzing. Then there was a throaty laugh, and the biggest woman that Lace had ever seen stepped into the light.

"Well I never, the Black Museum has come to call upon me. This is your lucky day, boys," she said.

The tall woman then flicked her arm. It was as though she were launching a frisbee or tossing an empty can into a waste paper basket but the two magical folk were thrown through the wall and disappeared.

"Don't worry about them, they will come to no harm – yet," she chuckled.

Sergeant Lace drew herself up to her full height, which was just about knee-high to the lady she was addressing.

"I take it that you are the woman known as ..."

Lace stopped for a second. She was wrestling with something. The tall woman, definitely a member of the Under Folk, had some magic and was obviously of high-standing. She was also very dark in colour and Lace was confused as to how to address her.

"Are you the *woman of colour*, called Maria?"

Black Maria started to laugh. She had a great big chest and a set of shoulders to make any heavy-weight boxer swoon, and from inside there came this church organ-sized bellowing. She laughed without taking a breath for at least five minutes but finally, she stopped and looked down into Lace's eyes.

"A woman of colour is it? Well, you may call me by my name, which is Black Maria, like the police trucks that they used to cart off the ne'er-do-wells and the unruly types in the good old days. Simple as that, easy-peasy-lemon-squeezy. The one, the only, Black Maria. So, you are the Master of the Black Museum's new sergeant then? I was told that you were formidable. It's nice to meet another strong woman, there are far too few of us left. Tea?"

Black Maria did not wait for an answer. She turned smartly on her heel, and wandered off down a brightly lit corridor strewn with packing cases of all shapes and sizes and rolls of bubble wrap that Lace had an urge to pop as she walked past.

"Give it a go if you like!" shouted Black Maria.

"If I could trouble you not to read my thoughts, thank you very much!" said Lace a little more sharply than she intended.

"In here," said Black Maria, pointing at a large metal door.

Sergeant Lace entered, and her jaw dropped so far she nearly tripped over it. The space was enormous. The boxes she had seen outside in the corridor were just the overflow. There must have been tens of thousands of crates stacked up in neat orderly rows running back into the darkness. Lace inspected a few and could read the markings quite clearly. Tokyo, Berlin, Machu Picchu, San Salvador, Greenland. Then there were the more fantastical locations: Emerald Isles, Dunsinane, Minitaurusel, Eden Under and so it went on. Lace would have continued reading the names of the destinations and wondering what was inside each box but the sound of a kettle coming to the boil stopped her.

Black Maria dunked the tea bags deftly and Lace was

An Ink So Dark

pleased to see that she made her tea properly, squeezing the bag against the side of the mug until it wept. It was dark and strong and Lace received hers gratefully with a nod of the head. Black Maria retired to a three-seater sofa next to a huge writing desk. This was her chair, and she settled back into it with her own vat of tea.

"So, how can I be of service to the Master of the Black Museum?" Maria asked.

"I have a note for you, from my DCI," said Lace.

Black Maria leapt up from her sofa so suddenly that Lace nearly spilt her tea, but she soon concluded that the giantess must move this way all the time. She was huge and daunting, that was obvious, but Lace saw something else, too. She was sharp, instinctive and no fool. No, she was not to be trifled with.

Lace held out the note. Black Maria took it, read it, then reclined once again. The sofa gave out a long airy wheeze as it took her full weight and Maria nodded as if hearing a silent question.

"What is that you do?" asked Lace, wafting her mug in the general direction of the crates.

"Import and export mostly, Lace. May I call you 'Lace'?"

Lace nodded.

"That's wonderful. Lovely. Smashing. As I say, it's moving one thing from one place to another. Only, I transport things from one time to another and from one world to another. Over there is a crate that will be going to that bunch of water rats the Ancient Mariners, and over there is a collection of smaller boxes that will be going to a vanishing village in Somerset. You won't find that kind of service at the Post Office!" Black Maria laughed again, and the sound of it made Sergeant Lace smile.

"Do you work alone?" Lace asked.

"Oh no, I have a workforce, lost buggers mostly but staunch, which is more important to me considering the places I send them off to. Your fancy man, the Mudlark, he often does a turn for me. A good sailor, not afraid of a wave or three."

"I said 'no' to the mind reading. Any more of that and I will have to take you in!" Lace was smiling as she said it and Black Maria nodded.

"And on that note, Sergeant, we should be heading back to the Yard. Your master has need of my assistance."

Lace placed her empty mug on the corner of the desk. It was piled high with paperwork and books, and she valiantly fought the urge to take a quick look at what was written down on them. The policewoman in her was naturally nosey but she liked Black Maria, so she closed her mind to the scribbles and moved away. Black Maria was waiting for her by the door wearing a black leather biker jacket and carrying a silver crash helmet under one arm. It looked like someone had cut a wrecking ball in half and scooped out the insides. Lace guessed that the contraption that Judas had warned her to be careful about was waiting outside and it went on two wheels by the look of Maria's helmet. Evans had broken the law getting her here, was she about to break the law getting back?

Black Maria walked back up the slope. She was halfway to the exit when she stopped and smacked herself on the head to indicate that she'd forgotten something. Lace heard the slap from ten feet away and was grateful it wasn't her own head. Black Maria started to rummage through one of the cases in the corridor, and after a few seconds she stood up, pulled out a full-sized stretcher, and casually put it in her pocket. Lace was stunned. The stretcher was long enough for a tall man to lay down on and she just slipped it into her pocket like a set of door keys. Black Maria didn't blink an eye. She gave the front door a push and stepped through it.

Lace followed, and just as she had suspected, *and feared*, Black Maria's favourite mode of transport was a Norton motorcycle with a sidecar that reminded her of an animated film featuring a plasticine man with huge hands and his sidekick, a clever dog with a grudge against penguins. Black Maria straddled the machine. It creaked. Then she put her wrecking ball helmet on and beckoned Lace towards the sidecar.

'*Join the Black Museum!*' they said. '*It will be fun!*' they said, Lace muttered under her breath.

In the sidecar, tucked under the seat, was another helmet. This one was human-sized but came with earflaps and a detachable visor that someone had already detached. Lace jumped into the sidecar, placed the helmet on her head and then held on for all she was worth. There was a roar of life from the Norton and then her lungs swapped places with her spine.

The return journey to Scotland Yard was a blur. Lace remembered seeing faces that comically stretched horizontally and cowering road signs, but she arrived back at the station in one piece. Lace directed Maria to the car park at the rear of the building and waived her warrant card at the duty officer. It could have been her supermarket rewards card for all the attention he paid to it, he was more interested in the rider of the motorbike.

Black Maria parked the Norton in the bay reserved for the Black Museum's Mondeo, which was still undergoing a revamp and retune. The giantess seemed to know the way inside and Lace gave up trying to keep up with her and eased herself into Black Maria's slipstream. They made an odd couple and many of the other officers stopped and stared at them. Black Maria noticed. Lace thought she might be feeling self-conscious, but far from it. Black Maria stopped, took a deep breath and began to sing.

"Turn around and watch the sky
Look about for paint to dry
See me not my lovelies
Dream for a spell of clouds rushing by
Or a stream with ripples drifting by
See me not my lovelies."

Everyone and everything in the Yard – the men, the women, the German Shepherds – listened to her tune and reacted in the same way. It was as if a light switch had been flicked. Their eyes rolled back in their heads and showed white, then rolled back down again and it was if Black Maria and Sergeant Lace had disappeared entirely.

"You'll have to teach me that one," said Lace.

Black Maria just smiled and replied, "Oh, that is nothing but a trifle, just a trick I learnt to quieten rowdy men down when they had taken one or two more ales than was right for them. I'll teach you some handy little tunes if you like, if your Master allows."

Lace was about to tell Black Maria where they were going but it was clear she already knew. This wasn't her first time at Scotland Yard. She knew it well and she knew the old Scotland Yard even better. Lace followed Black Maria not to the lifts and the 7th floor but straight through to the loading bay, where DCI Judas Iscariot of the Black Museum was waiting for them along with a dead girl on a stretcher, a rather dazed and confused looking young man, and a group of people that wouldn't have been able to tell you what year it was let alone which day.

"Black Maria, thank you very much for coming to our aid, it is greatly appreciated." Judas had taken some time to smarten himself up. He was wearing his dark blue Kilgour suit and had run a comb through his jet black curly hair. Even under the artificial lighting he looked healthy and there was a mischievous sparkle in his eye.

"Well now, Master Thief-Taker, how fare you? Sprightly by the look of you," Maria replied.

"The years have been kind to us both, kinder to you though perhaps..."

"Stop flirting with me or I'll take you up on the offer you made me at the Bucket of Blood all those years ago."

Judas looked startled for a second but then regained his composure.

"What offer was that, Sir?" asked Lace.

"Never you mind, Sergeant, a tale for another time," said Judas.

Black Maria chuckled but said no more. Judas stepped back so that she could see her cargo properly.

"Is this it?" she asked.

"I didn't want to burden you, and at your time of life I thought it might be one too many," he replied.

Black Maria did not take the bait; she knew the Master of the Black Museum too well for that. Instead, she just stepped forwards, picked the young man in the white forensics suit up and put him in her pocket. There wasn't even a bulge or a ripple in the leather of her biker's jacket. Then she lifted the dead girl on the stretcher up as if she were a feather and did the same. The rest of the people went in as well, and then there were none, save Judas and Lace.

"Easy peasy, lemon squeezy. I shall take them back to

mine and settle them all until you call me and let me know where you want them," said Maria, looking pleased with herself.

"Thank you, Maria, how many is it that I owe you now?" Judas said.

"There is no owing between you and me, but let's just say that if I wanted to chat with Sergeant Lace here, and maybe teach her a thing or two, that wouldn't go amiss?"

Judas looked at his Sergeant then back at his old friend.

"Something like this was always bound to happen. If Sergeant Lace is okay with it, then I am okay with it. One word of warning though, Black Maria. If Lace falls, or steps through the wrong door without the means to get back, I won't be best pleased."

Black Maria nodded and held out her hand. Judas stepped forward and placed his own hand on top of hers. When he removed it again, Lace saw that he had placed his silver coin in her palm.

"Silver to make her shine," said Judas.

"Silver for a long, safe and steady line," Black Maria responded.

"Silver to cross the realms of time," said Judas.

"Silver to bring her home just fine," said Black Maria.

The giantess closed her hand around the coin and then winked at Lace and departed. They heard the roar of the Norton from the loading bay and when it had faded, they went inside and took the lift up to the 7th floor.

"Won't you miss the coin?" asked Lace.

Judas shrugged and sat down at his desk then reached into his pocket and retrieved another silver coin. This one was rough and still had some markings on it and the edges were more jagged.

"Miss what?" he replied.

An Ink So Dark

It was Sergeant Lace's turn to shrug but she added a raised eyebrow too.

"And Black Maria? Who is she, and what is she?"

Judas smiled and got up from his chair and said, "a picture is worth a thousand words as the old saying goes. Follow me." And he walked out of the office and into the Black Museum.

Judas did not go into the Key Room. Instead, he opened one of the glass cabinets that housed some of the old police memorabilia and removed a leather-bound book. The spine was still intact and it opened easily. Lace thought she heard a horse whinny and the sound of metal rolling across cobbles. Judas noticed it too. He flicked through the book until he found a page with a line drawing of a police wagon. It had high sides and a window framed with iron and bars of steel, four wooden wheels with metal hoops, and a large horse, possibly a shire horse, was harnessed to the front. Sitting on the board, *the seat* in common parlance, was a broad-shouldered police officer with fantastic whiskers and a vicious-looking whip in hand. Underneath the drawing was the title of the illustration, it read: The Black Maria.

Sergeant Lace tapped her finger on the drawing and then said, "she's named after a police wagon?"

Judas closed the book and returned it to the glass cabinet.

"No, Sergeant, the wagon is named after her," he replied.

Sergeant Lace was confused but she wanted to reason it out just like a good detective should.

"Black Maria is huge, she's a lady of colour and she seems to be able to carry lots of people?"

Judas smiled.

"Right so far," he said.

"I can see why the wagon is called a 'Maria', that seems logical enough, but the question of her identity remains. What is she, some sort of enchanted being? A witch? The daughter of a giant?"

"Right again, mostly," said Judas.

"Black Maria has been walking the streets of London far longer than I have, and that's a long time. Back in the day, when the taverns and the pot houses got a bit rowdy, the tavern keepers would send a runner to fetch Black Maria. She would arrive, knock a few heads together and then cart the ruffians away. Rumour had it that she used to throw them in the Thames to cool off. Where she came from is anyone's guess. She lives in all worlds, meaning she can cross over into the Fae or take a trip down memory lane if she chooses. I've bumped into her in some strange places, believe me. I came to her aid in the past, and now she won't let me forget it."

"And the duet you and she performed and the exchange of the coin?" Lace asked.

"In places like Tower Bridge Under, for the Fae, and in the lands under the sea, silver is considered to be more precious than gold or diamonds. It has a certain power and when it is passed between two beings and a song-bond is made – that was the song we sang – a special charm is created."

"A charm for me?" asked Lace.

"If you spend any time with Black Maria, and she teaches you anything or takes you anywhere unusual, then there is a chance that you could get lost or stranded, hence the charm. It will act like a homing beacon and I or ..." he was about to say Angel Dave but stopped himself, "...or someone else we trust, can come and find you and see you safely back here. As charms go, it's a good one, but it's not a protection charm, so you still have to be careful. "

Lace nodded and said, "Thank you, Sir."

"You're very welcome, Sergeant. Now, Black Maria has kindly agreed to let us use one of her rooms as a temporary morgue. Bloody Nora should be there by now and we can get her opinion on why these murders have happened, who is behind them and what the relevance of the tattoos are, aside from the obvious."

Chapter Ten

Mary Blood Red Maroon

The caravan went unnoticed by the general public as it trundled up Middlesex Street and when it turned away from Petticoat Lane and onto Commercial Street, no head turned as it passed them by. Only the dogs were aware that something was not quite right, sensing danger in the middle of the mayhem that was the busy and vibrant gentrified East End of London. They strained at their leads and suffered the wrath of their owners, who yanked them back into line, unaware that their hounds were trying to protect them. A mounted policeman was forced to rein his horse in when it unexpectedly bolted. It had been trained to remain calm, steady in the midst of a riot, and unflinching when spurred into danger, but for some reason, the horse had lost its head.

At the top of Commercial Street the caravan turned left and headed into Spitalfields Market, not to be confused with the sort of market that sell vegetables and fake watches. This was an upmarket market. The driver manoeuvred it through the trendy crowds and the tortoise-slow traffic deftly. There were stalls selling scarves, jewellery, retro football shirts, old film posters and glazed bowls. The bright young things were taking their ease outside the market's trendy eateries and sipping on coffee from the Andes and tea from China. A friendly game of ultra-competitive 5-a-side was being played out on the far side of the vast space, directly opposite a brace of ageing and unroadworthy Citroen cars. Someone had ripped the boot off one of the poor old cars and inserted a sandwich stall, and it was doing a roaring trade in baguettes.

None of these activities was of any interest to the man driving the caravan. He was looking for the entrance to White Lion Yard, in the hope that he might pass through it and set up his caravan in the ancient market, a special market where magical things can be attained with under-the-counter cash. Getting into St Mary's market was easier said than done though. The gate was hidden from prying eyes and the White Lion that guarded it was a fickle beast and quick to anger. After a few minutes of navigating the market, the horse stopped abruptly and the caravan lurched to one side as the lantern that swung from the caravan's canopy swayed in the air. The horse had sensed the opening before it came into view and had edged towards it like a four-legged moth to a flame.

The driver let the horse have its head and relaxed the tension on the reins, and the caravan was pulled through the gates. The noise of the outside world abruptly ended and the sudden quiet took Odhran by surprise. They trotted on, turned a corner and there, sitting in the middle of the lane was a huge lion. It looked as though it were made of marble, white in colour and motionless, but Odhran knew better. Many unfortunates had seen the beast and thought it a statue and attempted to pass it by without so much as a nod. They were all mistaken, of course, and a large pile of white bones was testament to their folly.

"White Lion, Guardian of St Mary's, and Keeper of the Gate, may we pass?"

Odhran spoke the words with the reverence that he knew the lion expected.

"Who walks in my lane?" asked the lion.

"Odhran of Clonfert, a son from the Emerald Isle and painter of stories, great lion." Odhran always added the last bit, just in case he had caught the gatekeeper on one of his many bad days.

"Odhran of Clonfert, do you undertake to accept and abide by the rules of the marketplace?" growled the lion.

"I do your honour, freely and without question." Odhran placed one hand over his heart theatrically.

"Then pass by, and abide you may, but cause dismay and you shall encounter peril."

The lion snapped the last words, raised itself up onto four legs, and casually ambled to one side of the lane, leaving Odhran free to slap the reins on his horse's rump. Seconds later they were trundling into the heart of a very busy Under Folk market.

Montague Huxley, the famous Sin Eater, was hammering the last peg of his newly acquired velvet tent into the ground when he felt a searing pain at his temple. The sharp pain hit home quickly and Huxley missed the peg he was aiming at and hit the hand holding the peg instead. He stood up and dropped the hammer, which landed on his foot and caused him to hop around in front of his lovely new abode with his thumb in his mouth. He was still hopping when the caravan pulled into the vacant space beside him.

An Ink So Dark

The caravan's owner did not greet him, preferring instead to unhitch his horse and feed it first from a heavy-looking nose-bag. Then he set up a wooden board at the bottom of the steps at the rear of his mobile home and disappeared inside.

Huxley picked up his hammer and tapped the peg down into the soft earth with deep concentration. His thumb was turning blue and his headache had suddenly turned nasty.

"Careful now!" said one of the sins that he had recently eaten, from inside him.

Huxley Montague's job was to attend to the dying and consume the sins they had committed during their lives. They could then shuffle off to Heaven, Hell or whichever other appropriate realm without the baggage they had acquired in the mundane world. He ate the sins, for a fee of course, and they stayed inside him until he was able to free them at a place where he felt comfortable, which for Huxley, was a church in Battersea that looked out onto the Thames.

His foot had stopped hurting so he lifted the flap of his tent and went inside to lay down. He hadn't felt this bad for a while so he removed a damp cloth from his washing stand, laid down on his cot and applied the cool, soothing fabric to his forehead. It calmed him and eased the pain directly but he could still hear voices, and he knew instantly that these voices were not coming from inside him, but from the recently arrived caravan next door.

Odhran busied himself in the caravan. He had stowed all of his belongings in secret hidey-holes, cunningly built into the floor and the walls of the caravan, and it took him a little time to retrieve them all and unpack them. His most-prized things were always packed away first and unpacked last, for safety and security, and once he had stacked them all on the neat shelves he had commissioned, he felt comfortable again. He didn't like his treasures to be locked away in the dark for too long. He feared he might miss one of the glass bottles coming to life and therefore miss the pleasure of consuming the evil ink; but they were all still dormant, just waiting for the pain of others to bloom.

Once a fire had been lit and his lanterns were aglow, Odhran checked through his inventory of pens, scalpels, wipes and antiseptics, and found that he was running dangerously low in all departments. He counted some of the gold coins he kept in his secret horde into his palm, the money that the mundane folk said would not be accepted in the market next door, straightened his neckerchief and donned a waistcoat. Then he unlocked the back door, stepped down from the caravan, and made his way into the throng to look for the supplies he needed.

Huxley writhed and groaned on his bed and pressed the cold compress to his brow. It had lost most of its soothing properties but he continued with it until he could take no more.

"Is there nothing you Sins can do? I carry you and care for you and the least you could do is drown out those wretched screams for me!"

"You had but to ask, Sin Eater, it is easily done. Wait, there you go," said the combined voices of Hairy Legs Steve, an elderly fawn, and Winnifred Half-Hazel, a water sprite from Bermondsey.

And, as they had promised, the screams and the shrieking died away instantly.

"Thank you, both," said Huxley.

He was able to stand again and his head was much clearer than before. He threw the not-so-cold compress into the soapy cold water of the basin and took a series of deep breaths. It was silent inside his head and inside his tent, thankfully. But Montague did not like to hear of souls or creatures in pain, hence his calling, so he slipped out of his blue velvet tent, crept down the side of the caravan and pressed his ear against its wooden panels.

What he heard inside frightened him at first. The voices coming to him were stretched and thin, then he felt the first signs of revulsion. His stomach flipped and he drew back swiftly. The voices inside were crying out for help, to be saved, or in some cases, to be put out of their misery. He found it unbearable so Huxley Montague decided on a course of action that was very unlike him: he was going on a rescue mission. Huxley moved to the rear of the caravan and climbed the three short steps to the door. Once there, he lifted the catch and was not surprised to hear the tell-tale thud of an immobile latch. He persevered, but to no avail. Then he had an idea.

Hairy Legs Steve had been a little bit dodgy in life; he was known to pick the odd pocket, and he was on good terms with the Dodger family, which would have normally attracted the attention of the Black Museum straightaway. But Hairy Legs Steve had another role, a role that paid handsomely. Hairy Legs, as he was known by the masses, was a dab hand with a feather-pick and a barrel-tickler, the tools of a safebreaker. Huxley had all the help he needed to spring the lock on the caravan door, and if that failed, well, he also had Winnifred on board and he may just be able to channel her and lift the lock by spell or charm.

Both Hairy Legs and Winnifred were more than happy

to help when asked. Huxley placed both hands on the part of the door where he supposed the lock to be, then Hairy Legs took over. Huxley felt a strange sensation. It was like someone writing words on his back with their fingernail. If he didn't concentrate the words would just feel like swirly patterns instead. After a few seconds had passed, Huxley heard Hairy Legs Steve's past sins speaking to him.

"Easy as pie, Master Montague, simple as the back of my hand. That's no physical lock, there's no tumbler or mechanism to speak of; it's an old gypsy wooden press plate. Just place your hand a bit lower on the door ... just there is good ... and then with the other, stick out your index finger and the one next to it – I forget what that is called – and then push them into the wood just above your other hand."

Huxley did as Hairy Legs had instructed and the wooden door clicked open.

"Well done, Hairy Legs Steve! Thank you, I'm going in."

Huxley pushed the door open and seeing no guard, guard dog, cat or weasel, he took a deep breath and crossed the threshold.

The Parchment Man did not like the look or the feel of the man who had sidled up to his stall at the market. He had a mean way about him; his face was pinched and his eyes were telling lies long before he opened his mouth. But business was business and it had been a hard few months of late, so he put on his best smile and tried to ignore the way his latest customer ran his hands over the paper. It put him on edge and he hoped that this trade would soon be over.

"How much for the very fine double weave cream paper, Sir?" the man asked.

"That would depend on how you are paying ... sir," said the Parchment Man.

"Is *old Irish gold* still good in these parts?"

The Parchment Man reached across the table and held out his hand, and seconds later, two heavy gold coins were placed into his palm. They felt right, definitely heavy enough and the markings were correct, but the Parchment Man knew more about coins and measures than most, a handy skill when plying your trade around markets. He took out his proof jar, dropped both coins inside then replaced the stopper. They didn't have long to wait before the air in the jar began to change colour – to a very pleasing orange. The gold was of the highest quality. If the air had turned yellow, or brown, then something had been added to the coins.

"One coin of that quality will get you five large rolls of the standard paper. You'll need a horse and cart to take that much away. And at the other end of the scale, two coins will get you five boxes of my very best. There is nothing like it in this realm for weight nor weave, it is the best money can buy," said the Parchment Man proudly.

"Do you have any *angels-wing* mix?" said the man.

The Parchment Man took a step back. The expression on his face, which only seconds earlier had been open and positive, was now closed and his brows were furrowed.

"You'll find none of that filthy stuff on my stall. I've never traded in it, not now, not never. You can take your coins and spend them elsewhere. Please, take them before I speak to one of the constables."

The man on the other side of the table snatched his coins back. The action of taking them was so aggressive that a stack of paper was knocked from the table and fluttered to the ground.

"You watch your words, paper man, or I'll put something on you that will make you regret it! Here, take the coins, I will take five of these."

The man threw the gold coins back across the table and before the Parchment Man could alert the market's constables he was gone, along with five boxes of his very best paper. He had the gold coins in his hand, payment had been made, and the man had taken exactly what he was entitled to, so no constable would waste any time on him. He pocketed the coins, rearranged the stacks and boxes of paper on his stall and then set about collecting the white sheets from the brown cobbles. He felt dirty, and he shivered. He would watch out for that man in future.

Huxley stood in the silence of the caravan. His eyes had adjusted to the light quickly and he was scanning the small space, eagerly searching for the voices of the poor souls he had heard. The caravan creaked occasionally, and he jumped at the sound, but it was nothing sinister, just the wood it was constructed from swelling, then shrinking. At the far end a little fire was breathing softly in a metal bowl. To Huxley, it looked like a small heart beating and he feared the worst, but it was just a fire.

"Huxley?" whispered Winnifred.

"What is it?" he replied.

"They're in the glass jars on the rack," she said.

Huxley turned to the rack on the caravan's curved wall and saw the neat lines of glass jars. Each of them contained a coloured liquid. Some were half full, and others had barely enough to cover the bottom of the jar. A label had been affixed to each one in neat and precise handwriting.

"Russian and Prussian Boys Blue. Mary Blood Red Maroon. Francis at the Festival Fawn?"

Huxley continued to read them all, whispering their names to himself.

"They're inside," said Winnifred.

"Inside what?" said Huxley.

"The voices of the tortured are inside the jars," she whispered.

Huxley needed time to process what he was seeing and hearing but he was out of luck because the next thing he heard was Hairy Legs Steve, and he sounded scared.

"Something's coming, Huxley, get out of there fast! Something dark and cold! Be quick or someone will be eating *your* sins for their tea!"

Huxley was not a brave man and whatever it was that had imprisoned these poor souls was far more powerful than he was, but he had a stout heart and he did not panic. He calmly reached across to the shelf and removed the jar with the most liquid in it. Then he crept out of the caravan, closed the door softly using the double-handed gesture he had only just learnt to lock it again, and speed-walked back to his tent. He entered, closed the flap, and waited for all hell to break loose. But it didn't.

The following morning, the caravan was still there. Huxley watched it from the safety of his tent and decided after a short while that the coast was clear. He pocketed the glass jar and went in search of one of his good friends, a man-sized boxing bull terrier that went by the name of Bullseye.

He would know what to do with the jar, and if Huxley needed protection then who better than the undisputed light-welterweight champion of the Under Folk.

Chapter Eleven

The Fear of the Fae

"I'll put a pound on the cove in the blue shorts!" shouted one of the punters.

"You do that, my friend, and I shall be a pound the richer!" shouted another on the opposite side of the boxing ring.

A raucous cheer went up and another exchange of insults went round. The crowd were in good spirits. Most of them were actually *in* spirits; gin, rum, or some fairy brew that looked harmless but packed a bigger punch than the local heavyweight. A small giant, only ten-feet tall vomited due to overindulgence, drenching two rows of fellow fight fans in front of him. The giant also had an accident in the trouser department, coating the row behind him with something that smelt even worse than his vomit. The constables were called and managed to talk the inebriated behemoth into accompanying them to the stables nearby where he could get a bath and a bed.

The patrons who had been violated by the giant's excesses excused themselves for obvious reasons and went in search of a toilet of their own. It looked as though the whole seating area to one side of the ring would be empty for the fight but a team of market folk swarmed over the wooden benches with mop and bucket and soon the seats were retaken and the noise levels went from ear-splitting to nose bleed very swiftly.

Huxley wandered around the ring. An old pug who had fought his last, or at least that was what it looked like, his ear the shape and size of a firm young cauliflower, his nose a pancake, and his eyes mere slits in a swollen and puffy face, was being stretchered away and the victor, arms aloft and bathing in the adoration of the creatures he had just made richer, strutted around the boxing square like a bloody peacock. Huxley followed the stretcher to the dressing tent. It was here that the fighters prepared themselves for combat, and to have their wounds dressed by the healers. He entered, and on one side of the tent, he saw the pre-carnage fighters, skins shiny with oils and liniments, eyes sharp and focused, bobbing and weaving and trying to disguise their thunderous uppercut or sneaky new fighting style from the other boxers.

On the other side of the tent sat the broken and the bruised, heads in hands, coughing up blood, lamenting the loss of feeling in an arm or a leg, and appealing to their trainers to seek out the referee and ask him how much he was paid to throw the fight. Here was desolation and blood. Also here, sitting with his back to the canvas was a seven-feet-tall bull terrier wearing a very fine tweed suit and waistcoat, a cravat at the neck and a beautiful yellow flower in his button hole. On his head, pushed back so that it sat at a jaunty angle, was a pork-pie hat. All that was missing was a shooting stick and a silver flask full of the best brandy.

Huxley caught his eye and the bull terrier leapt to his feet and pushed through the crowd, engulfing Huxley in a dog-hug so fierce that Huxley thought his eyeballs might pop.

"Huxley! Huxley! Huxley! You is a sight for a sore eye, yes you is!" said the big dog.

Bullseye had a funny way of speaking. When he was excited or happy he let out the odd little yelp, or a short sharp bark. He pushed Huxley back but kept him at paws' reach to look into his eyes.

"What brings my dearest friend here? Eater of sins, carer for those that has been wronged and cut up bad by heathens and winged freaks?" shouted Bullseye.

Huxley had not seen his old friend Bullseye for some time. The hound was a tough nut but he had a good heart, and a vicious temper if crossed. There were many tales told of his ferocity in the ring, and out of it. Huxley had tended to Bullseye's wounds one dark night after he was set upon by a gang of Fae folk at one of the summer festivals. Huxley had done what little he could do and feared the worst, but fortunately, he was owed a favour by one of the healers attending the festival, and by hook or by crook they had saved him. Bullseye recovered fully whilst in Huxley's care and swore to protect him if ever Huxley needed help, which was what he was doing right now.

"Can I buy you a drink and ask a favour, Bullseye?" said Huxley.

Bullseye shifted from one leg to the other and his triangular-shaped eyes twinkled.

"Yes to both," he said.

Bullseye led Huxley through the milling crowds. He was stopped occasionally and asked why he was not taking a turn on the canvas, or whether he remembered someone who had seen him fight at some famous venue. Bullseye was always polite and made time for his fans but enough was enough and he grabbed Huxley by the arm and slipped between two tents. They passed through the narrow passageways between the tents and behind them, another world was happening. The servants and the actors, those that supplied the sellers and the strong creatures that guarded their takings, all were here, drinking and smoking, performing sleight of hand tricks and doing a little bit of black-market trading. No one batted an eyelid as they passed and soon both were ensconced in a booth at one of the refreshment tents on the opposite side of the market.

Chandeliers constructed from dead cart wheels swung in the air gently above them. Lampads, strange little creatures, said to come from far across the sea, danced from one to the other, touching any candle that looked as though it were wilting with a tiny hand, causing it to shine brightly once more. A large woman stood behind the makeshift bar and Huxley marvelled at how she could produce barmaids from the pockets of her voluminous gown. Bullseye caught his eye and winked.

"Watch this," he said mischievously.

Bullseye barked a deep, booming collection of ruffs.

Suddenly the barmaids that had been waiting tables – lovely young girls, dark-haired, ginger-haired, Asian, and one practically bald and wrinkly – dropped their trays and turned into cats. Huxley was intrigued. The cats ran like lightning across the floor, darting between the other patrons' legs, and leapt into the landlady's apron folds. Bullseye started to laugh a long, wheezing laugh, yelping occasionally, and Huxley could see his rounded stubby tail wagging furiously.

"Very good, Master Bullseye!" shouted the landlady, clearly angry but trying not to show it.

"Pardon, my lady, I was just giving my good friend here the laughing tonic, as he is a bit down in the dumpings. If you will allow me, I should like to propose a round of drinks, on me of course, and a donation to your cats home, back at the London Bridge Under."

"Seeing as it is you, Master Bullseye, I shall let you buy two rounds for the good folk here. One for the drink that the floor is supping on now, and one because you is a flash cove, and should know better," said the lady.

She winked at the dog though, and once the girls reappeared he made sure to tip them all in turn and apologise.

"It was but a wheeze, please forgive me," said the dog, flattening his ears to show that he was being contrite.

Huxley did notice, however, that his old friend let out a little growl under his breath when one of the young girls wandered past and yelped when he saw her jump. They drank in silence. Well, Huxley drank in silence, preferring to sip his wine. Bullseye was both greedy and somewhat lacking in social graces, and had foam from his ale all over his whiskers in next to no time.

"So then, my friend, what troubles you?" asked the dog.

Huxley shifted in his seat so that he could reach into his trouser pocket to retrieve the glass jar.

"Bullseye. You know how it is that I can hear the sins of others talking to me, and to each other sometimes, which can be a bit of a bore, especially if they don't get along with each other?" he began.

"I has heard you tell me of it many a time, Huxley."

"Well, the thing is, Bullseye, a caravan set up next to my tent, here at the market, and I heard these voices, crying out

An Ink So Dark

to me they were. Tortured, sad souls, screeching and praying and wailing, if you will."

Bullseye nodded.

"So, I slipped inside and I found this."

Huxley reached inside his pocket and drew the jar out but did not place it on the table. He had the good sense to keep it under wraps. Bullseye looked down at the jar and then growled at it.

"What do you think, Bullseye? Should I show it to the constables?"

Bullseye called for another tankard for himself and asked for a bottle of red to be left at the table for his friend. They sat in silence for a while, drinking slowly and Huxley noticed that Bullseye's stubby tail was not wagging anymore.

"That is bad magic that is, Huxley. Old magic from across the water. Show it to me once again."

Huxley passed the glass jar to his friend. Overhead, the Lampads, sensing the proximity of something evil, flittered away into the darkness at the corners of the tents and the landlady looked around, watching her patrons ever more closely. She too could sense that darkness was near at hand. The dog read the label and tapped at the glass with a manicured claw. The liquid inside started to glow and Bullseye's hackles bristled.

"Now, now," said the dog. "Back to sleep for you, my lovely."

Bullseye hid the jar inside his jacket and patted the pocket. He smiled at Huxley and quaffed his ale, and then he laid a paw on top of Huxley's hand.

"Never fear, Huxley, I knows someone that will be very interested to see this. A person that speaks with demons and angels alike. He'll know what to do with it, trust me, my friend. Now, I shall be away with this poor soul. You shall never see it nor hear it again. But be careful of that caravan. No more rescue missions, no matter what you hear, and if the previous owner comes looking for his lost treasure, you don't know nuffink!"

Huxley nodded. He understood and he wished that Bullseye could come with him but the old dog knew a lot more about the darker arts than he did, and the glass jar would be safer with him. He would just have to try and be brave and maybe even sleep with a pillow over his head to muffle the voices calling out to him again. Bullseye stood up. He neither wobbled nor slurred his words even though he must have consumed his own weight in dark ales. In fact, he looked even more chipper than when Huxley had met him. Bullseye looked down at his friend.

"I is going to take this here torture device to the Black Museum. The Master there will take it and get to the bottom of this caravan and the creature that rides in it. You know the Master?"

"Yes, I have met him. He has helped me in the past," Huxley replied.

"This wasn't the only jar was it, Huxley? There were more of them, right?"

"A whole shelf of them. Blue, red, yellow, as many colours as there are stars, I'm afraid."

"Well, we shall have to put a stop to this thing's capers then, Huxley, won't we?"

Bullseye weaved back through the tables towards the entrance and just before he stepped out of the tent, he donned his little hat, slapped a handful of copper coins on the bar, barked once, and slipped away into the throng.

Huxley nursed his wine for a little longer and listened to the sins he had consumed arguing about whether a South Paw could beat an Orthodox right hand.

Odhran was angry at the Parchment Man for speaking to him as though he were some sort of deviant, but he had had the last laugh on the dry old man. He had slipped a few quills into his pocket when he wasn't looking. Armed with his new supplies, he pushed at the crowds when they dared to get in his way and snarled if they didn't move fast enough.

"I'll draw that dusty old man into my book and then I'll set fire to his precious paper, and let's see what the constables can do about that!" he mumbled to himself.

He was nearly home. The caravan was where it should be, and his horse was standing nearby, thick neck bent and muzzle trimming the grass in front of him, but Odhran sensed something was amiss and his blood ran cold. He quickened his pace, ran up the steps at the back of his caravan and tugged at the door. It was still locked. Or at least it appeared locked. Odhran had been touring the Isles for a very long time. He had passed through the land of the Picts in the North long before the Romans built their wall, and paddled his tiny coracle across the lakes to shelter with the Christian Monks. Odhran had slept in the shadows of the standing stones, and he had learnt to protect himself. He knew without a doubt that someone or something had been inside because the strand of horse hair he had stuck to the door with his spittle was gone.

Odhran opened the door, stepped inside and closed it behind him. If the creature was still inside it would not be escaping that way. The ashes in the small fire gave off an insipid glow that turned the shadows into deep voids. Odhran searched the caravan, throwing his cushions off his bunk and lifting what little furniture there was quickly and aggressively, to startle anything that tried to hide beneath it, but there was nothing and he found no evidence of their passing either.

"A thief that does not take is not much of a thief!" he said.

But then Odhran saw it. Or, more importantly, he did not see it. There was a gap between the glass jars on his shelf. A space! An empty space! Odhran planted the palms of his hands against the wooden plank above the shelves and he roared so loudly that the horse stopped eating and flicked her tail in agitation.

"Stolen!" Odhran shouted.

And then he began to rant and rave, calling out to his dark gods. Then he cried, and began to smash his own little world into small pieces. Everything was cast down. Everything apart from his glass jars.

The little boy arrived at the long, low building where the constables were located. The front door was an old stable door. The bottom half remained closed at all times but the top half was always open and there was always a constable leaning upon it and gazing out as the market people came and went. The boy was winded and clutching his flat cap in his hand.

"Constable! There's a madman running up and down the market shouting and screaming at everyone, calling all and sundry dogs and such. He says that we're all thieves and footpads and something about his 'Dark Navy Blue Blade'.

An Ink So Dark

Mistress at the House of Pleasure wants you to come and sort him out as he's frightening the customers, and says your cut of the taking will be very slight if you don't."

The constable disappeared from the doorway. There was the sound of cabinets opening and doors slamming, and then the stable door was thrown open and the constables, all of them, raced away. They found Odhran howling at the old Parchment Man, accusing him of revenge and theft in all manner of languages, all at the same time. He was frothing at the mouth and pulling at his own hair. His eyes were red and the constables were concerned that dark forces were at play so they acted decisively. Odhran was cudgelled and carried semi-conscious on a plank of wood borrowed from a nearby tavern, back to his caravan.

The constables pitched him up and onto the seat at the front of the caravan none too gently, then they positioned Odhran's horse inside its yoke, and encouraged the horse – a slap on the rump here, the offer of a shiny green apple there – and when forward motion had been achieved, they escorted the caravan and its unpleasant owner to the White Lion. As they turned out of White Lion Lane, the great beast was waiting. One of the constables whispered urgently into its marble ear, and as the tale wound to its conclusion, the market's gatekeeper began to growl, and the cobbles he paced across began to vibrate and shudder, causing a few dark grey slates on the roof of the buildings nearby to rain down and shatter on the ground.

Anger made the White Lion swell, and it grew monstrous. The constables started to draw back, and one hardy soul ran for his life.

"I shall eat your horse and chew on its bones until there is naught but powder on the streets; you have come into **my** market and sullied it with your outlandish behaviour! I shall eat it, and then you, but I shall leave your head and place it on a pole at the centre of the market stalls so that all can see what happens when you break my laws! All you possess will be forfeit, and what cannot be sold shall be burnt!"

The White Lion frothed at the mouth, and its great white teeth, sharp and savage, could be seen clearly now, and all that did were forced to cower.

The sergeant of the constables, a brave man and true, was the only creature there that dared to move. He approached the beast, hat in his hands and head bowed, and when he was as near as he thought safe, he took his life in his own hands and addressed the Lion.

"My Lord, keeper of the great gates and protector of the market. If you eat the horse, the caravan will be unable to move, and we shall have to keep it on market grounds; there is bad blood amongst the merchants and the travellers now, and they will surely find a way to cause more trouble if they believe that he is still within the borders. The man there, sitting with the reins in his lap, is not well; he must be mad to create such havoc here. We all saw him in the market, carrying on, speaking in foreign tongues, jerking, and with a fire in his eyes that made him look unnatural. Could we not just send him on his way? The horse took no part in the incident; why should it pay with its life?" he pleaded.

The White Lion, not famed for his patience, roared so loudly that within seconds the lane was clear, and the horse had fouled the cobbles from both ends. Only the constable who had spoken up remained. The White Lion prowled around the caravan. It sniffed at the horse. The constable feared the worst, but the marble sentinel instead produced another great roar and the caravan, Odhran, the lucky horse and the shelf of glass jars and bottles vanished, reappearing many streets away.

An Ink So Dark

. . .

Odhran woke later that afternoon; night had started to fall, and he felt sick to his stomach. He sat upright and surveyed his new surroundings. He was on a filthy side street. The buildings on both sides were mostly derelict, and litter and crows tumbled across the empty road, the one chasing the other for scraps. A wire fence hung like a drunken man from one of its wooden supports and beyond it was a small patch of waste ground. All that was missing from this scene of idyllic wonder was a lit brazier, made from an old oil drum and surrounded by those that had fallen into the abyss between life and death. The sky above was dark grey and getting blacker by the minute, and from somewhere high above, a light rain began to fall. The horse felt it first, then Odhran began to sob and wring his hands.

He rocked back and forth on his seat and began to tremble like a junkie at the starting gun of the cold turkey run. He felt that need again, and the desire to savour the pain of others. It grew and grew inside him like a hungry hole; he needed to replace the blue glass jar quickly because his supply of misery and despair was running short. The other jars would blossom soon, but they were just small hits. They would take the edge off his cravings, but nothing more.

Odhran made a clicking sound and the horse pulled away, and as it clipped and clopped down the street Odhran began to scheme and plan. He had new pens and some wonderfully crisp new paper, and more importantly he had space on his shelf. His situation was not nearly as dire as he first imagined. Odhran cracked the whip unnecessarily as he pondered his lot, and the horse sped up for a few strides before reverting to its natural, steady pace. It walked on purposefully as if following some unseen map and soon the caravan reached the old Roman Wall.

The roads were very busy; four lanes of traffic sped past, two heading into central London and two others escaping to Canary Wharf and the buildings where the money was made. Odhran joined the moving masses and paid no heed to the horns and insults of the white van man and the couriers that informed him using sign language that he should not be travelling along this route. But none of them knew there was a hidden junction here leading to an invisible road that took you to some very strange places.

The Church Roads were created by the ancient druids long ago so that they and the Fae, the monsters, spirits, forgotten tribes and giants were free to travel across the country in safety. Powered by Albion's great Ley Lines, the Church Roads were invisible to the mundane folk and enabled those who used them to travel great distances in a short time. This was where Odhran wanted to go. He could drift and forget on the Church Roads. He would not be interfered with there, and could get on with his work unobserved.

The speed of the caravan had caused the traffic behind to draw to a standstill. The Black Cab drivers were performing three-point-turns in order to save as many minutes as possible on the clock, and motorcyclists had started to weave through the deadlock, infuriating the other road users. Soon the flashing blue lights of a police car could be seen in the distance, alerted by the traffic controllers that something had blocked the road.

The police car made use of the pavements whenever it was safe to do so, and before long it was approaching the Roman Wall. Odhran had missed the marker on the road that told him exactly where the opening to the Church Road was, and he was becoming agitated and edgy. He started to panic and when he saw the police car's blue lights approaching he despaired, but then something occurred to him. He had a glass bottle inside the caravan that contained the eyesight that he had stolen from a young woman not two weeks ago! All he needed to do was drink it and then he would be able to see the gateway clearly.

He retrieved the glass jar quickly, removed the cork stopper, and then drank the honey-coloured liquid down in one go. It tasted so good; his throat warmed and the heat in his groin increased. His right hand twitched and then suddenly he saw the opening, as clear as day. He grabbed the reins and flicked them, hard. The horse detected his master's impatience and bolted. Behind him on the road, the angry drivers suddenly realised that the road ahead was clear, obstruction free, and waiting for them. Afterwards, when the police interviewed the drivers of the front three cars, they discovered that all of them, and their passengers, believed that they had seen a caravan with a green metal roof, pulled by a grey horse.

The noise of the outside world was quickly muted, and its structures and forms faded until only shadowy and blurred versions of them could be seen through the grey translucent walls of the Church Roads. Odhran had travelled along the road for about ten minutes and then stopped, unhitched the horse and set about making himself something to eat and drink. After he had washed his tin plate with water he had collected in his scuttle, and drained the last of the gin he was partial to from his mug, he removed a small notebook from the folds of his cloak and flicked through its pages. He had made a comprehensive list of the festivals that the mundane folk attended and all he needed was one that was happening sooner rather than later. He must get there quickly.

He needed victims – or *fresh canvasses* as he preferred to call them.

Chapter Twelve

Nora Knows

They found Black Maria standing in front of a large metal shipping container, which had been cleverly customised by Black Maria's elusive workforce to act both as a holding cell and an interrogation room. The young man they had arrested for the murder of the family in Tooting earlier that week was sitting on a chair inside the container, still wearing his white paper suit and a vacant expression. He made no sound, and his chest did not appear to rise or fall, as if his breathing had stopped. He was staring straight ahead, his eyes unblinking, his mouth closed and his hands on his knees.

Black Maria had installed some crude lighting inside the container – very crude. It was a single bulb hanging from a nondescript flex, secured to the roof with black masking tape. In the corner, she had placed a large fan that moved like a geriatric, tilting and turning oh so slowly and sending small wafts of warm air out into the world of the warehouse.

Her considerable figure was swaying ever so gently, and

she was humming a sad tune. Judas had never seen her like this before. Normally she was a force of nature, always moving, never happy being still, so this caused him some concern. He watched her for a while longer and then cleared his throat. She turned around quickly and there was a strange look on her face.

"There you are. Let me tell you, Warden of the Museum, or whatever it is that the Under Folk call you this century, this is not good, Judas. There is something inside that boy, and it is hungry; I can feel it, and it is speaking with him, whispering such dark words and promising so much pain. I know the language it uses, and I haven't heard it since the old days," she said.

"Hello, Inspector," said Bloody Nora as she appeared from behind the shipping container, a clipboard in one hand and a dictaphone in the other.

"I've been examining the young lady. We have her at the back of the warehouse, it's much colder back there."

Bloody Nora was wearing a very large navy blue Crombie coat that reached down to the floor and a natty-looking little butcher's boy cap. It made her look like a well-dressed urchin from a black and white movie about street kids in Chicago. As she approached, she noticed that Judas and Lace were staring at her wardrobe intently. Sergeant Lace was also doing her very best to suppress a broad smile. She shook her head.

"My *friend,* Wulfric, the Warden of the Church Roads, with whom I have been sharing a bed these last few months was a proper gentleman and offered me his coat and hat so that I did not freeze to death inside that hellish ice box back there," she said haughtily.

"Whatever you do in your spare time, and whomever

you choose to do it with, regardless of how many centuries he might be senior to you, is not for me or Sergeant Lace to criticise. Isn't that right, Sergeant Lace?" said Judas.

"That's right, Sir," she said.

Bloody Nora shook her head once more and showed Black Maria her clipboard and they nodded in agreement.

Bloody Nora turned to Judas.

"I've been over all of the evidence and the tapes from the club, Sir. It's some form of magical mind control, nothing unusual there, but then there is the tattooing. The girl had the symbol for Truth drawn on her and then lo and behold, she walks into a bar full of complete strangers and tells them all that she knows their deepest and darkest secrets. The lad here had these knives drawn on him and then he goes and butchers a perfectly innocent family with a great big hunting knife. Identical M.O. The girl's tattoo was there, clear as day, and then it disappeared. The lad here had a tattoo, and guess what, it's disappeared too. My good friend Black Maria here thinks that the time between the fading of the tattoos may have something to do with it. I'm still trying to work it out, Sir," said Bloody Nora.

Judas looked at her. She had dark circles under her eyes and looked tired.

"Can you furnish the doctor with something sweet and restorative, please Maria?" he said.

"Of, course," she replied.

Black Maria escorted Bloody Nora away in search of a hot pot of tea and possibly, if the planets aligned, some orange-flavoured Hob Nobs.

Judas walked into the container and pulled up a chair alongside the young man. He had intended to speak with him but the boy was not really there. So he sat and removed his silver coin from his pocket and started to rub it with his thumb. There were lots of dark magic practitioners in London that had the power to construct a spell of this complexity, but there was always a reason why they attacked and what they wanted afterwards. This was different, and the question was, what would any of them gain from torturing complete strangers? There were secret organisations and sects that made sacrifices to some deity or other out there, but there were dates and times of the year when they occurred. These incidents felt random, and that made the situation even more dangerous.

He couldn't be sure how long he'd been sitting there. It could have been five minutes, it could have been an hour, but suddenly the young man sat bolt upright and turned his hands palm upwards. Judas stepped away from him. Sergeant Lace had been leaning up against the wall of the metal container and was on guard instantly, her hand reaching for her ASP. Then the lad's throat began to glow. It was a red glow to begin with, then it changed colour and became an intense blue. Judas tried to speak to the boy, to help him, to try and bring him out of his current state, but there was nothing he could do for him.

Black Maria and Bloody Nora appeared. They placed their mugs of tea down and started to advance into the container but Judas waved them back. He wanted to see where this was heading; the killer or the creature responsible might show their hand or make an appearance. This was their moment, their opportunity to crow and preen; but this murder was going to be silent. The light flared in the young man's throat and his head tilted upwards. The blue fire inside him erupted and he produced a ball of flame that scorched the metal roof and caused the bulb overhead to shatter.

The light in the boy's throat flared once more, then it died, and as it drew back inside the body of the dead boy, Judas heard the sounds of monks chanting and beyond that, he heard the scratching of a quill on parchment and maniacal laughter.

"I think we're in trouble," he said.

Chapter Thirteen

The Dog and Bone

Judas left Bloody Nora to complete the autopsy on the boy. Black Maria had her own business to attend to and Sergeant Lace looked as though she needed a cooling beverage with her Mudlark, so he returned to the Yard on his own.

Ensconced in his chair and sitting by an open window with a small glass of vodka, he was off the clock now, and thought about Nora and that fop, Wulfric the Warden. It made him smile because they made each other happy. And there was Lace and her beau. Hopefully, they were happy with each other too. Then his thoughts turned to the White Witch, but he did not allow himself to dwell there because it made him despondent.

Judas reflected on his time here in London. He still didn't understand why people stood by him, or with him come to that, but he was glad that they did. He looked up into the sky. It was full of clouds shot through with hues of pink, purple and red. It was a truly beautiful evening and he raised his glass to the Heavens.

"Time off for good behaviour? No. Didn't think so!" he said.

Judas finished what was left of the bottle of vodka, heavily laced with lime and tonic, of course, and was feeling if not merry, then at least warm and less bitter than usual. He was just about to leave and had decided to visit his favourite public house, The Lamb and Flag, just off Long Acre, or the Bucket of Blood as it was known long ago, when his mobile phone started to vibrate against his rib cage. The number on the screen was not one that he knew and he was just about to mute the phone when he remembered that he was a policeman. Someone might need his help, so he answered it, and got the shock of his long, long life.

"Hallo, Inspector Judas! You will never guess what pug is on the end of this 'ere blower. It is none other than Bullseye, he what delivered that shameless blackguard Bill Sikes to you that night and what helped you find your good friend, Mr Charles Dickens," said Bullseye the walking, talking bull terrier.

Judas shot up. He couldn't believe his ears. Bullseye had done the dirty on his accomplice Bill Sikes and absconded with a ransom that had been raised for Charles Dickens after he had been kidnapped by the devious pair. And, now here he was, hundreds of years later, carping on about his role in bringing that bruiser and murderer Sikes to heel!

"Bullseye! You had about as much chance of helping to solve that case as I had of growing wings. The fact that you're still alive and not cooped up in some prison beyond the wall of the Fae is a surprise in itself. What do you want?" he snapped.

Judas heard the snuffling and gnashing on the other end of the line. For some reason the image of the old bruiser speaking on a state-of-the-art mobile made him smile.

"Inspector, Inspector, now, let's us be the gentlemen we know each other to be. Let's have no harsh words or curt oaths! I has been wanting to speak with you about a man what does nasty tattoos and is causing a lot of upheaval on both sides of the Underworld. I has proof in my paw this very moment, which I was hoping to give to you as a sure show of my good-natured self. To you, the bright beacon of the law, *yus*," said the bull terrier.

Judas was instantly alert. Regardless of what Bullseye had done long ago, and the relationships that he had had, the burly cove had information that Judas wanted, badly.

"Go on then, *Bullseye*, make your pitch, but don't take me for a fool, you'll regret it. And by the way, Charles Dickens gave me a really good account of what actually transpired between you."

He heard the dog chuckling down the line and Judas pictured the strange ugly man-dog, smiling.

"I should like to meet with you again, Inspector, dog to man as it were. I has something to show you, and what I wants in return is such a small thing, a trifle, you'll be overjoyed with the exchange," said Bullseye.

"I very much doubt that," said Judas.

Chapter Fourteen

Festie-Bestie

Lace rolled off the bed and tentatively placed her feet on the floor, but there was no shock to be found underfoot because the new underfloor heating had done its job and the carpet felt toasty warm. She took a long shower, longer than usual, dressed at her leisure, and then decided on muesli instead of some sugar-filled pop snap hexagonal-shaped cereal. After breakfast, she dressed in her usual police-friendly outfit, complete with a MACE canister, ASP extendable baton, nylon hand-cuffs, and a whiff of 'Don't Fuck With Me' dabbed just behind the ear.

Lace was dressed and ready for action and her hand was raised to grasp the latch on her door when her mobile phone started to ring. Her arm dropped like a 10th Dan karate champion and with the other, she reached inside her leather jacket and removed her phone.

The voice she heard was very excited.

"Hey! Sergeant Lace of the weird and weirdos department, it's WPC Evans, your mate from police school and your personal taxi driver come chauffeur of the last week asking you if you are free to come and have something akin to a good time with an old friend? I have tickets to a really good London-based festival. All of the music, all of the young Australian guys, all of it under canvas with no ID checks and no questions asked about what put the smile on your face. You interested?"

She didn't need to be asked twice.

Chapter Fifteen

A Place of Beginnings

Judas was angry with himself. The girl had died, she had been murdered, and now the boy too. When he had been sworn into the Police Force and taken the shilling as it were, he had promised to protect both sides of London's underworld, *without fear or favour*, as the old saying goes. But, here he was, filling in a report that no one would ever read with the details of a young man's end, a life snuffed out by some manner of evil creature with links to a monastic set, somewhere in the past. He took the file to the wall of metal cabinets, pulled out a drawer and placed it inside. Closing the drawer felt like the lowering of a coffin.

He made himself a coffee, moped about the office for a minute or two, and then gave in and turned to the window and the skyline. In the middle distance, somewhere over the city, an airship was plastered against the sky; it had been a fairly decent day's weather and the wind had died down, so the airship was left hanging. He watched it turn and disappear behind another building, possibly the Walkie-Talkie or the Gherkin. He had no idea why they chose to build these fantastic structures, knowing that once they were completed, they would be given the name of a vegetable, or worse, a piece of redundant technology.

The airship drew closer; it had discovered a breeze and was making use of it to give the passengers onboard a different view of the great city. The grey sky sausage turned about, and Judas saw that there was a poster running along the side.

"Stuck? Waiting? Need to Move On?" it read.

Judas smiled; every word could have been written especially for him. But then he looked again, and somewhere in the depths of his vast memory, there was a flicker, which turned into a flame, and suddenly he was running to the Black Museum. Simon the Zealot was nowhere to be seen, as usual. It bothered him that Simon was always busy inside the Time Fields and ready with some story about making an inventory or mapping the further reaches. He would have to spend some time in the Museum and find out what Simon was really up to, but that could wait.

He passed through the outer room with its glass cabinets full of knives, bottles of poison, death masks and old photographs of the criminals and the desperate, and entered the Key Room. Once inside, he walked down one side of the great table. The Key Room was just a rectangle on the architects' plan of the Yard, but there was magic here, and the dimensions of the room were surprising. The great table was so long that it took him ten minutes to find the key he was looking for, and if he had decided to walk on another ten minutes, or even forty, he would still not have reached the very end – not by a long stretch.

The key he was looking for was placed at the centre of the table, surrounded by a collection of the strangest objects. It was a tiny silver bell, thin and covered in dust. Judas lifted it gently and then gave it a shake. The bell produced one single, clear note, and then somewhere, lost in the midst of the mists of time it sounded again, and Judas closed his eyes.

When he reopened them, he was standing in the middle of a drawing room in a Victorian house. The curtains were closed and constructed of such a thick, dense material that had it not been for the oil lamps, of which there were many, it would have been pitch black inside the room. A silver fire crackled in the hearth, flames and wisps that should have been yellow and gold looked cold and hard, and above it, on the mantlepiece, were thousands of pictures in silver frames.

In each frame was a woman, and instead of a broad smile, or a shy grin, there was only sorrow and despair captured there. Judas waited for his eyes to become accustomed to the gloom. A thin sheet of hanging dust divided the room in two; the particles moved so slowly that Judas had to keep reminding himself that there was life here. Sitting next to the fire was an elderly lady, white-haired, a string of pearls at her neck, cotton ruffles at the end of her sleeves and in her arms a dog, so dead that only its skeleton, a few tufts of hair, and the collar that it was dragged around on remained. The lady stared out into the room, unmoving. And then she sensed his presence, twitched, and forced her hand into the flames of the fire.

"Come again, come again, you watchers above! Come again, come again, and tell me of love!" she chanted.

Judas watched as she removed her hand; it was not even singed.

"You are the Lady in Waiting, I have need of a favour," said Judas.

The old lady sniffed the air like a dog on the scent.

"Oh, it is you, the Warden of Lies, the Master of Deceit and Betrayer! What do you want of me this time, Judas?"

Judas crossed the room and placed his hand upon a chair that was tucked into the folds of a round table, then he dragged it very slowly across the thick carpet and placed it directly in front of the old lady. He settled himself upon the chair and crossed his legs, then removed the silver coin from his pocket. The old lady recoiled immediately and hissed, but Judas pretended not to notice her reaction and turned the coin over and over in his hand. The clock on the wall turned its tick and tock into the beat of a bass drum, and Judas watched and waited for the dreaded beast that guarded the Place of Beginnings to come forth.

He turned the coin over, stopping occasionally to rub his thumb across the smooth side, and then he turned it over again, and again.

"What is it that you want, gatekeeper?"

Its voice crackled, and Judas was reminded of a great fire that has raged and is now spent and sputtering.

"I would like to visit the *Place of Beginnings*," he said.

"And would you pay the toll?" The old lady stroked the bones in her lap.

"I don't think so; you've eaten far too many already," said Judas.

The old lady hissed again, and then, casting off the crusty old bones that were once dressed in the skin of a Fox Terrier, she reared up and became the beast that guarded the gateway to the Place of Beginnings. The bones flew across the room, white feathers in the gloom, and then hit the floor and were swallowed immediately by the deep shag pile of the rug.

"I bet those bones are not the first that the carpet has

tasted, are they?" quipped Judas.

His attempt at some low form of wit or humour earned him another hiss from the monster; this time, the hiss was so loud and deep that it reminded him of the London Necropolis steam engine.

"Enough!" shouted Judas.

"Oh! Well, thank you very much; it's not every day that I get a visitor, and I have been practising that for ages; I didn't even get a chance to show you my new wings properly, or the tail. It's magnificent if you'd only let me give it a swish," whined the beast.

"Much as I would love to watch your performance, Millie, I don't have the time; I'm sorry. The wings looked rather good, though; why not make them a bit thinner, so you can see through them almost? The bile was very good. Unexpected," he replied.

The beast shrank in size before him, but it did not revert to the body of an old lady. Millie took on her true form this time; she was an ancient creature, fierce and deadly if cornered or threatened. Half lion, half man, and with a tail that could take on the characteristics of a poisonous snake. She was the stuff of nightmares and had killed many. Millie was a confused Manticore and had lived peacefully and contentedly in the Time Fields for a very long time, thanks to Judas.

"The thing is, Millie, the people that were after you all those long years ago are no more; you could leave any time you wanted, you know? I could help you get settled, find you a job, get you a flat, sort out your Council Tax and HMRC."

Millie shuddered and brought her large paws together like a parish priest who had just fallen asleep for the third time in the middle of a service.

"You wouldn't! Look at me; I can't hide this; I'm half *lion* and half *woman* on my good days! And how would you live with yourself if those creatures came back for me, and don't say that you'd sleep fine. I'm no good out there, Judas, I'm all twisted up here in the noggin. I jump at the slightest thing. That lamp over there, the one on the Grand Piano, that stays on all night. The dark bothers me, there are evil things hiding in it."

Millie was clearly troubled by the concept of venturing back into the world of the Under Folk. Judas always teased her; he thought that she liked it in a strange way. He imagined and hoped that it made her feel more like a person than a feline. She was a savage creature by nature and powerful, but when he had come across her in the cellar belonging to a very powerful priest of a nasty sect called the Shining Mirror, she had looked like a greyhound on a crash diet. Her teeth were brown, and her claws were more like rounded stubs. Millie had been drained of her magical powers, and the priest, an idiot called Udo Hammerhein, had experimented on her to the point that she was more dead than alive.

At the time he had only been in post for a few decades and was still getting used to the job and what was expected of him. If there was any pity left in him after the Archangel Michael had given him a crash course in ethics and compassion, he spent it all on Millie. He carried her away from that infernal hole and brought her back to the Black Museum. He had to hide her, to begin with.

The half-light of the Time Fields suited her, and she didn't seem to mind eating meat that she hadn't killed herself. After a short time, she was well enough to slink around and help herself to what food she could find in the station. Judas had decided to give her a place in the Time

Fields because she was too scared to leave. He hated looking at her then; she was an apex predator. In her prime she would have been magnificent, but they had cut her to pieces, and what heart she had once possessed was now lost. His pity tortured him, and he wanted to find Udo Hammerhein and feed him to Millie. She would have probably turned her nose up at him, though.

"I'm only joking, Millie. You're not going anywhere. I need you here," he said.

"I know that, silly!" said Millie.

Judas collected the bits of bone that he could still see from the rug. They weren't bones, of course; it was a rib cage whittled from the half-burnt logs in the fire.

"How long did this take you? Not bad at all, they actually look like bones this time. Do you remember that half-eaten baby you made from a turnip, an old cushion and some soot from the chimney?"

"I was just practising, Inspector. I have got better though, haven't I? You had to look twice at these here bones, don't lie now!" said Millie.

"They are very life-like, Millie, though I don't believe I've seen a dog with two spines and an extra rib cage?"

Millie scampered across the floor, snuffling for the remainder of her wooden bones and when she had retrieved most of them she padded across the room and sat down on her chair.

"What do you need, Inspector? How might Millie the Mighty Manticore serve thee?"

Judas sat back in his chair and rubbed at his temples.

"A young girl died recently. She was manipulated and then killed with a rare form of powerful magic, so that makes it my business. And because of the nature of her passing, she'll be waiting in the Place of Beginnings, wondering what the hell she's doing there. I need some information, Millie. In fact, I'm desperate for it. And, if she agrees to do a little bit of surveillance for me, maybe I can help her along the long road – and she can do me a favour at the same time."

Millie's long tail flicked and swished.

"I can take you to the stepping-off point, and if you need me to watch your back, just say so," said Millie.

Judas stood up and flicked a small piece of wood from his jacket. It flew towards the fire and would have surely perished but Millie moved with incredible speed and caught the chip in her paw.

"That's the dog's second vertebra!"

"I'm sure it once looked that way," said Judas.

"Funny," said Millie.

Then she turned away from him and jumped into the fire. Judas waited for a second, then followed her.

The Time Fields are vast. They are a spiralling, ever-changing mass of moments; a combination of spaces and places where killers, convicts and the evil are held in limbo, watching the world they knew and the innocents that they wanted to slaughter passing them by, just out of reach. It is the ultimate punishment.

The Place of Beginnings is where the newly dead are forced to congregate. There is no boatman here to take them on, nor is there any giant standing guard over a bright pathway through a forest of ancient oaks with riddles that require answers or inscrutable beasts ready to weigh the measure of your soul with a feather or a gem that can see into the depths of your soul. This place is far from that in every way; instead of a jetty or sea of doorways, there is a giant black flattened rock face, riven with the scars of brutal thunder and vicious lightning. Near the top is an opening, a vast black spot that goes deep into the stone.

A thin spur of rock protrudes directly underneath; it reaches out into the silver air like a jagged finger pointing to a horizon that none can see. Wisps of something grey hang from the underside of the digit, blowing from side to side like a beard on a dead man's chin. If the throng waiting at the base of the spot in the stone looked more closely, they would see that the wisps are the stretched and empty skins of those who chose to jump; if they looked even closer, they would see that the skins are still alive, their mouths forever forming the words 'help' and 'please'.

The Place of Beginnings is special; it is a place for those that have been touched by evil or involved against their wishes in some foul deed. Brainwashed, misled, controlled and conned, the reasons for their incarceration here are endless, because there is no clear division between their good and bad actions in life. They are trapped here, and they mill about with eyes glazed and memories dulled, dragging their feet in the black ash on the ground, mute and confused. The sky above them crackles with black lightning that makes no sound, and sporadically, there is movement and the crowds jostle; the grey clouds roll away, and a black shaft of dead light shoots out of the gloom and connects the rock face to the Time Fields. One of the dead hears a silent call and shuffles forward, places one foot on the black light and then they are gone. The remaining dead continue to carve their presence into the ash with their heels.

The land that surrounds the rock is marsh and desert; pools of black water reflect what little light there is so that they become small discs of silver. Fell and foul creatures roam the grey rivers, and evil spirits dress in the raiment of the mists. To walk here unaided is pure folly, and the ground underfoot squelches not with mud and dew but with the fleshy remains of the foolish.

Millie loped ahead, her paws disturbing no stone nor causing any pool to ripple. She had been here many times before and read the signs and pathways of the marsh grass as though she was reading a child's picture book. Judas could see her in the half-light, moving with the ease that only her kind possess. Occasionally, the manticore stopped and sniffed at the air but found nothing of interest in the breeze, so she gave a little snarl, snapped her jaws at the false scent and moved on. Judas followed behind, making sure to follow in her footsteps. Millie found the opening to the stairway that led up to the Place of Beginnings with ease; when Judas caught up with her, she had started to whittle at a piece of dark wood that she had found on the ground.

"That isn't wood, Millie," said Judas.

"If it isn't wood, then what is it?" she asked.

"The people that climb these stairs still have some connection to the real world, and when the reality sets in that they are not heading to Heaven or Hell, they have a tendency to panic; to get angry; to question their place in the great scheme of things. It is at that moment they feel the greatest hurt. They realise that they have been wronged in the real world, and cheated and lied to in the next. It is not the image or notion of Heaven that they imagined. And so, they argue and shout at the sky, they call everything into question – their faith and all of the good things they have done – and then they break down in tears."

"And what has that to do with the whittling of a stick,

Judas?" said Millie.

"Well, Millie, it is to do with the discovery that you are in a place you didn't deserve to be in and the realisation there is a long, hard walk through a cold, harsh land ahead. And, when that fact lands on them like an overweight Sumo wrestler, they have a tendency to get a little overwrought. And they panic. And then they empty their bowels. Over time, their brown purges turn to dark, wooden-like cigars. Often mistaken for bones, I hear."

Millie dropped the brown bone she had been whittling, and if a manticore ever looked angry, Millie did.

"That was very helpful, Judas; I thank you," she said.

"It's a pleasure, wouldn't want you to start exhibiting your latest creations and then be told that they're shit – actual shit," said a very smug Judas.

Millie scuffed her paws on the ground and sniffed at them. Then she looked up at Judas, hissed, and loped away into the mist. Judas smiled once again and started to climb the stone steps carved into the rock face. He reached a landing where the stairs led into the mouth of a dark tunnel and the sky above disappeared.

The stone walls of the passageway had been rubbed smooth by the hands of the countless climbers that had used it before him, and set at irregular intervals in the deeper handholds were small brass saucers with a candle at the centre. The light they gave off was blue and it took Judas a little time to get used to it. When he reached the top of the stairs there was another landing and at the far end of it was an opening. Judas walked towards it, and that is when he started to see them.

. . .

There were hundreds of people milling about; some were looking up at the strange sky, and some had taken to sitting with their backs against the rough stone. A few were standing at the very edge of the promontory, looking down and struggling to find the courage to leap. At any other time, and in any other place, Judas would have acted like the policeman he was, and he would have gone to their aid, but these poor souls were newly dead and could not be saved. It pained him to see them there, but he had work to do, and he needed to find the girl that had been weaponised and sent out to cause mayhem.

Judas pushed his way through the crowd; it reminded him of an exhibition he had attended featuring the works of the fashion designer Alexander McQueen; some of the women were wearing court costumes, huge gowns with peacock feathers and lace.

The men wore smocks for working in the fields or grey pin-stripe suits for the City. A few held nosegays to their faces. There were even a couple of men that looked like a tribute Bowie band, with platform boots on their feet and bouffant hair. It was clear that some of them had been waiting on this ledge for a long time.

He was beginning to think he might have missed her; maybe she had decided to jump, or she had not climbed the stairs at all; if she had chosen another path, this line of enquiry would be closed, and he would have to do things the hard way. He turned around and retraced his steps; Millie was waiting for him at the opening, and she had the girl he was looking for in her mouth. As he drew near, Millie dropped the girl onto the ground and placed one of her huge paws on the girl's back.

"I found her on the stairs, curled up in a ball, hiding," said Millie.

An Ink So Dark

"How did you know she was the one I was looking for?" said Judas.

"She smells the freshest, she's a dead girl, and she's been beaten rather badly at some point recently, all the clues you'd ever need to find someone that DCI Judas Iscariot was looking for." Millie lifted her great paw and helped the girl up.

"Hello, I am the man that Millie here is referring to; she won't hurt you, by the way, she's trying to go vegan, aren't you, Millie?"

Millie snorted loudly and the girl flinched.

"A little bit of desiccated flesh every now and again won't hurt ..." Millie growled.

The girl drew closer to Judas.

"Stop that, Millie," said Judas.

Millie snuffled; it was her way of giggling; then she turned around and disappeared back down the stairs.

Judas reached over and placed his hand on the girl's shoulder.

"I need to ask you a few questions I'm afraid. Do you know where you are and how you got here?" he asked.

The girl shook her head, it was a small, almost imperceptible movement. She was confused, that much was clear, as you would be if you had been tattooed, placed under a magic spell and then kicked to death by a group of trendy types in a private club in the heart of Soho. Judas led her to the stairs.

"Come with me and I will try to explain what has happened to you," he said.

The girl nodded meekly and followed him. When they reached the bottom of the stairs, Judas led her to the trunk of a fallen tree and invited her to sit.

"Now, this is going to be hard to understand and even

harder to take in, but I'm going to try and speak clearly and there will be moments where I may come across as being a bit blunt, but that's for your own good. Okay?"

The girl closed her eyes and placed both hands in her lap. Judas took this has permission and started to talk.

"You are dead. You will have looked about you and realised that all is not as it should be, but even so, you might have thought yourself to be asleep, possibly in a hospital, the victim of a hit and run perhaps. Regardless, this is where you are now. This rock and the marshes that surround it is called a Place of Beginnings; it's a sort of crossroads, if you like. But not the stepping-off point that you may have hoped for or imagined. In most religions, there is a place where the blessed and the damned congregate before they take the road ordained. The bad go left, the good go right. This is not that place. You were put under a magical spell when you were tattooed recently. The symbolic meaning behind the tattoo affected you in some way so that you were able to discover other people's secrets and then use them to cause pain. I really need to know who gave you the tattoo, where you received it, how it felt, who else was there. Anything that you can recall will help me to catch the creature that caused your death."

The girl twitched at the sound of the word 'tattoo'. There was a part of her, locked away, that recognised it and knew it had something to do with her current predicament. The girl had been used; he pitied her, and he wanted to make amends. When God had lifted him up from the floor of the olive grove and put him back together, this was what he had wanted from Judas, surely? To save people like this girl. Judas reached into his pocket for his silver coin and waited for the girl to settle and speak.

Millie was hunting nearby. He caught flashes of her

powerful flanks and tail in the mist. She was circling around them; constantly on the move, hunting for something, not because she was hungry he imagined but because that was what she did, when not masquerading as an elderly spinster. He heard a pounce and a splash, then the reeds parted and he saw a dark pool behind them. Something small and wounded squealed, then came the sound of powerful jaws snapping and ... silence.

Judas imagined she did it to remind herself that she was a predator, or maybe it was just muscle memory. It kept her busy, nonetheless. The sky above grumbled and changed colour a number of times, followed by a silence that sounded more menacing than the lightning. Judas looked at the girl. She was motionless, staring at something a hundred years away. He sighed and pocketed his silver coin. She was damaged, and he realised he had made a mistake in coming here; she would be of no use to him and he felt guilty about pumping her for information. He stood then, brushed a couple of grey twigs from his trousers and was about to whistle for Millie when the girl spoke.

"He had a caravan. It was old, wooden, gypsy, Romany. Under a tree it was. The sun dipping behind it, magical. It was hot and there was music coming from beyond the trees. The boy I had met earlier ... he smelt nice, we made love. The man with the ink ... short dark hair ... kept saying 'Clonfert' under his breath like he was trying to remember something. He smiled too much and trembled as the pen scraped over my skin. It was weird but not uncomfortable ... there were bottles, glass bottles on the shelves. I think I heard voices, crying and screaming. *"Don't do it!"* they shouted, but it was too late. We were in a dream, we smelt of sex, and we were free. Then we went to sleep – and I never woke up again."

Judas laid his hand on the girl's shoulder.

"Can you describe the man who did this to you in any more detail? Did he have an accent? His horse – what colour was it? Did he have any tattoos?" Judas could see some light in her eyes now; there was a chance that she was coming back from the brink.

"Anything? The smallest thing might help me find him," he said.

"Can I come back, away from this? Can you save me?" the girl asked, but she knew the answer already.

"No," said Judas.

"I was going to ask what was in it for me, but I presume the answer is nothing?"

Judas squeezed her shoulder then removed his hand.

"You'd presume right, but there is something that I can do for you. If you choose to help me and accept my offer you will have some sort of life, and you will have a purpose, a reason for being, I suppose. It will mean that I will call upon you to help me on occasion. If you can do that, I can offer you a way out of this. Not the entire way, but some of the way."

The girl opened her eyes again and Judas could see that some colour was returning to them.

"He had a soft Irish accent, green eyes, pale skin, and his hands moved constantly. His fingers twitched as if he were searching for something in the air, something invisible, but when he took up his pen and paper, he stopped fidgeting and mumbling and became still. I saw a boat, small it was. There was a man with a map, a navigator in a sea, rough and dark. And a mysterious island, undiscovered. And there was a traitor – and someone that wanted him dead." The girl closed her eyes again, she was spent, and Judas knew that he would get no more.

Judas whistled to Millie. Her head appeared from behind a clump of bullrushes, and then she padded forwards and sat down in front of them both.

"Catch anything, Millie?" said Judas.

"Oh, loads, Inspector. The pools hereabouts are teeming with life, hadn't you noticed?" she said sarcastically.

The girl did not step back or flinch at the sight of the manticore. Instead, she lifted her hand and allowed Millie to snuffle against it.

"Mmmmm, dead flesh and old ink, lovely!" said Millie.

"Don't be rude; smell me again; there's a festival and fun, love and sex in there," said the girl.

Millie growled and bared her sharp jagged teeth, but she returned to the hand once more and sniffed hard.

"True, there it is, just beyond the present, a shadow's width from the now. Mmmm, I taste a young man. Dark, sticky beer, the sweat of dancing and the faint odour of fatty burgers and strong mustard. Let me lick your hand, my love," said Millie.

"Bugger off! said the girl.

Judas stepped in between them.

"There won't be any scrapping here; you can later, if it floats your boat, but not now. What festival did you go to? How many nights did you spend there? And did you pay cash or card for your ink?"

The girl glared at the manticore but when Millie reared up onto her hind legs and showed her teeth, she decided that she may not have much of a chance in a fight, even though she were already dead.

"We both paid in cash, the festival was in Brockwell Park, and I was there for two nights. What will happen to me now then, DCI Judas Iscariot? What will be my payment for the information?"

Judas signalled to Millie and the manticore loped off.

"There is a place nearby; it is called the Time Fields. The inmates call it by many other names but it is a prison, a very harsh and unforgiving prison. All of the worst criminals that have ever breathed are there, reliving their days over and over again in a savage, never-ending cycle. They live and exist in close proximity to their prey, but the people they once stalked, harassed, tortured and murdered are always just out of reach. It is a prison of temptation and constant rejection. A hard place indeed.

"But there are also spirits and the ghosts of those that meant no real harm in there. Some of them help me to solve crimes in the real world, and for that they are given their freedom. They can live a life away from the scum and the villainy of the Time Fields, and move between time zones, eras and centuries. This is what I can offer you."

The girl straightened.

"What is it that you want?" she said.

"I will give you free rein to come and go as you please within the Time Fields, and also inside the Black Museum, a place you will come to know in time. I ask that you watch – no, spy on – a man, who has, I believe, explored some of the distant parts of this place and started to map them, a man called Simon the Zealot. He has close ties with Jack the Ripper, and is not to be underestimated. As a soul that has no real connection to any of the Time Fields you may move amongst these places and follow him. There is real danger in this undertaking though, and I am asking a lot of you, because if Simon discovers you and he manages to lay his hands on you, things might go very badly."

The girl gave him a weak smile and sighed.

"I am dead. Brutally murdered by people I didn't even know. Trapped at the top of a godforsaken mountain by you, the man who betrayed God's son. And you ask me to trust you! Then there is this hellish place, like something on Netflix, full of savages and serial killers held in some sort of limbo. And you say I can have the keys to the kingdom if I spy on one of your 'friends' there, but if I get caught, things 'might go badly' for me! How much worse can it get?!"

Judas had to smile.

"It's a brilliant offer, isn't it? I have the contract right here, and you get 25 days' holiday a year, free smoothies on a Friday and a choice of Yoga or Pilates!"

The girl did not respond at first, so Judas waited for his words to settle, and for her to think them over. She sat very still, her eyes darting here and there. Occasionally, when a swirl of ash floated in front of her face, she tried to flick it away like a moth. Above them, another fork of black lightning spiked and speared the rock, and as they looked up they saw another figure, tiny against the clouds, walk along the lightning and disappear into the blur of the Time Fields.

"Are there many like me?" said the girl.

"There are a few humans. There are also a couple of horses, a parrot and some hounds – you can work out what sort of hounds. And there are the ghosts," said Judas.

"And are they approachable? Can I speak to them? Will they tolerate me?"

The girl had a quick mind. Judas could sense that she had already come to terms, or at least partially, with her current situation. Black Bess, Dick Turpin's faithful steed, had galloped away from him for many years. She had taken a long time to settle in the Time Fields.

"All of them are wayward and can be troublesome at times, but they are, on the whole, good villains," he said.

The girl gulped and turned her head away. Judas saw her shoulders sag and she sobbed for a few minutes. He wanted to reach out to her and put an arm around her shoulders but the time was not right. Then, she rubbed at her face and took a deep breath.

"Okay. I will do it. I will spy on this man for you. But I know so little of this place. How it works. What I am allowed to do and what I shouldn't. I have so many questions. I think you need me to help you right now, but I'm not convinced I can. I'd probably take a wrong turn, or say the wrong thing. I can't walk into this ... this Place of Beginnings and the Time Fields without knowing more about them," said the girl.

"That's wise, and not unexpected. Time works strangely here and fluctuates from one Time Field to the next. I can take you somewhere and to someone that can help teach you more about what happens here. She's a bit strange, at first, but there is nothing more she likes than an audience, and she is a good soul – and won't attempt to eat you," said Judas.

The girl sniffed and then stood up. Judas rose with her.

"Where are we going then?" she asked.

He pointed into the mist in the direction that Millie the Manticore had taken. The girl set off. He fell into step next to her and thought about engaging her in further conversation but decided that any more words now would not work well. So, he waited and when they had been walking for a few minutes he spoke to her about the Black Museum, broad brushstrokes only, and how it worked and whom she might meet there. Her mood seemed to lighten and Judas decided that it was time for her to step into the fire.

Judas reached out to her with his hand open, palm uppermost. She nodded then laid her hand on top of his. He

An Ink So Dark

gripped it tightly then stepped into a dark shadow hanging in the air. She followed, and seconds later they were standing in a large, dusty drawing room with a grand piano, tall bookshelves crammed with first editions and as much dust as you could handle.

Millie the Manticore lay before the fire, her snake tail swishing back and forth and her ears flicking as if to dislodge some invisible fly.

"Millie, my love, I have a guest for you. She will need your help, and wisdom," said Judas.

"You are so pompous, you know that? Leave her with me and I'll see to it that she understands exactly what snake oil you are pedalling. Now do one!" said Millie.

"Do one?" he replied.

"I heard some of the rough lads, the boys who used to work the streets, using it. It means 'get lost'." Millie purred like a scooter.

"You're hanging around with the wrong crowd, Millie, you're becoming very uncouth," Judas replied.

Millie roared. The girl stepped backwards, her eyes wide with terror.

"See what you've done, Millie?" he said.

"Oh, don't be so silly, girly, come over here and warm yourself, and I shall tell you all about DCI Judas Iscariot of the Black Museum at Scotland Yard. And of the angels, the devils, and the deep blue sea where the dead swim, and of the great bridges that connect all of the places in all of the worlds."

Judas watched the girl settle, then he turned away. Seconds later, he was back in the Key Room.

Chapter Sixteen

Legionnaire

She had slept badly again. At first, she thought that it might be the wine or the late night dining, or it could just be that some of her old life in Whitechapel was trying to remind her that although she was no longer part of the old Whitechapel, those streets were still part of her. Meg sat up and after rearranging her pillows into a silken upturned 'V', she reached for the water jug on the side table, poured the contents into the large glass beside it and then drained it. The water was crisp and cold and as it travelled down her throat she felt the scar on her neck twitch. Meg tried to snuggle back down into the bedsheets but she was awake five minutes later. She stared at the ceiling, becoming angry and frustrated that sleep eluded her; and to add insult to injury, the jug was now empty.

She swung her legs across to one side, eased herself off the bed and stood up. She grabbed the jug and started to walk across the bedroom floor towards the bathroom. Meg was naked, save the silk scarf that she always wore around her neck; the only time she was without it was when she was in the shower or the bath. Her long legs and broad shoulders could have belonged to an Olympic rower and her dark brown hair, almost black in colour reached down to the middle of her back. To a stranger, she would have been beautiful – a woman of certain years, perhaps, but still handsome and fair.

Unfortunately, the young man who had been hired to kill her, and who was hiding behind the super-heavy Heals velvet curtains, did not know that she was one of Jack the Ripper's victims, brought back to life by the Silent King of the Resurrection Men, and head of a very powerful, all-female gang that were incredibly rich with connections all the way up the societal ladder to certain members of the Royal Court. He was capable – five years in the Legion had turned him into a killer – but he was outmatched and woefully underprepared for what was about to happen to him.

Meg had been slaughtered once already. She had also been burnt, tortured, shot, stabbed, and a few creative souls had tried to eliminate her with a JCB. One of them had tried to feed her to his dogs, and then there was the head boy of an East London Roadman collective that had purchased 100 gallons of acid and made a metal coffin for her. When the police found the Top Boy, just two teeth remained, and they only survived the cleansing chemicals because they were hidden behind the gangster's diamond rail that he wore over his pearly whites. It was safe to say that she was hard, tough as a gypsy's dog and ferocious when she, or any of her girls, were attacked.

The young man waited until she was almost at the bathroom door before he slipped out from behind the curtains.

He brought his right hand up with his dagger pointed towards the target, as he had been taught by the experts in Marseilles, and leapt forwards. He was going to stab her underneath the arm first, then when she searched for the new wound with her other, good hand, he would stick her in the neck. It was an old, yet reliable form of attack. You hurt, they react, then you hurt them again. If you can get one hand to cover the wound, the rest of the body is yours. The only problem with his current strategy was that the target had disappeared, and the only thing he could see was a triangle of moonlight that hung in the centre of the room.

"Hello, lover. Is that for me?"

The young man froze. The voice was coming from behind him, and in front of him. He knew better than to spin around or make any sudden movements. His instructor had warned him again and again that in a knife fight nerves were sharper than any blade. So, he waited.

"You're awfully young for this kind of business, aren't you? Barely thirty, I'd say. Proficient with a knife, three horizontal creases ironed into the back of your shirt, healthy tan, March or Die tattoo. I'd say we have a French Foreign Legion man here, am I right?"

The man did not move. He knew he was in trouble now, and he needed to find a way out.

"The Falcon Brothers approached me through an intermediary. They want you dead. I was around. I took the job ... I failed. I can return the favour and take out one or both of the Falcons, no fee?" he pleaded.

"So, the Falcon Brothers, London's most powerful Real Estate company, want me dead? Tell me Beau Geste, am I the only target? I hope for you and your employers' sake that I am, because if any of my girls are in this same situation, their would-be assassins won't get off as lightly as you."

The voice was everywhere. He could not pin it down, and a bead of sweat ran down the back of his neck and slipped between his shoulder blades.

"You are the only one ... that I know of," he said.

"That would make sense," said the voice.

The bathroom light clicked on, and a solid yellow bar appeared at the bottom of the closed bathroom door. The young man had a choice now. Slip away as quickly and as quietly as he could and hope that she did not follow; or take a chance, slip across the room, kick the door open and let his steel do the talking.

He may have been young, he may have only done his five years in the Legion, and he may not have finished top of his class at school, but there is something that all soldiers know, regardless of how long they have been carrying a rifle and how many war zones they might have survived. You never go into combat if the terrain is unknown or has changed recently, or you are up against a superior force. So, he took one step backwards, sheathed his dagger and reached out behind him for the shelter of the curtain. His hands met steel instead of velvet.

"That was the right choice to make, little boy."

The voice was in his ear, so close that he could feel the warmth from her breath on his neck. He tried to pull his hand back but it was caught in a vice-like grip.

"Veux-tu mourir, képi blanc?

"Non."

"That's good. I haven't been sleeping so well of late, and that does make me a bit cranky. Now, how about you drop the dagger point-first into the carpet, then you remove the cheese-wire garotte from your top left pocket, and drop that on the floor next to the blade. You follow?"

The young man took his dagger out and, holding the hilt

between forefinger and thumb with the tip pointing downwards, released it and heard it 'thunk' into the carpet. Then he flipped up the flap of the chest pocket on his jacket using his only free hand, slowly reached inside it and pulled out the garotte.

"A nasty weapon, young man. The choice of the assassin," said the voice.

He was somewhere between panic and confusion now. His world had turned upside down. He was supposed to be speaking the chill words of death into the ear of the target, and yet, here he was, the victim. Time moved so slowly; every moment lasted an age. His heart was thumping, and he realised he was dead.

"Now, before you get any ideas of doing the secret service thing and trying to turn this situation to your advantage, with action or deed, please don't.

"You are out of your depth, which makes me wonder why you were sent. I'm sure you're very good at your job, but you aren't up to this one. Either you've been sent by someone who doesn't realise who they're dealing with, or just to warn me that I might be over-reaching myself. I'm going to go for the former. And that is why I'm not going to let you live."

The voice was strong and it was so close now that it seemed to be inside his head.

He felt the grip on his wrist tighten, and then he was pulled backwards so quickly and with such force that it reminded him of the night jumps he had done over French Guyana.

The plane's door opened, the green light went on. You stood up, hooked yourself onto the static line that ran down the length of the aircraft, shuffled forwards and then, when you were in the opening with the world tearing past at 1,000 miles an hour, you took one step forwards and the hand of God grabbed you by the shoulder and threw you into the sky.

That was what this felt like. He was pulled, lifted and turned all in one swift, fluid movement, then he felt his head being pushed up against the cold glass of the window. Pressure was applied to the back of his head and with the force of a giant wave he was pushed through the glass. It shattered all around him and he saw perfect triangles spinning in the moonlight like a kaleidoscope.

Then he saw his own hand, writing the letter that he left in the halls of residence with his only friend. The letter that told his grandfather, the only one of his family that ever cared for him or showed him anything like love, that he had decided to join the French Foreign Legion. Then he saw the white gloved hand of his commanding officer taking his dark blue beret – the mark of the would-be soldier – from his hand and with a flick, casting it onto the dusty parade square, to be forgotten. He had passed the course! A real, French Foreign Legionnaire. He was hard, tough, strong.

Before he hit the ground, the young man saw many other things. His friendships with fellow loners and outcasts. The first stirrings of love with the girl from the diving school in Grenada, and his disgust at the pawing of the older gentleman that was so happy to hear his story and wanted only a little physical recompense in return for $200. But there was not much more. The end of a life is quiet. There are no fanfares. The young man had only one last thought: he wished he had never entered the room of the woman with the scarf around her neck.

. . .

Meg watched the boy fly out of the window, propelled by her own hand. She saw him spin and turn in the air. The lights from a nearby housing block illuminated his fall. He spun and flashed in the night sky – first dark, then yellow, then dark again. All the way down. All twenty-two floors.

"Try and kill any of the Women of the Chapel and that will be your reward," she spat.

She returned to her bed and pulled the Egyptian cotton covers up. She was tired now, or at least she felt she could sleep at last. But there was something not quite right. The shattered window was not a major issue, of course. She knew it was there, she'd just thrown an assassin through it. The soft billow of the velvet curtain was quite nice; it gave her the impression that she was not alone, that there was something in the room with her.

Meg untied the silk scarf at her neck and cast it away. It floated across the room like an airborne gossamer snake. When it landed on the thick carpet, it sighed ever so lightly. It was almost apologetic, a mere silk hiss. Her neck was exposed for a second and her left hand came up instinctively to cover her scars, but there was no one here to see them anymore.

She lay back against her pillows and stroked the purple, knotted scar around her neck. For some reason it created a not unwelcome sensation. Meg pulled her hand away, feeling that she had somehow betrayed herself with sensual and sexual thoughts. She had been a prostitute long ago, during Jack the Ripper's time, and had been used terribly by the scum that roamed the streets of Whitechapel, and the scum that floated into Whitechapel onboard the ships that came in from the sea. This old wound just reminded her of pain, not love.

There were other marks on her body, of course. One of

An Ink So Dark

the many scars she carried started at her suprasternal notch and ran all the way down. Not in a straight line, sadly. The drunken police surgeon's knife had wavered and strayed as it cut her open down her trunk, finishing just below her belly button. Jack the Ripper had painted her with his fury then consigned her and her friends to Hell and history. 'Why' was still a mystery, even now, hundreds of years later.

Meg and her sisters were the butchered prostitutes of Whitechapel. The dirty and the desperate, the weak and unfortunate, slaves to gin and to the surge of progress, victims of a world where only the privileged survived. If they had looked in the mirror and seen past the familiar, they would have seen themselves anew; as drudges, with chapped lips and bloodshot eyes, gin-soaked and hungry, happy to debase themselves for the price of a bottle of grog and a kind word. Jack the Ripper had tried to destroy her, and he had failed, then this little amateur hitman had wormed his way into her apartment and tried to slice her open. Meg punched the pillow and made herself comfortable. She sighed and thought about what had happened, then smiled.

That worked out well, didn't it?

She rolled over onto her side and tried to sleep again but there was something else. Not an assailant – he was gone. They would be scraping him off the pavement in the morning. There was something else here. It was softly scratching at her from somewhere deep in her past. She could feel it inside, goading and spiteful. A memory. A connection that she had tried to destroy many years ago.

Meg sat bolt upright, as though she had heard a sound. Her eyes were wide open and her pulse began to beat like a muffled drum. The realisation was an alarm that sounded first in her heart and then her mind, and she quickly reached for her mobile on the bedside table and called the others. She already knew what she would ask them. She knew how she would try to elicit the truth – suggest rather than imply, cajole and then focus – but in her heart of hearts, she knew that they would all have the same answer.

"I have been dreaming of him. He is still there, just at the periphery of my vision, watching and waiting for me to lift my chin so he can slice at my neck."

This is what they would all say.

Meg spoke to each of them in turn, dropped her phone, then took out a pack of rolling tobacco from the first drawer. She opened the plastic wallet and reached inside; she had already rolled a few and she selected the longest and most well-constructed. Meg hated smoking, but what she disliked even more was a flimsy roll-up.

She was the strongest of them all. It had been her responsibility to lift the others and will them into existence. She was totally happy with that, she felt comfortable in that role, but she was afraid now – and if *she* was afraid, something bad was afoot.

The Women of the Chapel (with the aid of Judas and the Black Museum at Scotland Yard) had destroyed Jack the Ripper. Or at least they thought they had.

Meg took a drag on her roll-up then tried to create a Gandalfian smoke ring. She tried again and again until just a centimetre of cigarette paper remained between her fingertips, but failed – miserably. The bedroom was now full of silvery-grey plumes moving in slow motion, gently making their way into the ether like disintegrating strands of thought. Later that night, she dreamt of Judas and saw him locked in mortal combat with a huge bear of a man with long lank dark hair and porcelain white skin. Their fight was bloody and shocking but when she woke, she could not remember which one had been victorious.

In the morning she would go and pay a visit to the Yard and request a favour from the only man she really trusted, and the only one she was truly afraid of.

Chapter Seventeen

Gone to the Dogs

Rylee was nearly one and a half years old. He had been returned to the Home twice that year already and the staff were becoming concerned about his welfare, and his future. There were only so many times that Rylee could misbehave and blot his copybook. Rylee was a German Wire-Haired Pointer and his current abode, and probably his last if he didn't get his act together, was the world-famous Battersea Dogs Home. Rylee didn't want to live in the city. Nor did he want to share a house with noisy children. And he *hated* cats. These requirements had reduced the number of potential new owners month on month, and a one-way trip to the vets was on the cards.

Rylee was energetic and he loved other dogs, sometimes a little too roughly, and on occasion, rather too passionately. He could run all day, didn't mind the rain or the cold, and he had a good nose on him. It was the nose that got him into trouble.

It was early in the evening when Rylee picked up the scent of something that excited him. He started to pace. Then he started to scratch at the door. One of the helpers heard him and came to his door to find out why he was acting so strangely. When she opened it Rylee made his bid for freedom. He raced across the Astroturf where he was exercised most days, evaded not one but three other members of staff, and casually leapt over the fence, using one of the outside kennels as his escape platform.

Rylee's nose led him down Lockington Road. He took a sharp left and was approaching Newton Preparatory School when he found the beast he had scented, and attacked. The fight did not last long. One of Rylee's legs was found halfway down the street under a bush, by a local lad. His head was mounted on one of the steel barbs on the top of the school gate and what was left of him had been stuffed inside a dark green box that belonged to the telecoms provider for that area of London. Back at Battersea Dogs Home, a candle was lit for Rylee and his name and lovely photographs were quietly deleted from the website.

The Mason's Arms is a well-attended and popular public house, just around the corner from the prep school and only a short way from the dogs home. There is a Snug at the back, reserved for rather unusual patrons. The door to the Snug is located behind the barrel room. Once through it, there are two flights of steps that take you down to another door, covered with a thick velvet curtain, and beyond, is the Mason's Arms Under.

Standing at the bar on his hind legs is Bullseye. He's wearing a rather fetching two-piece suit from Gieves and Hawkes. He has a friend on Savile Row that runs him up a tailored version of whatever the current trend in men's suits happens to be. The giant dog is necking his third pint of

Guinness and lamenting the tear in the cloth of his jacket to the barman, a cyclops named Gerald.

"Out of nowhere, Gerald! Completely unprovoked, great hairy German thing. I thought it was a friend of Herr Gut, come to try and rinse me for that money he swears I owes him from the Camberwell fight back in March. Which I doesn't owe, as you well knows, Gerald! Another black and white for me will you and have something for yourself whilst you're there, my good man."

"And that is why you are having the tear in your coat, Mr Bullseye?" said the cyclops.

"This is not a coat, it is a jacket, Gerald. But yes. You is correct. The great hound tries to go for me so I has to act," said Bullseye.

"So, are you telling me that ripping a dog to pieces so small that they had to be removed from the street using a dust buster is self-defence then, Bullseye?" said a voice from the back of the room.

The fierce-talking dog spat his freshly poured Guinness out all over the bar. Gerald reached under the counter for his cudgel, an instinctive response to the possibility of a fracas, but when he saw who had spoken, he left it well alone and went back to polishing his pint pots.

"Why there you is, Inspector Judas. You got my note then?" said Bullseye.

Judas, who was sitting in the darkness of one of the leather banquettes, leaned forward so that his face could be seen in the light of the candle that flickered in the centre of the table.

"Yes, Bullseye, here *I* is," said Judas.

. . .

Gerald made three trips to the banquette in under fifteen minutes. That dog was thirsty. He had a tendency toward the theatrical. Long years of solitude and loneliness had taught him to stretch out every conversation to its absolute maximum. His previous life had not been an easy one, and he had fallen into bad ways and learnt to hate far too easily. But, Bullseye had been reborn under the lights of the fighting pits and on the canvas squares of the boxing booths. He was a famous fighter, and with fame comes money and with money comes hangers-on and sharps who give love and interest for monetary gains. Bullseye had learnt to separate those who wished him well from those that wished to make their purses bulge. Judas didn't mind the beast's thirst for contact and smiling face. He had lived in the gutters shunned by all mankind for much longer than the dog.

"You've been dancing around the reason you called me at the Yard and asked to meet up, Bullseye. When you said that you wanted to meet me here, down the road from the Dogs Home, I thought you were pulling my leg! But then, you love to pull a leg don't you, Bullseye? The only problem with that is that you also like to pull the arms off, and the head, and then—"

"Now, now, Inspector. I was the one who was attacked!" said Bullseye.

"It was all a matter of self-defence, yes, I heard you. Now, what is it that you want to tell me?"

The beast shifted uncomfortably in his seat and pushed his empty tankard around with his meaty paw.

"Another?" asked Judas.

"Don't mind if I does, thank you kindly, Inspector."

Judas caught Gerald's single eye and motioned towards the dog's empty pot. The cyclops quickly pulled another pint of the black stuff and placed it upon a circular tray that looked suspiciously like a man-hole cover. Gerald growled his way through the crowd and placed the dog's beverage down in front of him.

"Well then?" said Judas.

"I has some information that I knows is of value to you and I wants something in return." Bullseye was good at fighting but not much good at negotiating.

"How will I know if it is of value to me if you don't get on and tell me what this piece of information is?" Judas was getting impatient now and he reached for his overcoat.

"I has a bottle of ink that screams, Inspector. The ink inside is cursed and holds the life property of some poor soul what has been tortured. I has come across it by the hand of our friend Huxley, who tells me that there are hundreds more of these here bottles with hundreds of poor, damned souls inside them. The creature that has all these dreadful things has a bad mark on it. He's got some bad signs over him, Inspector. I can tell you more about him, and I has one of these here bottles for proof."

Judas sat forward and rested his elbows on the wooden table in front of him. The thin white scar that circled his neck began to warm and throb.

"Ink? In a bottle?" he asked.

"That is correct, Sir. Huxley can hears it, and if he says that he can hear the screams of the unfortunate, I believes him, yes I do," said Bullseye.

Judas removed his notebook from the inside pocket of his overcoat. He had draped it across the seat next to him to deter anyone from sitting too close and listening in.

"You're going to have to give me this bottle and tell me everything you know, Bullseye. Now!" barked Judas.

Bullseye raised his paw to signal for another beer. Gerald placed the glass he had been cleaning with his apron under the pump but he did not pull his friend Bullseye a pint. The look that Judas gave him sent him ambling away to wipe the tables down and make small talk with the remainder of his punters. Bullseye turned on Judas, and snarled at him.

"I drinks when I wants, Inspector, not when anyone tells me I can!"

Judas pushed his empty pint glass away from him, then looked into the old pug's face. He was calm and very still, and it began to unnerve the fierce creature sitting opposite. Bullseye growled and lowered his snout but his ears remained up and pointing towards the ceiling. A witch at another table cackled at some unheard joke and all around them merry was being made, but the atmosphere at their table was tense and there was danger lurking. Judas moved his left hand very slowly and started to twist the small metal bar at the back of one of his Paul Smith cufflinks. Then, faster than any punch ever thrown at Bullseye in the ring, on the cobbles or anywhere else in the Underworld, Judas reached out and grabbed the beast by the neck.

"Carry on like this, Bullseye, and you and I are going to fall out. You might be a good boxer, but I've fought with angels, so put a lid on it and tell me what you know, or we can take this outside and let's see how tough you really are," said Judas quietly.

The softness of his voice was a direct counter to the growling intensity of the dog's, but Bullseye, so confident and so strong, knew that he was out of his depth. There were stories about the Black Museum and the magic that went on inside it. He also knew that Judas was a lot older than he looked, and had come through more than his fair share of scraps and battles.

Judas felt Bullseye's shoulders tense as he prepared

himself for the blow, but none came; Bullseye's shoulders relaxed and he released his throat.

"You should have got in the ring, Inspector, you would have made yourself a mighty purse. I hasn't been surprised like that since I was a pup! And those hands of yours, they looks soft and clean, but there's iron in them! I apologises for my behaviour. I means no disrespect to you."

"That's okay. Now, tell me more about this creature and his collection and I'll have a word with Gerald about setting up a tab for you and I will cover it," said Judas.

Bullseye produced a series of little yaps, and his large tongue unrolled like a pink carpet.

"I will tell you all you asks and more, Inspector, and I won't go on drawing it out like before, but I must ask for payment for my precious knowledge. To let it go for naught would make me an informer and I hates one of them like a plague of ticks."

Judas waved to Gerald and two pints of Guinness arrived swiftly.

"Okay then, Bullseye, what is this information going to cost me?" said Judas.

"What I wants, more than anything, is a Royal Pardon for crimes committed in my youth, like that scrape you and I, and a certain Mr William Sikes got into one white, snowy Christmas in the Rookeries. That is all I wants. To be free, and know that I is respectable once more."

Judas nearly choked on his Guinness and set his pint down quickly to save from spilling it everywhere. He pointed to his throat and pretended that the heavy liquid had gone down the wrong hole. Luckily, Bullseye was snout deep in his pint and didn't notice a thing.

"You want a Royal Pardon, Bullseye? I don't think there's a warrant out for you, or anything linking you to any

An Ink So Dark

of the Black Museum's old, unsolved cases. What makes you think you need a Royal Pardon?" said Judas.

Bullseye finished his pint then raised one of his meaty paws to his mouth and wiped it. The roughness of his paw passing across his face made a sound like grinding metal.

"I knows I has done a lot of heinous crimes, Inspector, some of which you is aware of and some you has no clue as to who or what done the deed. I wants a pardon for them, for the ones that I wished I had been caught and hung for but wasn't. I might not have many years left on the canvas and I wants to know that I doesn't have to watch over my shoulder all the time, or shift where I sleeps every other week," said Bullseye.

Judas took his time over what remained of his pint, and when he finally finished it he set it down and signalled to the cyclops to bring another round over. The pub had filled up considerably since their last beverage and Gerald was pulling pints with two hands and wiping his one enormous eye with the third. Judas tried to engage Bullseye in small talk but it was one-way traffic and he was relieved when Gerald barged his way through the crowds with their drinks.

"And I don't suppose you'd part with this information now, and I'll promise to get you your pardon tomorrow?" Judas asked the question but knew the answer already.

Bullseye's small, dark eyes twinkled then he yapped again.

"You knows the rules, Inspector, no prize before payment. Why, my old trainer, Bones McGinty, the fiercest pug pugilist to fight his way out of Ireland and into the Golden Ring Boxing Finals, which he won on a split decision from the cheating whelp, Fast Hands Freddie the Dagenham Destroyer, said that you risked all for nothing if the gold weren't placed in your purse beforehand," he said.

"So, that's a 'no' then, Bullseye. You want your pardon before you'll tell me who it is that's going around murdering the mundane folk?" said Judas.

"I doesn't want to see no life lost, Inspector, but the rules is the rules. If we don't fight by them, then we is nothing less than beasts, is we?"

For the second time that night, Judas had to pretend he had choked on his Guinness. Bullseye was in fine spirits by the time Judas left. He had put some money behind the bar with Gerald for him as he was leaving, and he made a big deal of pretending he was looking for someone else amongst the crowds, quietly pleased when a number of the patrons tried to hide from his gaze. It was a small victory, but Judas had learnt long ago that a good reputation for being a nasty piece of work sometimes worked wonders.

It was getting late and Judas didn't see any point in going back to the Museum, so he walked on. As he made his way through the darkening city he tried to imagine what the Chief Superintendent was going to say when he told him that he needed to secure a Royal Pardon for a very unusual character. The Chief would want to know more and then Judas would have to explain, in great detail, who and exactly what, Bullseye was. He didn't mind some of the responses he got from the brass at the Yard after he had asked for more operational funds, or enquired as to the possibility of more manpower, but this request was going to raise the Chief's eyebrows, and then when he'd finally thought it through, he was going to laugh so hard that Judas would be able to hear it all the way down on the 7th floor.

Chapter Eighteen

Blood and Skulls

It was one of *those* pubs, the ones with pretensions, and delusions of grandeur. The lonely dartboard was still there, a black and white bloodshot eye glaring out from the newly painted Farrow & Ball walls. It was occupying a dimly lit corner of the room, and it was clear to see that it was being starved of darts and fading fast. The new manager of the boozer didn't want to encourage the old locals to come back in with their shabby clothes and monographed dart flights. The new locals – the ones with the money and the children, the chocolate labrador called Archie, or a pug called Inky – those merry little units of well-to-do, who needed a Sunday roast cooked for them by a proper chef, were where the future of the pub lay. The hot plate with the glass front that was home to the steak and kidney pies and the greasy sausage rolls had been retired, for health reasons, and replaced with boxes of Risk, Global Toxic Panic, and other fashionable board games involving widespread panic and death on tsunami scales.

. . .

Odhran had chosen this pub because it looked quiet and a little down at heel, but as soon as he stepped inside he realised he had made a mistake. If he were to leave suddenly it might cause some to remember him, so he stayed. He secreted himself in a corner far enough from the door but close enough to the window that he could keep an eye on his caravan. Someone had been inside, and he didn't feel at all well. He felt exposed and violated, and worst of all, one of his treasures had been stolen, and he was choked by the loss of it.

Deadman and Phillips were squaddies. Young squaddies. Neither had been out of basic training for long, so they still felt immortal and rather powerful. Their regiment had selected them from thousands of other wannabee tank commanders, shaved their heads, beaten them down, shaken them about, and then lifted them up. Now they were soldiers, and if some terrorist cell was looking for an easy target, a pair of stupid, macho-meatheads, then look no further. Dave and Simon were as daft as two brushes and stuck out like a giant's thumb.

"Two pints of your finest," said Dave.

"And some of those bar snacks too, the ones that look like wood shavings and are supposed to be crisps," said Simon.

The barman, dressed in a waistcoat over a checked shirt and sporting the finest moustache this side of Shoreditch put on his number three smile, the one saved for idiots and chavs, and poured two pints of their microbrewery's most expensive pale ales. The crisps he threw in for free. Dave and Simon paid then navigated their way through the tables to an empty booth nestled against the exposed brickwork of the wall. They chose this seat because the only people nearby were a

An Ink So Dark

little chap with a sketchpad and an older lady that looked as though she were recovering from her latest black eye. Even Woolwich, one of the fairer boroughs, had its meaner streets.

"So, Dave, did you get that tatt you were talking about?" asked Simon.

Dave necked half of his beer and then let out a soft, secret burp.

"I couldn't find anywhere near me that had a good enough range, and I want to have something big, something that looks serious, not just my blood group at the top of my arm, you know? Something a bit tasty," he said, and when Simon looked away for a second he let another cloud of belly gas slip away.

"That's the problem though, Dave, isn't it? I want a big tattoo too, but I'd like to sort of see what it looks like first, if you know what I mean," said Simon, pretending that something had caught his eye to avoid breathing in Dave's burps again.

The barman with the Belgian detective's facial hair served them five more times in just under three hours. The boys were starting to get a bit merry now and their mood had changed from jarring to obnoxious, with a twist. Regardless, the pub was making lots of money and long may it continue. If the bar staff had to suffer the odd idiot or two then so be it. The insults and the one-liners kept coming, and the ale kept flowing. Everyone was happy.

It was shortly before 11 p.m. when the boys realised that the bloke with the drawing pad was looking at them. He had been listening since pint number three, but had actively taken an interest in them now. Simon kicked Dave under the table.

"That bloke keeps looking at us," he said.

Dave placed his empty glass down on the table, shattering a carrot and oregano-flavoured piece of wood shaving.

"What you looking at, Leonardo? See something you like?"

The strange-looking little man just smiled and stood up. He was not threatening at all. The fact that he had approached them would normally be the proverbial red rag but they just didn't get the feeling he was dangerous and so they gave him a seat at their table and soon they were talking about tattoos.

"I can draw anything you can see in your mind's eye, whatever the design, and then if you like, I can offer you a free, gratis, non-permanent tattoo. It will fade in a couple of weeks, and if you like it, and want it forever, then I can recreate it for you, and you will not regret it," said the little man with the sketch pad and ink-stained fingertips.

Simon and Dave were intoxicated, but not with the microbrewery's finest. As soon as the little man had opened his pad of rough-edged paper and started to scribble across it they started to get boisterous. They felt taller, and wider, and there was something about the drawings that the man was creating that loosened their tongues. Simon started to describe a skull he had seen in a book all about the Mexican Day of the Dead celebration. He loved how the skull looked so dark and deadly, and fearsome, and that it signified rebirth. He really wanted a pair of pistols crossed underneath the skull too. They would make the tattoo appear even cooler, and guns were good, especially for a soldier.

Dave was not to be left behind either. He wanted a knife. He'd seen an old film on one of the streaming platforms about a crack troop of mercenaries going up against a shape-shifting alien that could become invisible when it wanted to. The toughest soldier was the only one to survive, and he had lopped the creature's head off with a wicked-looking knife. Dave wanted a really big knife. In fact, he wanted a sword, a proper blade and he wanted some creepy-looking demon reflected in the shiny steel of the blade.

The scratching of the nib of the man's pen grew louder and louder and then it stopped suddenly. The pub was nearly empty and the barman was looking over at them. Either he wanted them out so he could start cleaning up, or he wanted to beat last night's bar total. Simon wanted another pint but Dave was mesmerised by the drawing of the knife.

"My mobile studio is parked just there. I have not been imbibing, as you can see, and would be more than happy to draw these fine creations tonight if you have the time?" said Odhran.

He already knew the answer, but he loved seeing the conflict in their eyes. They knew that they shouldn't, but they wanted it so badly. They always chose badly, but that was nectar to him because he loved drinking in the pain that his drawings caused to others. They had always brought about suffering and pain, and he consumed it like air.

"Let's do it!" said Simon.

"Hell yes!"

They wandered out of the pub. The barman waved them into the night, and they disappeared under the branches of a nearby tree.

Simon and Dave woke up on the bus. They had been superstars and showed some good skills obviously because they had somehow managed to get a kebab with plenty of onions and chilli sauce from somewhere, and they both felt supersonic. The Duty Sergeant at the barracks waved them through the gates with a cursory glimpse at their ID cards. His only condition of entrance was that they split one of the kebabs with him. They did this happily and returned to their rooms, where they consumed their lamb shish and congratulated each other on their incredible, double-hard bastard tattoos. The skull looked cruel and the knife, which was as long as a sword, looked brutal. The last thing that either man remembered was a lantern swaying overhead, the sound of the sea and the singing of monks.

On Shooter's Hill, a long and well-used stretch of the King's Highway, a black cab indicated then pulled out to pass a wooden caravan, pulled by a lovely grey horse. It coasted past then pulled back into the correct lane. The cab driver looked into his rear-view mirror just to make sure he had not spooked the horse, saw that he hadn't and then accelerated away. He did not see the caravan disappear into the fog bank that had just miraculously appeared, even though the forecast was for clear, open skies.

Later, Odhran fed the horse an apple then attached its nose bag so that it might munch on it at its own speed. Then he climbed the steps and slipped inside his home. The two idiot boys had been a gift and he was so very grateful for them. The hollow dark space that had widened with the loss of his precious ink was full again. Odhran lifted the spent pens that he had used to draw the inks onto their skins from his wastebasket. He caressed them and inhaled the delicate aromas that came from them like perfume from a bottle, then he placed them into the brass bowl he always used. Brass was by far the best conductor for his magic. He warmed the base of the bowl with fire.

An Ink So Dark

Into the bowl, he placed the drawings he had used to trace the details of the skull and the knife onto their arms, then the tissues he had rubbed over their skins, wiping away the special ink he had used and the globules of blood he had drawn from their skin with his cursed nib. The bowl glowed as its contents reduced down and created a liquid that Odhran quickly spooned into two glass vials.

He wrote one name on one label and affixed it to its bottle. He repeated his actions for the second glass bottle then he carefully placed them both on his shelf. Odhran sat back on his bed and gazed lovingly at them all. The silence inside the caravan was beautiful. The pub had been noisy and it had hurt his ears. So much shouting, random noise, electronic interference and piercing conversation had occurred between the mouths of the silly drinkers and the synthesised lullabies of the fruit machine.

It made him sick and he wanted to draw an axe onto each of their backs and chop them all down like dead branches, then build a bonfire that would warm the stomachs of the clouds.

Chapter Nineteen

The Pen That Was a Mountain

Surprisingly, Judas did not wake up with a hangover. In fact, he felt really good. He had had one of those night's sleep where he had woken up in exactly the same position as when he had closed his eyes the night before. The flat was still and the light had not quite managed to find its way inside, and he had the rare pleasure of turning the alarm clock off before it kicked in. He rose and prepared his favourite working man's breakfast: two fried eggs on marmite on toast, two sausages from the butcher on the high street, one rasher of bacon, a handful of grilled mushrooms and a vat of coffee. As mornings went, this was a five-star special.

He left his apartment building with a full stomach and a spring in his step. As he walked to the bus stop he tried to imagine the magnitude of the hangover that Bullseye was suffering from and nearly burst out laughing when he visualised the great hound holding an ice bag to his brow and howling "Never again!"

The bus was fairly busy today. It was not quite at the madness level of rush hour, so Judas took a seat on the upper deck, about midway down the vehicle on the right-hand side. Many years of commuting had honed his senses to the quiet places of buses, tubes and trains. It was a pleasant journey with only a few stops. The general mood of his fellow travellers was good too. He even caught one chap laughing out loud to something he was listening to. Could be a podcast, or an audiobook narrated by a failed actor. Judas settled back and watched the people performing their show of life. He drifted for a couple of stops, taking the world in, consuming it, enjoying each moment and appreciating the general contentment of his fellow travellers. He smiled broadly when he overheard one young lady remarking to her friend that she had better lick her lips; he understood this to mean that she had somehow got the cream the night before.

Judas loved the mortals. He admired their fortitude and their everlasting optimism. It didn't matter how many times the party in power performed its latest U-turn or raised taxes, they kept moving forward, sometimes at a shuffle, sometimes at great speed. No matter what happened, they kept going. There was war in Europe, conflict in Asia, and nothing new on the telly. Money was tight, but still, they smiled and made the best of it. He liked that.

He was about halfway to Scotland Yard when he heard a thump on the roof of the bus above him and caught the flash of feathered wings out of the corner of his eye. One of London's angels was hitching a ride on the top of the bus – again. The drivers turned a blind eye to these winged fare dodgers; it was rumoured that the angels brought luck to the service. A rumour started by an angel, no doubt.

For all their power and grace, their stoicism and beauty, they were a bunch of stingy so-and-sos, and if they didn't have to put a hand in a pocket, they certainly didn't.

. . .

The main desk at the Yard was strangely quiet this morning. He passed through it without drawing the attention of the Duty Sergeant and took the lift up to his domain. He was still full of light and purpose but if the wheels could come off his perfect start to the day, this was the place for it to happen.

Judas took off his coat. He had retired his trusty Frahm City coat for a while and was breaking in a dark blue parka from a brand he had recently discovered called Shackleton, named after the great man himself, the explorer and stretcher of maps. This new coat was lighter and supposedly much harder wearing than his other coat. He would have to take a trip into the Far Realms to test its strength and insulating capabilities for real. Half of these technical garments were designed for the arctic but would fall apart this side of the Scottish border if put to the test. Still, it looked great and it hung well. Judas draped it over a wooden coat-hanger and hung it up.

He checked his desk for any messages from Lace. She had been acting a little strange lately; maybe her love affair with the Captain of the Mudlarks was not as plain sailing as she had suggested, or maybe there were other factors that he was unaware of. He made a mental note to sit down with her and have a chat over a pint. She had proved herself many times since he had invited her to join him at the Black Museum.

There weren't any messages from her. Usually, there would be a sea of Post-it notes on his desk, the older ones curling at the ends and looking like little yellow waves, but not today. Judas wandered over to the big map of Greater London on the wall. It was still covered in pins. There were more red pins now. The older blue pins indicated a sighting and it didn't take a genius to work out what the red ones were for. Red spelt blood, murder, and nasty things that shouldn't be roaming the streets. He scanned the map and noticed there was a larger concentration in West London now. Previously, it had been East London. He needed to get over there and take the pulse of the underground.

He looked at his watch and realised that he had been subconsciously avoiding the task at hand, so he picked up the desk phone, took a deep breath and dialled the number for the man at the top of the tree – the Chief Super. Judas had had run-ins with some of his superior officers in the past but he liked the current owner of the big chair. They had very little to do with each other on a day-to-day basis and that was possibly why they enjoyed such a good relationship.

He was ushered into the Chief Super's office by a lowly police sergeant who knew Judas by reputation only. He kept his eyes down and Judas caught the whiff of disdain, or it may have been the smell of fear, as he retreated and closed the door behind him. Judas was offered a seat, and he took it. He looked around the room and saw the faint stain on the carpet where he had accidentally-on-purpose nudged a pot plant onto the Worcester shag pile carpet after a rather unpleasant meeting with one of the former men in charge of the Met. The carpet had been ruined for all eternity. The Chief Super noticed him checking out the stain.

"That thing just won't come out. I wouldn't mind so much but I was in Forensics at one point long ago and I can't keep from seeing it and wondering if it's truly soil damage or something more sinister."

The Chief was from the Midlands and very proud of the Black Country. Many moons ago, a regional accent would have meant that the highest rung on your ladder was approximately ten below an officer from the Home Counties. That's why Judas liked the man. He was an outsider of sorts, not a member of the establishment, and something of an oddity – just like Judas.

"Coffee, Inspector?" said the Chief.

He was a tall man with an easy smile and there was a brightness to his eye. He played rugby and football for the police and wasn't a bad opener for the Force's cricket team. He was referred to as a *Red Brick Don* by some of the Eton types; it was about as far from the truth as you could get. He had taken Classics, or should that be, *read* Classics? Judas never knew which way that went. Regardless, the Chief had a powerful frame and a powerful brain to go with it. Most of the time you got one or the other, but not with this chap.

"I'm a bit of a coffee snob, Sir," said Judas.

"So I hear," the Chief Super replied.

He pressed the buzzer on his desk and seconds later the sergeant reappeared with a tray, two china cups, a cafetiere and a small jug of milk. As he passed, the aroma of the freshly ground coffee beans wafted down and stroked Judas across the cheek like a Burlesque dancer with an ostrich fan.

The Chief saw his reaction and smiled.

"I asked one of the officers to find out where you got your coffee from. Sometimes the scent of it wafts up the side of the building and drives me mad. Absolutely delicious, isn't it? I was shocked that there weren't queues running around the block, but then the importer is not registered on any paperwork that I could find. Funny that, isn't it, Inspector?"

Judas accepted the cup that the Chief offered him and

An Ink So Dark

held it under his nose. He inhaled the aromas and then sipped at his brew sparingly.

"The chap I use is an old friend, or I should say his great, great, great grandfather was an old friend. I buy his coffee beans because they remind me of a place that I once knew well. The smell is familiar to me."

Judas took another sip of the delicious coffee.

"Mathematics was never a strong point of mine but if you knew his great grandfather, then you must be of fairly advanced years yourself, Inspector. You look very spry if that is the case," said the Chief.

"I don't really remember my parents very well, Sir, but I'm told that my mother had good bone structure," said Judas.

The Chief blew softly across the surface of his coffee cup and smiled.

"Well put, Inspector. Once a policeman, always a policeman. I shall stop prying and take a step or two back. Forgive my clumsy questioning, I have always had an insatiable curiosity and the things that cannot be explained I find the hardest to leave alone."

Judas sipped at the delicious brew and nodded.

"It's always been hard to explain or elaborate on the things that happen downstairs on the 7th floor, Sir. On the whole, your predecessors preferred not to know too much. A little was often far too much, and I have learnt to keep myself to myself and my superiors at arm's length – for their own good. I apologise if that sounds arrogant, Sir," said Judas.

"Not at all, Inspector. I wish my dealings with other members of the Force were as easy and straightforward as this one. What can I do for you?"

Judas swallowed hard and placed his empty cup down on the table in front of him.

"I need to obtain a Royal Pardon, Sir," said Judas.

"A Royal Pardon?" The Chief placed his cup down too.

"Yes, Sir. A Royal Pardon for a very tall, ferocious bull terrier, called Bullseye, who undoubtedly has done some very nasty deeds in his time, and will not be offered a place in whatever Heaven he is trying to buy his way into." Judas waited for the laughter to begin.

"Bullseye? As in the Bullseye that belonged to William Sikes, the character that Charles Dickens invented? Oliver Twist's Bullseye?" spluttered the Chief.

Judas sat forward and helped himself to some more of the Chief Inspector's coffee. He surmised that being ridiculed and laughed off the top floor warranted finishing it off.

"That is correct, Sir. He's close to being seven-feet tall, talks with an East End accent, most likely Poplar, circa 1600, is a rare talent in the boxing ring and has a tendency to yap like a puppy when amused," said Judas.

"Good God!" the Chief exclaimed.

"If you wouldn't mind, Sir. That name doesn't sit well with me," said Judas.

The Chief Inspector sat forward. His eyes were bright and his eyebrows were threatening to disappear into his hairline.

"Do you mean to say that this creature exists? That he ... it ... is real?" said the Chief.

"He is, Sir. Very real. He has some information that I need and has decided that the price for what he knows is a Royal Pardon for past crimes and sins committed."

The Chief sat back in his chair and shook his head in disbelief.

An Ink So Dark

"Absolutely astonishing!" he exclaimed.

Judas remained silent.

"And how on earth does he think that you, or I, can secure a Pardon from the Palace?"

"I'm at a loss, Sir. It's not something that I've ever had to consider or contemplate before. I thought that you might have access to someone who might be able to obtain something akin to a pardon. The one thing that Bullseye isn't, is a fool. He'll know if we've just printed something off on the Met photocopier, and I really need this information, Sir. The case I'm working on has some overlap. There have been casualties from both sides of the London we try to serve, if you get my drift."

The Chief Inspector drummed the fingers of both hands on his desk. He was alert now, his features were more pinched and the light in his eyes had dimmed. Judas made a mental note of this. He liked to study people, and his new Chief was a formidable man, there was no question of that. But he had a 'tell', something poker players know all about, and that meant his actions could be anticipated, something that might be useful in the future.

"Are we talking about fatalities, Inspector?" said the Chief.

"I'm afraid so, Sir," Judas replied.

The Chief Superintendent reached across the desk and lifted the handset of his desk phone from its cradle. Everything was happening at a quarter speed; the Chief seemed to be in a mild daze, but as soon as he opened his mouth Judas realised he was thinking two moves ahead instead.

"Get me Inspector Howard of Special Branch, please."

Seconds later Judas heard a voice responding, and then the Chief spoke quickly.

"I know that you are well in with one of the royal family's equerries. No, don't deny it, you've met him on the *Square*, I expect, down at the Lodge."

The Chief Super placed a hand over the mouthpiece of his handset, looked across the table at Judas and whispered *"Freemasons"*.

Judas nodded, and the Chief removed his hand and continued talking to the Special Branch Officer.

"I want you to get your friend to obtain a signed Royal Pardon from whomever signs them at the Palace. I know that they sign all of these forms in advance to save the Royal wrists. It has to be blank but signed," said the Chief.

The person on the other end of the line tried to weasel his way out of calling in a favour of such magnitude but the Chief had him over a barrel for some other misdemeanour and refused to let him off the hook. The conversation ended abruptly and the Chief slammed the handset down in triumph, looking pleased with himself.

"I can't tell you how many times I have been offered an apron, Inspector. But the Freemasons are not my cup of tea. They do come in handy sometimes though. Your Pardon will be here first thing in the morning, Inspector."

"Thank you very much, Sir. I thought that you might react differently, have me turfed out of your office, or laugh me all the way down to the 7th floor. I appreciate your help, Sir."

The Chief Superintendent stood up and offered his hand to Judas. Judas shook it and turned to leave the office. His eye was drawn again to the stain on the carpet and for a second, he thought about apologising for it all over again. He heard the Chief chuckle and turned to face him. His superior officer was smiling and he pointed down at a silver pot with a lid on it next to the new plant in its white plastic pot and the old, dirty stain.

"Try not to kick that silver pot over will you, Inspector? It's got the ashes of my old German Shepherd, Judy, inside," he said.

Judas stepped away from the silver pot theatrically, opened the door and made his way back to the lift. It was only after the doors to the lift had closed and the metal box had started to descend that he remembered he had forgotten to thank the Chief for the delicious coffee.

Chapter Twenty

A Change in Course

The Irish Sea was in a contemplative mood; it was neither angry, throwing large hull-shattering waves around in all directions, nor was it village pond calm. Occasionally, a rogue wave would defy nature and raise its white head high and take a look around. Finding nothing worth breaking against, it would slide back down into a deep grey trough and dream of warmer waters and energetic currents that drag and propel. If it had taken another look before giving up it would have seen a strange vessel hove into view.

The small ship had a bright green sail flying from the mainmast, and when it caught the sunlight, it brightened and turned a vivid emerald. It was an old design, roughly 40 feet in length, with a beaky, angled bow, and a rather stubby stern, making it very solid in the water and also very fast. There were no gun ports dotted along the side, nor was there a flag or a name painted across the transom. And, if a spyglass or telescope were fixed upon it by a pirate or a member of the Coast Guard, they would have seen that there was only one sailor on board.

An Ink So Dark

Brendan of Clonfert was tall, and his hair was a dark chestnut colour. His facial hair was magnificent. It was long and he tied it with a beard bead that he had acquired when trading with a German U-boat. Most of the current depictions of him in churches, or in the glossy pages of historical guides to Ireland showed him almost bald and white-haired, with some sort of halo hovering over his ears. It was far from the truth but it did allow him to move freely without eager types searching for Saints appearing in search of wisdom, of which he had lots, or spiritual guidance, of which he too had his fair share, but was too busy to ladle out. Brendan of Clonfert, *the real* Patron Saint of Travellers, was on a mission to discover the Sacred Realm, and he was growing restless at neither finding it nor a clue as to its location.

Brendan scanned the horizon. It was growing dark and the line that separated the sea and the skies was beginning to smudge; the moment of the penumbra was near.

"Another day, another league of leagues travelled, and still no sign of the path," said Brendan.

There was a tiredness in his voice now. He was weary and he knew that he must make land fairly soon to recharge his batteries, both spiritual and physical. He took one last look around at the sea and checked the rigging before taking the ladder down below deck. After removing his cloak and hanging it on an iron peg driven into the bulkhead, he studied his maps for the time it took for two candles to wither. The cartographer who had given Brendan the map had stolen it from the great library in Alexandria. There was only one of its kind, and it showed the Old Land, the Forgotten Paths, the secret gates, and the doors that led down into the Hollow Earth.

The only thing it did not show was the location of the Sacred Realm. This, rumour had it, was an island that came and went like the mist and the fog. There were tales of the beings that lived there – incredibly ancient and far-seeing. Many sailors called it Atlantis or the Submerged Kingdom, but its true name was the Sacred Realm.

Brendan wanted to walk upon it and spend time there. He found the New World, with its machines and grey steel ships, its borders, some disputed and others long forgotten – boring. The people of this time were regressing, not moving forward. Science and technology trumped magic and spells, and this constant desire to unlearn something, to reduce it to its basic form and then disregard it, angered him. There were wonders everywhere but not many to champion them.

Brendan rolled the map up, placed it carefully into its long leather tube and placed the water-tight stopper in the end. The container was waxed and oiled and even if – Brendan reached out to touch the side of the ship – if the ship were to go under, the maps, all of them would be saved. He climbed into his hammock and once his body had fallen in with the rhythm of the sea, he fell asleep.

He rose early, breakfasted, then took a tour of his ship. All was well, the rigging taut and the sails curved outwards like a straining shirt across the belly of a jolly fat man. Brendan lifted his chin and breathed in the pure clean air. It was heady stuff and he felt fully awake now. He sailed on for the rest of the morning. Two container ships passed him by, heading for Liverpool, or further north perhaps. As the afternoon sauntered in he spotted a Royal Navy warship, a destroyer, surging away, cutting the sea in half, searching for shadows in the depths. Then, Brendan saw two Cornish Luggers. Both were Mount's Bay Luggers, ships designed to be very quick and slightly larger than their smaller cousins, the plain Lugger. They had reinforced holds to combat the heavy swells of the Atlantic, or cram in more barrels of smuggled whisky or other such contraband. He knew both by sight, instantly.

One was captained by John Carter, the King of Prussia Cove, and the other was captained by Carter's close friend, Cruel Coppinger. Brendan reduced sail and watched as the two very experienced Cornishmen brought their ships to a halt on either side with scarcely a bump of his hull.

"Well met, Captain Carter and Captain Coppinger! Will you come aboard and dine with me?" shouted Brendan.

"It would be a pleasure, Captain Clonfert. Just as long as you don't sit me anywhere near that great stinking barrel of offal!" said Carter.

"Offal, is it, my beauty? Well, we'll see about that. My men say that there is nothing sweeter than my company, isn't that so, Captain Clonfert?" Coppinger cackled, and his men, a small crew, laughed at his witty retort.

"I take no sides in disputes at sea, gentlemen, you both know that and you both know that you and your men are more than welcome to whatever I have. Come aboard, I am absolutely ravenous, both for food and for information," said Brendan.

The three captains retired to the main cabin. The men drank, danced, wrestled and sung and eventually grew quieter and fell asleep. Brendan's holds were stocked with some of the best victuals ever stowed, and his reputation for being a quality host was unrivalled; there would be many full stomachs tonight and sore heads in the morning.

"Gentlemen, how have you been since we saw each other last?" asked Brendan.

"The winds have been strong and the sea has been fair to me," said Carter.

"I wish I could say the same. I've had to work my men to the bone due to the sheer size of the cargo I've picked up from the Ghost Fleet. We'll all be rich men after we unload, hard work it has been, Captain Brendan. If only we'd had a small cargo like Carter there," said Coppinger.

Both captains were great friends and loved to bait each other. Carter did not take offence and laughed out loud and raised his glass to Clonfert and Coppinger. The bottle was passed around. Course after course arrived at the table, although no servants or deckhands were seen. They talked of other ships, and the latest gathering of the Ghost Fleet. There had been a prize fight, a dance and the usual trading of illicit cargo, but Brendan was more interested in something else – gossip.

"Have either of you come across the Flying Cloud? asked Brendan. "She's a clipper, and she moves fast, even for a clipper."

"I doubt any captain has come across her. Some tell a tale of seeing her, hull up on the horizon, heading south, but I've never met anyone that has actually seen her close up," said Coppinger.

"One of my lads tells of a night he spent in a Malay ship, during one of the Ghost Fleet markets. He'd been supping with a cousin who had ended up shipwrecked in Java Straits, and pressed onto a Malay pirate ship, and he says that his cousin had not only seen it but had been aboard," said Carter.

Brendan sat forward and reached for the decanter of port. He filled both of his guests' glasses and urged Carter to continue.

"I thought at first that it was just a deckhand trying to

elevate himself amongst his mates, but I heard him speak of it a second time and he said something about a line in the sea, and that the Cloud, once upon it, drew away like a flare from a Customs House mortar."

Carter looked a little embarrassed at the disclosure of what surely had to be another tall tale from a bored sailor, but Brendan was excited and pressed Carter for more information.

"Might I speak with this man, with your blessing, of course, Captain Carter?" Brendan asked.

Coppinger drained his glass and helped himself to another. Brendan continued.

"I am searching for something called the Great Sea Path, gentlemen. There are many stories about it, you know most of them. The tale I am most concerned with is the one that tells of a secret island. I am desperate to learn more about it," said Brendan.

"Alas, I know nothing of this island, Captain Clonfert, other than, as you say, the bawdy tales of drunken sailors and the whisperings of turncoat customs men. I have heard about something that might interest you though. We've been doing a fair few runs along the coast, heading toward the chops of the channel, towards the white cliffs, there and thereabouts." Coppinger struck a match and wafted it underneath the end of his fresh cigar.

"As we were loading up in Poole at the midnight moorings, some of the lads got talking to a few of the boys that work the harbour. Apparently, there have been murders of the human folk, by something nasty from ours," said Coppinger.

Carter puffed on his cigar and then blew the smoke into the brandy glass that he was drinking from. It was a neat trick and the grey smoke sat on top of the beautiful amber and gold liquid until he sniffed it back in, and then took a sip of the brandy, all in one smooth, effortless movement.

"I heard that and more. They are saying that the victims are drawn upon with runes and shapes that have not seen the light of day for centuries now, and that soon after, they lose their minds and start killing anyone near them," said Carter.

"When you say they are drawn upon, do you mean that the shapes are smeared onto their bodies with paint, or ash?" asked Brendan.

"I heard that the victims pay to have the symbols tattooed onto their skins, but then the images fade away, leaving no trace behind," said Coppinger.

Brendan shuddered and finished his drink in one go, then he filled it once again and repeated the same action.

"Does it mean something to you, Captain Clonfert?" asked Carter.

"I'm afraid it does, Captain, I'm afraid it does," said Brendan.

The rest of the evening passed swiftly and captains Carter and Coppinger, both inebriated above and beyond the call of duty had to be gently eased over the side and back into their own ships, both singing loudly and swearing that they had been slighted by the other and that a duel must be fought at the earliest convenience.

Brendan smiled as both vessels departed. It had been a successful evening in some respects, but the news of the murders and how they had been committed left him cold because he remembered, long ago, how a boy with a book and a quill, and a dark manner, had honed his unholy skills on the innocent, and butchered them. Brendan looked up at

An Ink So Dark

the stars. It was a clear night and the sea looked like a black mirror coated with foam that resembled a mid-morning frost. When the skies were empty the world was even fuller because a traveller could see forever. Brendan thumped the handrail with the flat of his hand. He winced then chuckled because he had always wondered why people hit inanimate objects in anger, when clearly there was no release of that anger, no passing it on, just pain.

When the Cornish captains had spoken about the Flying Cloud, the vessel he had sought for so long, his heart had leapt and started beating like a ringmaster's drum inside his chest. It was only with great self-control that he had stopped himself rushing from the cabin and interrogating the sailor that had purported to have seen the *Cloud*. He would have done it if they had not then spoken about these bloody murders. His mind was in turmoil because of it. He wanted to unhear what they had said, pretend to himself that he didn't care, and sail off after them. Once he had caught them he would obtain the name of the Malay ship, and then search for that craft. From there he would find the Flying Cloud, and then he would discover the Great Path.

But that was not to be just yet!

The wind raced in over the grey-blue waters. It had been steady and constant for days now, pushing Brendan further and further away, always heading in one true direction. But now it seemed to him that another force was acting upon it. A force mighty and undeniable, stronger than any storm and impossible to resist. Destiny had caught up with him and it was this power that filled his sails and set his course. Suddenly, the boom swung from Port to Starboard, the ship leaned over as the sail caught the air and the bow moved slowly to point towards the shores of England. Brendan sighed, grasped the wheel with two strong hands and turned it. The ship kicked like a horse straining to be released from the reins of its rider.

The tides appeared to be with him. But time, he feared, was not.

Chapter Twenty One

A Dark Dream

The Western Cemetery was, for want of a better word, the *attractive* side of Highgate cemetery, and at its heart was Egyptian Avenue. Entrance to the avenue was through a vast gate, carved in stone with four columns, two on either side. The stonemasons responsible for coaxing these fake Egyptian roof supports from the raw materials they were supplied with were well remunerated for their efforts, and one local newspaper, renowned for its anti-Empire stance remarked that they looked so real, they could have been liberated from the people of the Nile by red-coated soldiers – with muskets and bayonets. Spindly, curious branches hung down from the trees above, trying to escape the darkness at the base of the canopy, searching for light and possibly even adventure, but they did not touch the stone or rest their leaves upon it; some of the cemeteries nymphs and fairies said it was out of respect, whilst many other creatures said it was fear.

Regardless, the gateway was beautiful to look upon and yet there was something sinister about it. Beyond the gateway and Egyptian columns were rows of vaults, the final resting places for some – but not all. There were the dead that wandered here. One of these unsettled and unyielding characters was John Asherly, formerly of the Royal Household, a horse slaughterer by profession, and unbeknownst to his employer, a lover of blades and blood. Recent improvements to the cemetery by the Highgate Committee, both structural and aesthetic, had trifled with the stability of the old walls. Hairline cracks and tiny fissures had appeared everywhere, and ancient doors and rusting gates had become less secure. Through the gaps in the stone and the steel, impatient and evil spirits rose.

John stepped out from the shadows of his vault and looked up at the moon through the branches of the trees. He was hungry; he always was, but not for food or drink. There was a deep, empty hole inside him that could only be filled with misery and flesh. He had killed half a dozen badgers already; slow they might be, but they were ferocious and he had come off badly more than once. John wanted more, though. He wanted to hear the pleas of his victims and drink in their desperation. The beasts of the cemetery were good practice, but they did not make him replete. Twice now, he had ventured to the edge of the graveyard and seen the new, real world through the bars of the fence. It was so alive and bright, noisy too. But John could not pass through the railings; that way was locked to him, so he searched out new prey. There were lots of the living visiting the dead, but he did not attack them. For now, he was a killer, but he was a clever killer and did not want whatever passed for the law sniffing him out and putting an end to his capers. So John searched for more beasts, and after clearing out a warren and a badger set, he chanced upon a pathway that led down to a place where he and others like him could pass without causing a disturbance. A city of the Fae.

An Ink So Dark

John discovered he could walk through the tunnels and the packed markets and squares without drawing much attention; occasionally, his presence would turn a head, or a conversation might stop mid-flow as he passed, but on the whole, he came and went as he pleased. If he caused no trouble in Highgate Under, then no trouble troubled him.

He was in a low drinking den called the Old Cedar, named after the giant 280-year-old tree that once stood atop the cemetery when the names of Gibbet and Hench came to him. They were graverobbers and suppliers of certain illicit goods, and they roamed far and wide and had great knowledge of the workings of the cemetery. John was intrigued and decided to seek them out. He was already weary of this place, and his nocturnal activities and insatiable bloodlust had almost wiped out the local wildlife. He would capture Gibbet and Hench and rip their secrets from them, and they would tell him why he could not leave the grounds of the cemetery and everything else they knew.

It took the horse slaughterer a week and a day to find Gibbet and Hench. At first, they were wary of his approaches and tried to placate him, feigning ignorance and adopting a surly manner; they did not like the smell of him and after a few curt exchanges, told him so. Then they threatened him with their knives and drove him off by pelting him with sharp stones and old broken bones. But he returned the next night, and he did not waste their time, or his, in talking; he appeared suddenly, had found a weapon of his own, and he immediately made it crystal clear that he was adept at using it.

Gone were the bravado and the bluster; Gibbet and Hench were skilled fighters, their diminutive size had forced them to learn to scrap lest they get bullied into submission by the big bad world around them, but they knew when they were outclassed, and when to run. Unfortunately, they did not get far.

Hench was in a bad way, and his best friend and lifelong companion was dead, opened from belt to chin. Hench had seen his guts slip out of him and pool at his feet like dead red snakes, bloated and coated with a sheen that caught the moon's beams and turned them silver in the half-light. Gibbet had sacrificed himself so that Hench might live, and Hench hated him for it. Gibbet had been his big brother for so long, caring for him, protecting him, and making sure that his belly and pockets were full. The thought of life without him made him sob. Gibbet had gone toe-to-toe with the monster and when he knew his time was up, he had pushed Hench backwards so he fell over a log and down the slippery slope into the lanes of the dead.

The last thing Hench saw was the lethal blow that felled his friend, then he was flipping over and over in the darkness. When he hit the ground his first thought was to rush back up and fight alongside his friend, but Gibbet was dead, so he crept away into the night, holding his shoulder tightly to stem the flow of blood. Hench heard the man pursuing him, but he was safe as long as he remained conscious. He knew Highgate much better than his pursuer.

Sergeant Lace was in a bad mood, and it was not getting any better because her rendezvous with the little graverobbers, Gibbet and Hench, was ruining her social life, and she had a hole in her boot that was making her left foot throb. She was about to call it a night when she heard the rustling of leaves nearby. At first she thought it might be a rodent, but it was no rat. It was a very bloody Hench, with a face as white as the snow that never fell on London these days. She raced across the clearing and caught him before he fell over.

"Hench Hench! Stay awake now, do not, I repeat, do not, fall asleep!" she shouted.

Instinctively, she reached for her phone with one hand and tried to staunch the flow of blood with the other.

"He's gone...poor Gibbet, gone forever," whispered Hench.

Lace heard the desperate sadness in his voice and her heart ached, but she could not allow herself to be distracted. Her professionalism, training and ability to react to any situation kicked in; she was a Sergeant in the Met, and that meant something. She had a duty to protect London's inhabitants, all of them, without fear or favour, and she was angry – even angrier than before.

Lace reached inside her black bomber jacket and retrieved her phone from the inside pocket. It came to life in her hand, the screen turning from black to a bright blue. She swiped quickly across the screen and as soon as she saw Bloody Nora's name she hit it with her thumb. The Black Museum's resident pathologist, and font of all knowledge concerning London Under, would not be at her post this late in the evening. But she did have a small staff of junior doctors from some of the top medical schools in the capital – sworn to secrecy, willing to work for nothing, and intoxicated by the realisation that fairies and monsters did in fact exist – manning the phones for her.

Lace held the phone to her ear with her left hand and clutched the small body of the graverobber to her chest with her right. She held Hench tightly; his breathing was rough and ragged, and she could already feel the warmth of his blood seeping through her shirt and onto her skin. She had to act quickly, but it would be no good running off like a headless chicken now. Whatever had hurt Hench and probably killed his partner Gibbet, was close, she could feel it, so she slowed her breathing and stayed as still as possible. Everything was silent, the commotion caused by the attack would have sent every living thing scampering to safety. Nearby, much closer than she expected, a stick cracked and she heard the sound of heavy breathing.

"It is mine," said a voice in the darkness.

"I don't think so. Step forward, identify yourself," said Lace.

"It's my turn to say 'I don't think so' now."

It was a man's voice.

"If you don't step into the clearing, identify yourself and lay down whatever arms you are carrying it will go badly for you," said Lace.

Lace felt Hench grip her with what remained of his strength. He hugged her and tried to get as close to her as possible; it was an instinctive reaction – he was scared – attacked, weakened and reduced by his attacker. Lace was protecting him, and he heard the strength in her voice, and felt safe.

"Come out into the open!" she said again.

"What makes you think you can stand against me, woman?" said the voice.

"Years of experience, and knowing that my fellow officers will rip you to pieces if you lay a hand on me. They're on their way right now. Give yourself up, or run and hide, we'll get you regardless," she said.

Hench coughed and then fell still. Lace scanned the trees and waited, but there was no answer from the cemetery.

"Hello? Hello? This is Roberts of the Black Museum. Is

this an emergency?" The voice on the other end of the phone sounded far too young.

"Roberts, this is Sergeant Lace. I need a car and a medical professional to meet me at the corner of Highgate Cemetery; I'll text you the exact location. Get them here as soon as you can, and tell them to run the blues and the twos if you have to, but get here fast. Can you let Bloody Nora know that we have an emergency on our hands? A person of interest, a G2; she'll know what that means."

Lace stood up and pulled Hench to her, and then she began to retrace her steps back down the path she had used to reach their agreed meeting place; she heard noises in the bushes and imagined the worst, but she kept moving, and soon she reached the bottom of the path and located the gate she had used to enter the cemetery earlier.

When Gwen Roberts turned the corner in the patrol car she had *borrowed*, and saw the figure standing with her back to the road, she let out a soft whistle. She had driven like a maniac through town. She was not even qualified to drive a police car but she thought that this was an emergency and was prepared to take the blame if she had crossed the line.

The woman's shoulders were hunched, and she was looking back into the cemetery. Gwen flashed the headlights and pulled to a halt beside Lace, then she reached over to activate the central locking that would unlock all of the doors in the patrol car. Gwen did not know Sergeant Lace personally; she had never gone for drinks with her and the other girls from the station or sat next to her in a briefing, but she knew of her reputation and that she belonged to the Black Museum.

Sergeant Lace turned around swiftly, reached over for the door handle and then wrenched it open and almost fell into the passenger seat. Gwen was about to ask if there was anything she could do but realised that she didn't need to.

"Get me back to the Black Museum, the rear entrance, as fast as you can!" said Lace.

The journey back to Scotland Yard was a blur for Roberts. Lace said nothing to her, and when they arrived at the Yard, Lace got out of the patrol car and carried the small body across the car park. She held it tightly to her chest, and to the casual observer it might look like a service wash or a bag of gym kit; no one would have looked across and wondered why a fellow copper was carrying the small body of a badly wounded grave robber through the back door and downstairs to the old morgue. Roberts followed her in silence.

They put Hench on one of the metal tables that the surgeons would have used for dissecting the bodies of the murdered and the murderers. He looked tiny on the slab. In the darkness of the cemetery, Lace could not see his face properly and she hoped that he had just fainted or passed out, but here in the harsh neon of the morgue he looked truly awful. His skin was grey and his eyes flickered but saw nothing. He was still in there somewhere but he had lost a lot of blood. Lace turned away to check the doorway – she desperately wanted to see it open and Bloody Nora to come striding through it. Then she heard Hench whisper and she turned back to him.

"Sergeant Lace...are you still there?"

"I'm here, Hench, help is on the way," she said as convincingly as she could.

"Oh don't worry about young Hench, Sergeant. My people know graves and death, they are our business. Can I tell you about a dream I had about you?" Hench asked.

Lace took his hand in hers and gently squeezed it.

"If you like," she said.

"All grave people like me have waking dreams," he said softly.

Lace tried to calm him but the little creature carried on.

"We have these waking dreams. We see so much death, you see? We are sensitive to it," he said, his voice almost gone now.

"Stay still, Hench, one of our healers is on the way," said Lace.

"They're too late, Sergeant. But listen to my dream now. Something bad is coming for you! I see a bird and a river and then darkness. Watch out!"

Those were his last words.

Lace saw the tiny, stubborn flicker of light in his eyes fade away and then that was that. Hench was dead. She hoped he would find his friend Gibbet straightaway, if that were possible.

"What do you make of what he just said, Sergeant?" Roberts had slipped back into the room and was standing behind her.

"Where's Bloody Nora?" asked Lace.

"Stuck in traffic on the Westway I'm afraid, Sergeant. She told me to activate the voice recorder and switch on the video cameras though," said Roberts, unable to take her eyes off the little cadaver.

"Can you put little Hench here in one of the cold boxes, please?" said Lace.

"Of course. I should probably take some photographs first though, it's procedure," said Roberts.

"I couldn't care less about procedure, just make sure you treat the body with respect. You can find me on the 7th floor if you need me," said Lace.

Roberts watched Lace walk away, then retrieved the

camera from the equipment store. After connecting it to a charger, she inserted a fresh memory card and made herself a cup of tea. The camera was on a fast charge and it took only until her tea had cooled to molten temperature for the small red eye on the camera to turn green. Then she carefully removed the sheet that covered the body of the creature called Hench, and started to document his demise. Flash! Flash! Flash!

Chapter Twenty-Two

To Arms

Dave heard the knife whispering to him in the night. At first, the voice was distant, it mumbled and hissed at the very edge of his consciousness, but it became more and more insistent, and suddenly it grew loud, and he could not keep the blade's words from slicing their way into his mind. He felt for the ink and caressed it, tracing the lines with the tips of his fingers, again and again, long into the small dark hours. When he awoke, still tired and with dark circles underneath his eyes, he groaned and reached for his pillow to block out the light even though it was still dark outside. He felt odd. He was usually such a good sleeper and he had not had to rely on an alarm clock for years, but try as he might he could not return to the Land of Nod.

Dave started to get angry with himself; he was uncomfortable and tetchy now. He looked at his watch but his eyes could not read the face of his timepiece properly, they watered and itched. Something was wrong. He decided to get up and go to the washrooms. Once there he'd take a shower and that would make him feel a lot better. Dave got up and rotated his shoulders to try and work a knot out, and then he had his morning cough and a quick scratch of his balls. He felt heavy and the back of his head ached as if it had been resting on a metal sheet rather than one made from cotton. Today was not starting as it should.

When Dave reached the showers someone else was already up and using one of them. The white plastic curtain had been pulled across and great clouds of steam were beginning to fill the room. Dave chose the shower furthest away from the one in use and stepped in. He turned the water on and waited for a few seconds for the temperature to level out somewhere between the Baltic sea and a launch pad in Florida, and once it was bearable he stood under the shower head and let the water wash over him.

At first it felt good but the feeling of normality was fleeting. His head was still aching and he was having trouble making out the colour of the tiles on the wall of his cubicle.

"Don't panic, Dave, let it come," said a voice he knew well.

"That you, Simon?" Dave asked.

"Of course it's me, you fool. Has your ink been talking to you?" Simon's voice sounded strange.

"I've got a blinding headache, mate, can't see too well either," said Dave.

"Oh, that will pass in a minute or two. Just relax, I'll wait for you. Just listen to the voice and you'll see," said Simon.

Dave started to hyperventilate and he reached out to grab the shower curtain but the voice told him to stay still and to calm down. Dave wanted to scream and struggle but realised he was no longer in control of his own body. The voice was in charge now and it told him exactly what it wanted him to do.

An Ink So Dark

Simon had dried himself and dressed in his army-issue tracksuit and was wearing his white gym pumps. He waited patiently for Dave to step out of his shower, dry himself, and then walk out of the washroom with his white towel wrapped around his waist. He returned shortly wearing his tracksuit and white pumps.

"We've been given a gift, Dave," said Simon.

"That is true, my friend, and a plan that we must follow. So now, we'll go on a recce to make sure that we can carry out that plan to the best of our abilities," said Dave.

"Let's take a look at the armoury first," said Simon.

"No better place to start," Dave replied.

Chapter Twenty-Three

Rough Repton

In 1884, Repton School set up the Repton Boxing Club. It is the oldest boxing club in the world and it has produced some very good – and some notorious – pugilists. Judas had to smile. Bullseye may have been a magical dog but he had a wicked sense of humour too. Repton Under was where he wanted to meet Judas and receive his Royal Pardon so that is where Judas was heading. He got off the Tube at Shoreditch and tried to avoid being run over by crazy young things on electric unicycles and very expensive fixies painted to look very cheap. The number of coffee shops (mobile and stationary) had diminished of late, and so had the number of bike shops and pop-up shops – thankfully.

He walked along Sclater Street until it became Cheshire Street. The world-famous Repton Boxing Club was just a few doors down. Judas knew the club well, he'd been to see it just after it had opened. It looked just as it had done then, give or take a few improvements. The local area, on the other hand, had turned into a fun fair and he much preferred the old streets and the slums to the new *sanitised modern.* Judas was having a look round the back of the club when he saw an old friend.

Julius was an odd one. He was a fairy bastard, and he loved fighting. Judas had arrested him more times than he cared to remember. The last time he'd picked him up he was half dead. One of his wings had been ripped to pieces and his ears, normally pointed and delicate, looked like a pair of cauliflowers. Judas had introduced him to the head trainer at Repton Under and told him that if he had cause to arrest him again then he would be going into the Black Museum, and he took the hint.

Julius was wearing a long puffer coat and a Jack Nicholson, *One Flew Over the Cuckoo's Nest* sailor cap. He could have passed for anyone around here, but Judas knew who he was from a mile away. Julius had fairy ankles; they were ballet dancer thin and he had to pad his socks out so that they looked normal. As a result, Julius walked in a certain way and Judas could have picked him out of a crowd without thinking. Apparently, Julius did not enter the club through the front door. Here, at the rear of the building, he knocked on an old green door. A slit opened in it, he showed his club membership and the door opened.

Judas smiled and decided to go in through the front door to give the boxers a chance to get ready for him.

The tough-looking old pug on the door gave him a queer look as he entered and was about to tell him to clear off when Judas showed him his warrant card.

"Tell Mr Bullseye, Hound of the Ring, that the Master of the Black Museum is here to see him," said Judas.

"I couldn't care less if you were the King of Scotland,

mate! This is the Repton Boxing Club, not some fancy dress emporium! Now – sling your hook!" said the old boxer.

He was a spry-looking old bantam weight and could have held his own against a far bigger man in his time, but this was not his time and Judas was in a hurry.

"You're quite right, I'm not the King of Scotland, but can you carry a message through to one of the boys for me, please?" he said.

"No!" said the pug.

Judas put his warrant card away and stepped away from the table.

"I'll tell you what, *Punchy*. If you can land a punch on me, and I'll give you three chances, I'll walk away. And if you miss, you'll take my message in wearing your underpants on your head – deal?" said Judas.

The old man jumped up from behind his desk. No boxer can take being called '*Punchy*'. It's an insult that fighters won't stand for, which was why Judas had chosen it. The old man's fists came up, and he was around the desk and squaring up to Judas in a flash.

"*Punchy*, is it, my friend? Okay then, but just so you know, I have boxed some good fighters in my time, so you are warned and good night!" said the old chap.

He jabbed using his right hand; it was quick, much quicker than most men, but then Judas had been taught the Queensbury Rules in 1806 by Hen Pearce, the Game Chicken himself, and he ducked down and twisted at the waist so fast that the older man was punching the air instead of his chin.

"That's one! You get two more, and then it's underpants on the head, agreed?" said Judas, warming up.

The old boxer adjusted his stance. His hands dropped very slightly and he shifted his weight so that his jab would come from a completely different angle; he was a game old bird and must have been a fair fighter in his time. Judas admired him for his bravery and his pluck. The old fighter looked at Judas's chin again, signalling to his opponent where the blow would be landing and then quickly fired his left hand at Judas's midriff. Judas did not fall for that old ruse – it had floored him once before. He casually stepped to one side and allowed the blow to pass him by.

The old fighter nearly fell over, and more importantly, he'd seen enough and knew that a third try would only see him embarrassed, so he nodded in appreciation like all experienced boxers do when they see good honest boxing skills.

Judas felt for him then; he'd tricked the old boy because he thought it was the best way to impress him and gain entrance. He could have followed Julius in round the back but for some reason, his ego had egged him on into getting more macho than he should have done. Repton was a place that worshipped boxers and boxing, not violence and arrogance. He was ashamed of himself and wanted to try and make it up to the old man, but that might have been even worse. He scribbled his note down on a page from his police notebook and handed it over. It wasn't snatched but it wasn't taken with any sort of warmth either; it was what he deserved and he took it on the chin.

Judas waited and read the posters on the wall until the old boxer returned.

"In you go. At the back, Mick is the big lad with the bushy moustache and the 'I Love San Fran' t-shirt," said the old man.

"Thanks, Mr...?" said Judas. He wanted to at least know his name, out of respect.

"Chapman. Jim Chapman," said Jim.

"Is that you up there on the right?" Judas pointed to a poster worn brown with age.

"It is. I fought that lad twice – once in Borstal, and then again in the ring. We shook hands the second time, but I can't remember what we said to each other the first time! Good lad though, staunch, didn't know when to give up, good hand speed," he said.

"Not as fast as yours though?" said Judas.

"Not quite. You move like you've fought a couple of times," said Jim.

"If I told you where and when you'd throw me out of here!" said Judas.

"Not that club out in Dartford?!" said Jim.

"No, Jim, you wouldn't have heard of it. Thanks for the lesson," said Judas.

"But it was you giving the lesson, I couldn't touch you!" Jim was confused.

"You gave me the lesson in humility, Jim, and I thank you for it." Judas shook his hand and walked inside.

The smell of a boxing club is unique. Some people think it's a dirty, smelly and rough sort of place. It isn't. The good ones are spotlessly clean; they smell of leather and timber and determination. Repton was packed, as usual, with fighters of all ages and sizes, weights and levels of skill. There wasn't a lot of shouting or raised voices, everyone was focused and committed to their own training routine. The only voices heard today were the trainers at the rear of the club working with two young fighters; one of them was wearing a San Fran t-shirt.

Judas carefully threaded his way through the club, making sure not to encroach on anyone's space. It took him a few moments to navigate through them all and get to the back.

The man in the t-shirt saw him coming and bellowed.

"You have got to be kidding me! The immortal man! I haven't seen you down here since that business with the Resurrection Men and that lost Sprite Chieftain!" he exclaimed.

"It has been some time, my Lord Gwydion. How are you and the family?" Judas asked.

"Very well and fine. My good lady is still pining for that beautiful Welshman Williams! How is he?"

Judas frowned and was about to tell Gwydion that his old Sergeant Williams had died at the hand of John the Baptist in the battle of Wandsworth Common, but his face betrayed him and told the prince all he needed to know.

"You have ill luck, Inspector. Williams was one of my children, he will be sorely missed. Where is his body buried, Inspector? I shall send some of mine and it will be returned to the land of his fathers," said Gwydion.

Judas looked around, expecting to see all of the boxers standing still and listening to their conversation but Gwydion had already placed his wards around them both; life in the gym went on, and they were able to continue their conversation unobserved.

"He is not returned to soil, Prince Gwydion. Such was his bravery and his commitment to the law and in a way to *me*, the Archangel Michael, who fought alongside us, recognised his worth and offered him a place in the Host. He decided to accept the offer and is now a loyal sergeant-in-arms to another master. I have heard news of him and he is well." said Judas.

Prince Gwydion, son of Don, heir of Math, King of Gwynedd, and a keen middleweight who liked a good ruck and was hiding from his princely duties and responsibilities, nodded slowly.

"All the Welsh are angels, Inspector, as you well know. At least he is with others like him now. But you have business in the *other part* of the club, I understand. Master Bullseye is awaiting your pleasure. If you do get a moment, call on me before you go," said the man with the San Francisco t-shirt.

"It would be good to talk further about Williams."

"I shall do my best," said Judas.

At the rear of the club there were two doors. One led to the showers, storerooms and offices, and the other took you down a short, dimly lit corridor, at the end of which was another door with a sign on it that read 'Under Twelves Boxing'. Someone had put a line through the word 'Twelves' so that the sign read 'Under Boxing'. Judas smiled again. He was about to step into the Underworld's finest boxing club – Repton Under.

He opened the door and walked in. The difference in the smell and the noise was remarkable. Gone was the faint but pleasing aroma of well-oiled leather. Also missing was the huffing and puffing of the would-be champions. Instead, there was the scent of woodland and of something more primal; fire and heat, possibly? Judas closed the door quietly behind him and surveyed the scene. Repton Under was a mirror to its more famous neighbour but whereas Repton made use of steel girders to support the walls and keep the roof where it should be, and iron fixtures and fittings to keep the ropes of the boxing ring taut, Repton Under was constructed with wooden timbers and some form of hemp rope.

Nearest to him were two ugly gnome-like creatures sparring. They were not holding back and their gloves were moving incredibly fast; occasionally one landed a blow on the other and let out a sharp yap in celebration. One of the trainers, clearly identifiable in his Repton Under green polo shirt heard it and hissed at them.

"Fighters fight! Fighters don't talk as they fight!"

The two gnomes stopped sparring, touched gloves, nodded to the trainer and then started again. Judas spotted at least four fairies, one bulldog, a few demi-giants, a huge ram, a couple of demure witches, and a host of other races of the Fae. The club was packed and he heard the shuffle of leather-bottomed boxing boots on canvas, and the thudding of gloves on bags filled with sand. It came at him from all angles. No one was interested in him, they were all focused and fierce, and he had no trouble at all in making his way to the small office at the back.

He knew he would find Bullseye there with his feet up on the table, a glass of something expensive and very rare in hand, and a cigar, half-smoked and half-eaten clamped tightly between teeth sharp enough to put a hole in a shire horse.

"Inspector!" yelped Bullseye.

"Hello, Bullseye. Do you have the bottle and the information you promised?" he said, getting straight to the point.

"Does you have my Royal Pardon, Inspector?" Bullseye retorted.

Judas reached inside his coat and pulled out a hard-backed A4 envelope. Bullseye sat up quickly, the cigar disappeared inside his great maw, and he let out a very small but excited yap.

"Is that it?" he asked.

"This Royal Pardon was handed to me by the Chief

Superintendent. He requested it from one of the Royal Household – an Equerry, whatever that is – who had it drawn up and signed. It's a very fine-looking document, Bullseye. I'd hate to have to run it through a shredder, or set a match to it," said Judas.

Bullseye's hind leg started to twitch. He was clearly excited and he tried to hide it by finishing his drink and removing a bottle and a fresh glass from the drawer of the desk in front of him.

"Please be seated, Inspector. I has here a bottle of Glade Whisky from a mermaid friend of mine, triple distilled and kept in a wooden barrel in an ice-cold rock pool. There is nothing quite like it, I promise. Here let me fill your glass," said Bullseye.

He'd regained his composure now, and was back to the chatty, cocky old Bull Terrier. His paws were huge and hairy, and like others of his kind, he had fingers and a thumb, with clipped dark claws at the end of them. He was very precise in his movements and Judas was impressed by how he poured so accurately with one paw and scooped some ice from a bucket with the other, adding it deftly to the pale yellow liquid. When he was happy with the presentation of the glass he pushed it gently across the table to Judas.

"Thank you, Bullseye," said Judas.

He raised the glass to the dog, they clinked their glasses together, and then they both took a swig. When Bullseye had savoured the liquid and then swallowed it, he closed his eyes and very softly said, "To the first of the walking dogs, bless them."

Judas repeated the saying and continued to sip from his glass. Bullseye nodded his approval and set his glass down. He then lifted the bowler hat he had placed on the table when he had arrived and underneath it was a small glass bottle. Inside the bottle was a small amount of ink, but unlike the sort that you filled an ink pen with. This ink moved, and Judas could hear it screaming from across the table.

Bullseye helped himself to another glass of his mermaid-made whiskey and leaned back into the old chair he was sitting upon. Judas noticed that it had been upholstered with the leather from worn-out boxing gloves. It would have sold quickly in any of the King's Road furniture stores. Judas reached out for the glass bottle and he saw Bullseye stiffen.

"Be right careful with that, Inspector, it brings with it some fair awful bad luck. The hand that created it belongs to a dark soul," said the dog.

Judas retracted his hand and reached for his own glass instead. The liquor was good and he thought he could detect the spray of the sea and something earthy in it. He placed his glass back down and looked up at Bullseye.

"What do you know of the ink and the artist?" he asked.

Bullseye growled and bared his fangs.

"The *Beast of the Black Ink* is a story that you'll hear at any one of a score of fayres, Inspector, in the realms of the Fae and in our own for sure. Like all tales, it's been embroidered with little bits of fluff and colour to make it even more blood-curdling, but the heart of the story is still the same. There is a beast out there that draws pictures on the skin of its victims and takes control of their actions. It always ends badly with blood and carnage. Whole families has turned on each other, butchering their loved ones, and there has been fights between giants that has levelled villages, caravans of folk setting their homes on fire and climbing inside to be roasted. There was once a troop of ghouls that took it in turn to drown each other until there was only the one left. It threw itself off the nearest high-rise building it could find. Nasty stuff this is, Inspector, the blackest." Bullseye growled again.

"What form does this evil take, Bullseye?" Judas asked.

"Why, it can take any form, or that is what I has heard, Inspector. That is what makes it so dangerous. One tale I heard tells of a man, bearded and frail but with the strength of ten. Another told of a young girl with blonde hair, blue eyes and sharp teeth that she used to eat those that turned against her. What I has just heard from a close friend, who hears the voices of the dead and is not squeamish about blood and terror, is that this time it looks like a young man. Fresh-faced, with short dark hair and the greenest eyes this side of the old Ulster," said Bullseye.

A cloud had passed over the dog, and he was not his usual good-natured and truculent self. Telling Judas what he knew of this creature had awakened old wounds.

"And where can I find this man then, Bullseye, and what is his name?"

The old pug looked up, startled. He'd been drifting along on the current of his past.

"He was at the old market the last time I heard, Inspector. He'd had a run-in with the Spitalfields security and threatened one of the merchants there. He was banished from the market and had taken to the road. Where he is now I cannot say but there are plenty of openings onto the Church Roads nearby, and from there, he could be anywhere. He is travelling in an old caravan, the sort that the old Romany people's used, pulled by a grey horse. There can't be too many folks rumbling around in one of those, I presumes," said Bullseye.

"If that were only the case, Bullseye. And, he has a head

start and he knows or must suspect that there are those that cannot allow him to continue with these murders who have been alerted and are tasked with stopping him. I just have to get my skates on and find him before he takes another life."

Judas finished his drink and replaced the empty glass back on the table.

"That Royal Pardon, does it really mean so much to you?" he asked.

Bullseye's muzzle twitched and then he smiled his very widest Bull Terrier smile.

"You has no idea, Inspector. You might think me a bit punchy, too many bouts in the ring being clobbered around the head by monsters of all shapes and sizes, perhaps? But, this here slip of paper makes me feel like I has left one life behind and the door to another one has just opened before me. It won't cut any ice with any other cove or gain me passage anywhere for free, nor will it get me the best seat at the table neither, but I will know that it is in my pocket forever more, and if I *chooses* to believe that my sins are forgotten, then this old dog will take that. I might even start to believe that I was always a good dog, you never knows, Inspector."

Judas smiled.

"So, there is new life in the old dog now?" he asked.

Bullseye's eyes widened and he looked as though someone had just farted in his presence.

"That is a very poor joke, Inspector, very poor, you are clutching at straws there."

Then Bullseye let out a couple of his happy yaps and he drained his glass once again and refilled it.

"One for the road, Inspector?" he asked.

"Thank you but no, Bullseye. I want to show this bottle of ink to someone and then I have to find the creature responsible. If you can help me get started with a name, I would be most grateful," said Judas.

"I can't be sure of what it calls itself, Inspector. The only thing I can be sure of is that it will be called something to do with the colour black. Blackstone, Blacktown, Black-something or other."

Judas stood up and when Bullseye reached out with his oddly shaped hand, he took it and shook it. Then he left the old boxer to his thoughts and stepped out and into the gym. The fighters were still working hard hitting each other and the punch bags suspended from the wooden rafters above their heads. Here and there a head turned, a Centaur spat in his direction and a dwarf that was wider than it was tall tried to accidentally nudge a spit bucket over as he passed, but a hasty rebuke from one of the trainers stopped him and the dwarf pretended to move the bucket out of the way instead.

Judas passed through the gym but stopped at the door, then he turned around to face the boxers. One by one the pairs of pugilists stopped jabbing at each other and their hands dropped to their sides. When the gym was silent, Judas spoke.

"I am looking for someone who travels around in an old caravan pulled by a grey horse. He, she (or it) uses the Church Roads, and moves freely around in the Under World. Blood has been spilt, and if the carnage continues things will go hard for you and your kin. Believe me when I say that I will close everything down. This gym, the taverns, the Church Roads, everything! And all of you who believe that your crimes have gone unnoticed by the Black Museum – think again. Garnet Lathe! Don't try and hide behind that punch bag! I know that you are holding a small fortune in moonstones for a certain witches' coven. And you, Lakey

Brooks! Don't try and disappear, I can see you over there, and I also know that you have something in your lock-up that a certain ogre has been missing for the last two weeks. Maybe I should whisper in his ear that you have it? I'm off home. If you or anyone you know has some information that could lead to the apprehension of this killer, leave it for me at the Black Museum," said Judas.

He left the gym knowing that by the time he got back to the Black Museum, there would be some helpful information on the killer and if he was very lucky, something about its whereabouts waiting for him. At least, he hoped there might be.

Chapter Twenty-Four

What the Dark Brings

The Women of the Chapel, unbeknownst to the *Top Boys* of London's warlike drug gangs and to the older, more established crime families, controlled most of the crime above ground in the East End of London through a legion of shadowy intermediaries. Their real estate portfolio was the envy of many an Oligarch, and they owned enough *ART*, to fill the Saatchi Gallery ten times over. They had stocks and shares, gilts, bonds, numerous Swiss Bank accounts and owned two Swiss banks in Berne, but it was in the underworld beneath the Underground and in the mirrorlands that border the great city of London that they made their true fortunes.

It was the last day of the Moon's Quarter, and the Women of the Chapel met, as usual, at the Sign of the Silver Bear, a tavern located directly under St Paul's Cathedral. Their business interests ran themselves these days so the ladies lunched and partied – a lot. But at the end of each phase of the Moon they met to talk of new business or of threats they faced. Tonight they talked about the latter.

"We have all had the dreams, all of us, and we have all

felt the same way on waking. *HE* is still out there, he must be!" said Meg.

The other ladies nodded.

"So, are we all agreed then?" asked Meg.

Each of the other ladies present nodded once again, and then one by one they finished their drinks, removed coats and jackets from the shoulders of the wooden chairs they sat upon and drifted away into the night. Only Meg remained. She beckoned to the huge figure of Delilah the Ogress, owner of the Silver Bear, who shuffled over to her table like a hayrick on wheels.

"I'll have another bottle of red please, Delilah, and the bill for tonight. And before you start to mumble something about not wanting payment, please don't. Times are hard enough, and you run a good house," said Meg.

"As always, my lady, you are kind and just," said Delilah.

The ogress scooped up the empty glasses and the overflowing ash trays from the table in one broad, hairy hand, and then wiped the surface of the table with a bar cloth the same size as one of Meg's silk bed throws with the other. Once all was clean and clear, she ambled away to the bar, deposited the dirty glasses into a hogshead barrel full of hot soapy water and tipped the ash into a steel bucket. Then, she disappeared through a door behind the bar and went down into the cellar to fetch her mistress one of the best bottles in the house.

Meg tasted the wine and beamed back at Delilah.

"That is amazing, thank you, Delilah," said Meg.

The ogress blushed and performed a clumsy sort of curtsey. She did not have cause to perform the act very often and she was self-conscious, but Meg reassured her.

"The wine and your hospitality are payment enough for the Women of the Chapel, Delilah, you are too kind."

Delilah bobbed her great shaggy head and went back to the bar. The Silver Bear was still lively and it was clear that she would be serving into the small hours. A group of rowdy sailors would keep her on her toes but she was more than capable. Meg watched her and smiled. She had a fondness for Delilah, but then again, she had a fondness for any female who stood tall and did not flinch or buckle under the strains and the hardships of life. Meg relaxed into her chair, savoured the wine and thought about what she would say to the Master of the Black Museum in the morning.

"Has he lied to me? Was it all a show? A subterfuge? An act to get the Women of the Chapel onside?" she murmured.

There was no answer, just a howl of delight from the far side of the room and the creak of the front door signalling that the ogress had more thirsts to slake, so Meg finished her wine and left.

Judas remembered she liked to wear a very brightly coloured scarf around her neck and when the lift doors parted to reveal her, he saw that she had outdone herself today. She made the Met look very drab and grey.

"Meg, how are you? You look well," Judas said.

She did look good but there was a strange look on her face and she did not return his smile.

"It's good to see you again, Judas," she said.

They turned and walked back down the corridor towards the Black Museum in silence. When they reached the door to his office he reached for the handle but Meg stopped just outside his office with her head cocked to one side. She could hear the whispering and the mumblings of the spirits inside.

"They've been a bit fractious of late, Meg. Something has upset them, I think," said Judas by way of an icebreaker.

"Interesting," she said softly.

Judas turned the doorknob and the door swung open, then Meg walked in and waited for him to close it.

"Coffee?" he asked.

"Please," Meg replied.

Her voice was still low and her manner was beginning to concern Judas so he decided to cut to the chase.

"You don't need to be a detective to realise that there is something on your mind, Meg. Why don't we cut out the pleasantries and just get on with whatever we're going to be getting on with?" he said.

Judas knew that Meg was stronger than she looked. She was also handy with a knife and he had at least one unconfirmed report of a rather grisly murder that he thought she may have had a hand in, so he kept her in view at all times and decided to put his desk between them, just in case. Meg smiled. She knew what he was doing and why he was doing it, so she raised her hand with palm outermost.

"Fear not, mighty Master of the Black Museum, I mean you no harm – yet," she said.

Meg smiled more broadly now and Judas was just about to relax when she vaulted over the desk and kicked him in the chest. Judas used the force of the blow and fell backwards over Lace's desk and was back on his feet before the cup of pens that Lace kept her desk tidy with hit the lino. Judas watched Meg closely now. She reached across her body with her right hand and slipped it into her left-hand pocket, pulling out a set of small throwing knives.

"The sentence and punishment for attacking a police officer in the act of carrying out his duties has been upgraded, Meg," he said.

Meg replied, but not with words. Her arm flew up and when her hand was level with her chin, she threw the knives.

One hit Judas in the neck, just below his right ear. One embedded itself in the back of his right hand – he would call it a defensive wound and worth taking because he would have caught the tip of the blade with his eyeball; the others missed. Judas stepped backwards and then to the side. He would not be a stationary target again. Meg snarled and then ripped the beautiful scarf from her neck to reveal what Judas had long suspected to be one of the marks left on her body by Jack the Ripper. A trophy or a reminder? He didn't know which, and at that moment in time, he cared not.

Judas flicked his left hand and the motion of it dislodged the blade and it flew across the room and thudded into map of Greater London on the wall. Then he reached up and plucked the blade from his neck. No blood flowed from the wound, the skin closed swiftly, and in the blinking of an eye, Judas was left unmarked but slightly miffed.

Meg looked on. Time seemed to have stopped. Everything was moving so slowly, and then she heard the warrior inside, and she told Meg in no uncertain terms that she had picked the wrong fight. She realised that she would be made to pay for this mistake, but before she did, she would ask him the question that had kept her awake all night.

"The Ripper lives, doesn't he? That night, the one when you brought us all here, it was all an act, wasn't it." She mumbled the words and as she waited for the reply she plucked the silk scarf from the floor and re-tied it around her neck.

Judas stared at her. He was still wary and waiting for the next attack, but after a few thousand years of fighting dirty, he knew that this particular fight was over. Seeing a man remove a knife from his jugular right in front of you had that effect.

"The Ripper? He's no longer with us, Meg. His key, the white opera glove he used to wear disappeared from the table in the Key Room the same night he was turned into memory. And, as for it all being an act, I'm not that smart and I had nothing to gain from pretending otherwise," he said.

"Then why is HE back, Judas Iscariot, King of All Liars!" Meg spat the words out.

"It's not possible, Meg. Once the key goes, the link between the Black Museum and the entity is broken. He lives on in memory only," said Judas.

He righted his chair, which had been thrown across the room in the attack, and sat down in it. Meg watched him and then followed suit. Judas looked across the desk and registered her gazing at his neck.

"It's a good trick, isn't it? I feel the pain but only for a fraction of a second, and the scars disappear. Only the ones that *HE* made, remain." Judas carefully opened the top three buttons of his shirt to reveal the top of the thick scar that ran all the way from the button on his trousers to the suprasternal notch at the base of his throat. Meg's eyes widened.

"That's a pretty heroic scar that you carry too, Meg."

"It doesn't make us pen pals, Inspector," she said.

But her hand reached for the scarf instinctively regardless.

"It doesn't make us anything, Meg. But I'm going to do the right thing and just remind you now that I am a policeman ... sort of HIS policeman, if you like. Try anything like that again and your King will not be able to save you, or the other four." He looked into her eyes and saw the words hitting home.

"You may be as hard as a coffin nail, Meg, and you may have been around the block, metaphorically speaking, but raise your hand to me again and I'll snap it off. Are we clear?"

Meg nodded. She knew that she had overreached and even worse, she realised that she might be wrong about him.

"I apologise for my actions, Judas. The last few weeks have been stressful. There was an attempt on my life and the girls and I have been having the same dreams, over and over again. We cannot shake them, and they are exactly the same for each of us. Have you ever heard of anything like that? Mirror dreams? The only answer I could find, or the only answer for it to happen in this way, is that he must still be alive and reaching for us. We are unfinished business, it seems to me." Meg's shoulders dropped.

Judas stood and walked to the small kitchen on the other side of the office and made coffee for them both. When he returned, Meg was sitting more upright and she had a different look in her eye now; she was back to the old Meg. He placed the coffee in front of her and then sat back down.

"These dreams are all exactly the same?" Judas asked.

"Exactly, that's what makes the whole situation so frightening. Everything, from the clothes we are wearing, the place it happens, the time of day, everything is exactly the same."

An Ink So Dark

Judas drank his coffee slowly, watching Meg through the steam from his cup.

"Why would you think that I would stage something like this?" he asked.

Meg snorted and stifled a laugh.

"Why? You're a man, aren't you? All of our trials start with men – men in power, or those that want power. Century after century, it's always the same." Meg placed her coffee cup down on the desk.

"That's a bit narrow-minded if you want my honest opinion," he said.

"Honest, you? Please!" said Meg.

"That was a long time ago, Meg," said Judas.

Meg reached for her cup again and Judas could see that her hand was trembling.

"You have nothing to fear from me, Meg. I'm here to fight evil, whether I like it or not. We have something in common you and I. We're in it for the long run, whatever it is. And, as I said before, I'm a policeman." Judas smiled.

Meg held her cup in both hands now.

"So what is it? Why the dreams, why this feeling of dread, the same feeling we carried around for hundreds of years? It's so raw, Judas. This pain knows us, and we know it. Believe me, I wouldn't be here if it weren't so important, and I wouldn't have risked attacking you if I thought that there might be another way," she said.

"Well, let's put your knife-throwing extravaganza to one side for now, no harm done. If you'd put a hole in my suit mind you, things might be different. Will you trust me to look into this for you and the other ladies?" he asked.

Meg looked conflicted.

"My first and usual response to any man who asks me to trust him is to laugh and then to throw him out of the room, but that course of action doesn't work with you obviously, so I must bite my tongue and do something I thought that I would never ever do again – and trust you," said Meg.

"That's a wiser course of action, and one that I'm glad you've decided to undertake. The Black Museum will protect you, Meg. Just as we protect, without fear or favour, any of the folk that turn to us," said Judas.

Meg stood and placed her empty coffee cup on the desk.

"It was delicious, Judas. You must tell me where you get it from. And, I have to apologise once again, my behaviour was wrong. I will send you something to say sorry properly. Not a bribe, just a show of good faith on my part. When can I expect to hear from you, Inspector?" she asked.

"Let me look into it. Where can I find you tomorrow evening?" he asked.

"We have a new bar. It's one of ours, under the old Bow Street Court. I will leave your name on the door. Dress smartly," she said.

Then she turned away and was about to walk through the door when she stopped suddenly and turned around to face him.

"There is something else, Judas. You were also in our dreams, and you were battling a giant bear of a man covered in blue tattoos. His skin was like milk and his eyes cloudy. Does it mean anything to you?"

Judas sat upright and placed his elbows firmly on the table.

"Did the bear have the face of a man, or was it just a large, hairy man?"

"Hard to tell, Inspector. There was a lot of thunder and lightning," she replied.

Then she turned away and he heard her footsteps

tapping down the corridor, the ping of the lift door and then silence. He took his silver coin from his pocket and started to trace those small circles across it with his thumb. His mind quietened and he drifted for a time, but then he woke and when he opened his eyes he had a dreadful feeling he might have overlooked something.

Chapter Twenty-Five

Shooting Fish

It was nearing 03.00hrs and Dave and Simon were standing in front of each other in Simon's room. Both were naked and in the half-light, they looked like small, badly formed statues. Nobody would have queued or paid money to see them in a gallery or museum. Neither spoke. Simon applied some cam-cream to Dave's face and then Dave returned the favour. Then they stood to attention, saluted each other (their Drill Sergeant would have been proud of them) and then they slipped out of the room and made their way to the armoury.

Once there, they used a fire extinguisher to put the duty officer, whose job it was to keep an eye on the firearms, to sleep. Then they liberated the keys to the armoury from the now unconscious officer's pocket and entered. They reappeared moments later carrying an SA80 LMG each, and enough rounds to choke a donkey, or kill an awful lot of innocent people. They set their weapons up so that their arcs of fire would cover the barracks where their brothers-in-arms were sleeping, and also the main gate so that they could blow a fair few civvies away too.

An Ink So Dark

Dave lay down on the ground, attached a full magazine and adjusted the weapon's iron sights using the yellow neon sign above the door of the taxi firm across the road from the main gates as a marker. Simon checked his weapon and trained it on C Block, the closest of the barracks' sleeping quarters. Then they spoke, but not to each other. Both were having separate conversations with their tattoos about how many people they needed to kill and how much carnage they needed to create to make the ink happy.

Rory wasn't quite sure why he'd taken the fare. The last time he looked at the clock it was nearly 05.00 a.m., and he had done his time behind the wheel for another night. The taxi belonged to a mate, and so did the licence that was stuck in the window. Rory was just covering for him *again* and making a few quid to make the next term at business school a little more comfortable. He was on his way home, he was sure about that. He'd turned LBC off – the radio station was his favourite and kept him awake during the downtime between passengers – and he'd switched off the app on his mobile phone that sent him the fares, so why was he driving in the opposite direction with a bearded man that smelt of seaweed in the backseat?

Dave cocked the weapon and pushed the butt firmly into his shoulder. He could see the world through the scope; it looked strangely grainy and orange. Then he tilted his head so that his right cheek rested on the top of the butt. He was ready, the tattoo told him that he was ready, but something was wrong, and the tattoo didn't like it.

Brendan of Clonfert, the true Patron Saint of Travellers, did not like cars. He had heard about the electrically powered versions but he was not a fan, and he missed the sea already. He had moored his ship in a small inlet that he knew well on the coast of the Isle of Sheppey, and then once the craft had been hidden, he had stuck his thumb out and hitched a ride into London. He knew how to find the killers – he had done it before, time and time again – and over the years he had become very good at it.

Brendan also wore a charm around his right wrist that helped him to tune into the frequency of the spells. He could hear the ink talking now. In the beginning, it had just been a crackle like tiny twigs snapping underfoot, but now it was becoming a fuller sound. It grew louder until it boomed like giants shouting into the wind. As the driver weaved through the city streets, Brendan thought about the boy and wondered how and when he had come to know of this strange and powerful magic from the time of the first people of the Emerald Isle. How he had mastered it at such an early age, and who had taught him, were questions that had kept Brendan awake in the night on more than one occasion, but now was not the time to languish in the past, now was the time for action and to end the boy's life.

"Turn here, and park on the left please, driver," said Brendan.

The driver did as he was requested and Brendan waited patiently until the car had come to a complete stop before disembarking. As payment, he left the young man a pearl, and he touched the lad's forehead with his thumb and left him a memory that told him that the pearl was real. It would more than cover the cost of the journey.

Dave saw the car pull up in front of the main gates and the old man get out. His hand gripped the stock tightly and his finger moved from the safe position and hooked itself around the trigger. The old man appeared in his scope and his tattoo told him to open fire.

Brendan heard the tattoo order the boy to fire but did not panic. He had time, not a lot of it, but enough to counter the spell.

"Enough, Boy! Hear my voice and know me! The ink is false! It must not live, and nor can you! I draw you down, and I break the quill, no longer can you picture your malice and nevermore your ill," said Brendan in a very loud voice.

Dave squeezed the trigger, but nothing happened, and then he blacked out. Simon had fallen over and passed out too. Brendan walked through the main gates. No guard challenged him and even after the footage from the cameras was analysed by the MOD Police, no sign of him or image of him was ever recorded. Brendan kneeled down by the naked boy's body. He could see the nasty tattoo quite clearly; it throbbed and twitched and revolted him. How many times had he seen this before? How many times had he come across the body of an innocent that had been used as a weapon to kill and destroy?

"Enough..." he said softly to himself.

Brendan turned around and walked back the way he had come, and once he was through the main gates he raised his arm aloft and a car from the taxi rank across the road performed a neat U-turn and pulled up to the kerb in front of him. The driver activated the passenger side electric window, and when it was done he leaned across so that he could see the old man more clearly.

"It's your lucky day, sir. I have just come on shift and you are my first fare, and just because I like the look of you, this journey is on me. Where can I take you?" asked the driver.

Brendan smiled and opened the car door and got in.

"Can you take me into the centre of town, please?" said Brendan.

"Of course I can, sir. Just sit back and relax," said the driver.

Brendan settled back and watched the world go by. They had been driving for a few minutes when Brendan noticed the St Christopher's medallion hanging from the rear-view mirror. The driver caught him looking at it and said, "That's the Patron Saint of Travellers, St. Christopher."

"Are you sure about that?" said Brendan.

Chapter Twenty-Six

It Fades

Odhran retched so hard that he produced a gobbet of blood the size of a ripened plum, and then he coughed up bile for a full minute. He was not well and he was beginning to wonder what had caused this malady when two of his precious ink bottles shattered right in front of him. The small quantity of ink inside each one seemed to increase in volume ten-fold, and it spattered the wooden walls of his caravan. His head swam, and buckets of sweat began to roll off him. There was a thumping sound as though giant hailstones were falling on his roof all about him, and then Odhran heard a voice that he had not heard in centuries.

"Enough, Boy! Hear my voice and know me! The ink is false! It must not live, and nor can you! I draw you down, and I break the quill, no longer can you picture your malice and nevermore your ill."

Odhran shrank back and his eyes rolled up into his head. He felt like dropping to his knees and crying but then something stirred within him. The force that he had hosted for so long sensed that its puppet's strings were being cut away and reacted quickly. It would not go quietly, and it would not allow its human vessel to give in so easily. Odhran felt the presence of a cold spot in his guts. It swelled inside him and inched through his body muscle by muscle and bone by bone until it had filled him to the brim.

Odhran opened his eyes and saw the world anew. His vision was sharper and he could see colours in the air all around him. The sickness had gone and his head was clear. His clothes were still drenched in his own sweat and vomit, and the ink and blood from his recent attacks still decorated the interior of the caravan, but he felt more vigorous, and he was ready to act.

"So then, Brendan of Clonfert, my old teacher and betrayer, you have returned from the sea. How I wish you had drowned long ago. Well then, we shall see how this plays out," said Odhran.

He pulled out one of the small drawers below his collection of ink bottles and retrieved a handful of flyers and pamphlets from inside it. Each one advertised a festival or a county show. He chose the nearest one, he needed to give his old Master something to think about while he drew up his plans to destroy him. Then he cleaned the caravan until it resembled something less like a colourful abattoir.

Once the fire was lit and the horse fed, Odhran placed his precious leather-bound book on the small wooden table and flicked through its pages until he found the song that he was searching for. He sang to himself and traced the words with his fingertips. The paper felt soft and smooth, and he remembered a time long ago when as a boy, lonely and frightened, he had found the quill. It was larger than any that he had seen or heard about. That it was special there was no doubt, and it had talked to him and told him of the wider world, and it had promised him something if he would write of certain things. It had promised him power over others, great knowledge, strength and guile, and resistance to the magic of the Charmed Ones and the Monks.

He had guessed that it was the feather of an angel, and he had also realised, but not soon enough, that it was a feather from a fallen angel. He had used it and been abused by it for years before he understood its true purpose – to cause pain and spread evil. But it was too late, the quill was far too powerful to be cast away, and it needed to be fed. Its appetite was insatiable, and without the misery of others to keep it satisfied, the quill drained the life from Odhran instead. It was a magical parasite and it controlled Odhran at all times. If Odhran disobeyed the quill, it took a decade of Odhran's life away.

Brendan of Clonfert, the Abbots, the magicians and the Fae, all thought that the power came from the book that Odhran carried with him. They thought it was the spells written inside it, but the truth was very different. The quill made the words, and the quill drew the symbols. The evil came from within. Odhran heard the quill speak to him then, and he drew himself back from the mists of his memory to the caravan and his collection of small glass bottles.

"There are far fewer than before," said the voice.

"Yes, Lord, there are many empty spaces on my shelves," Odhran replied.

"No matter, I shall have some of your life force to keep me going." The voice was cold and flat.

"Please, Lord. Do not be too hasty with your servant, the return of the one who would destroy you has made things difficult, but not impossible," said Odhran.

"I care not for these holy men and their chanting. He is of no consequence to me. And as for you, you have had more

than enough time to develop a fine collection of tortured souls for me, and yet your shelves look famished!" The voice was stronger now.

"Lord, I know a place nearby where there will be no shortage of folk with an eye for some skin decoration. I can fill this caravan twice over for you." Odhran was breathing quickly, his chest rattled and his eyes began to hurt.

"Make sure of it, or you shall age a hundred days in an hour!"

The voice sounded very near and Odhran felt his hand begin to tremble. He looked down at it and saw liver spots forming on the skin of the back of his hand. The colour of his skin was grey, and his knuckles bulged with the onset of arthritis. He dropped the black quill and reached for the mirror. The face that looked out at him was his own, but he had aged and he looked sixty if he was a day. He sobbed for a time but all he heard was laughter, and when he had recovered himself enough to hitch the horse to the caravan he found it hard to tighten the reins with his bony hands. The pain was acute but it gave him an idea.

He picked up the black feather quill, took a deep breath and started to talk.

"Lord, I cannot hold the quill to draw the words and pictures onto the flesh of the new souls with these hands. Can you not but give me back some of the life you have taken? I fear that my current state would not appeal to the young people, and nor would they trust the dexterity of my fingers. They are asking me to make art after all…"

The voice returned to the caravan and this time it was loud and made Odhran's heart rattle around inside his chest like a bird in a cage.

"'Twas only for a moment, little scribbler. It was just to

remind you of what will happen to you if you do not fill those shelves with poison. You understand?"

"Yes, Lord. I do," said Odhran.

The next time he looked in the mirror the face he knew so well had returned, but now the clock was ticking and he must find a place to pitch the caravan. But before he did that he must buy a big bottle of vodka.

Chapter Twenty-Seven

Angel in the Middle

The flash came before the blast. That was all that Angel Dave could think about. He had heard the mortals talk of their short lives flashing before their eyes at the moment of death, but he hadn't experienced anything like that. He could remember the night of the fight between Gogmagog the giant and his nemesis, Corineus. In his mind's eye he saw the stampede of the crowd that had packed into the vaults below the Tower of London, and the fires and panic caused by the discovery of a magical bomb. Then, he saw himself as if through a misty lens, lifting the bomb and flying away, and hearing his old friend Judas screaming at him to stop. But he had carried on. Saving the lives of thousands of the Under Folk was all that mattered to him at that moment.

Why he had done it was still a mystery to him. Angel Dave had stopped standing up for others after he had been beaten half to death by a far-right religious anti-angel army. Judas had rescued him from their jackboots and their cudgels, and ever since they had been friends, and Angel Dave had always been there if Judas had called for his aid.

"The flash came before the blast," he said to no one.

That fateful night, Angel Dave had pulled in his wings; surprisingly they were complete and whole. He had expected them to have been burned to a crisp, along with the rest of him, but something had happened up there in the night sky above the Tower of London.

He had found himself sitting on a bridge and when he had turned his head he could see it stretching away in both directions; he couldn't tell how long it was because he couldn't see that far, and there was no ground below and no stars above, just blackness, a desert of the dark. Occasionally he fancied that there were things flying above him, or it could have been below, or both. But whenever he stood to look up or walk over to the edge of the bridge and look down, there was nothing. He was not alone, however.

Occasionally, the air had shimmered in front of him and a mortal man had appeared. Angel Dave had tried to talk to the people he had seen but they were unaware of him and could not hear him regardless of how loudly he shouted, nor could he touch them. Each time he tried they faded right in front of him, only to reappear ten feet away. Unlike Angel Dave, these people seemed to know where they were and where they had to go. Each time one of them appeared the first thing they did was exhale as if they had been holding their breath for a long time, and then once they had taken in their surroundings, they turned one way and then the other. He saw the look on their faces. Some would cry for joy and stride off full of purpose and with a spring in their step. Others, of which there were many, cried out in despair and shuffled away. He had seen thousands arrive and depart, but none like him.

Angel Dave had tried to flex his wings again and again and launch himself into the air, but his wings would not work as they should; instead, he folded them around his body to keep him warm when he slept and locked his feathers together when he felt scared, which was often. There was no sun or moon, and as a result, no sense of time. How long he had been there was a mystery; it could have been hours or aeons, he couldn't tell. But something occurred to him then and there. Angel Dave was neither alive nor dead. He was in a sort of limbo, and it appeared that there was no escape from it. All he could do was hope and sleep.

"The flash came before the blast," said a voice that was not his own.

Angel Dave woke with a start and stood quickly.

"The flash came before the blast. It keeps returning to you, doesn't it? That thought, you know something isn't quite right," said the voice again.

Angel Dave searched the gloom for the owner of the voice but he could see nothing. Then something huge flew past him and he was thrown to the ground. Angel Dave thought he saw streaks of gold and red in the air. He stood once again and edged backwards towards the edge of the bridge.

"The flash came before the blast," boomed a deep voice.

Angel Dave fell to the ground and covered his ears with his hands. His head was ringing and he could taste blood in his mouth. He cowered under his wings and shook with fear.

"Stand, little one!" ordered Lucifer, the Morningstar.

Angel Dave tried to crawl away, but the voice of the

First of the Fallen would not be denied, and he was lifted up and made to stand; his wings were pulled back and stretched outwards so that his back felt as though it were on fire. He tried to fight it, this invisible manhandling, but he was weak compared to Lucifer, control of his own limbs was no longer his own, and his heart was beating far too quickly. He had wished to see sunlight again, to bathe in it, to fly in a sky made warm by a sun, but the light that was emanating from Lucifer burned his eyes and made him shiver.

Lucifer was magnificent to behold. Terrifying but magnificent. His wings were enormous. Most of his feathers were jet black, but here and there could be seen flecks of gold and silver, and reds, lots of reds – ruby red, blood red and fire red. The rumours that Angel Dave had heard about Lucifer's armour were true; he could see it quite clearly now. The Morningstar had melted down the weapons and armour of the angels he had bested in battle and forged them into something else. But he had not stopped there. His armour was infused with the souls of those he had killed and Angel Dave saw their faces screaming and sobbing as light played across Lucifer's greaves and chest-plate. Underneath it, he wore a tunic the colour of cooling lava. At his side he wore a sword. There was no sheath for it though; Lucifer wore his weapon naked.

"Do you know where you are?" said Lucifer.

"No, Lord," said Angel Dave.

"Lord? I thought that those of the Second Fall had chosen not to worship *HIM*, nor to follow *ME*," said Lucifer.

"What should I call you then?" Angel Dave asked.

"What would you like to call me? How about, *sire, rescuer, leader, champion*, any of those will do. Stay with *Lord* if you wish."

Angel Dave tried to move but his body felt like stone and he could not force it to respond. Lucifer read his thoughts and nodded, and Angel Dave regained the use of his limbs once more.

"I can do so much more for you than that, little one. I can free you from this place, I can unlock any number of the hidden doors and see you on your way back home – wherever that is. Or, I can grant you a wish or two. The choice is yours. After all, we are kin, you and I." The Morningstar smiled.

Angel Dave felt the first feelings of warmth since he had been imprisoned on the bridge and a tear came to his eye. But he knew, as all angels do, that Lucifer, the brightest of them all, the most powerful, brave, wise and strong was also the most corrupt and what *he* wanted, was everything.

"You are kind, Lord. But I must decline your aid. I am here for a good reason; it has not presented itself yet, but I must have done something wrong, or maybe something right to have wound up here; time will show me the way out, perhaps," said Angel Dave.

"How predictable, little one; I have grown oh so bored of hearing the weak choose to be punished and tortured when all they need do is choose not to be. I can take you if I want. I could rip you apart and drop you into the void, or I could raise you up as a champion in my realm; the delights and the treasures are something to behold, believe me. Is there nothing that I can tempt you with?" Lucifer's voice was difficult to deny.

"I honour you, Lord Lucifer, and thank you for your offer, but I cannot accept," said Angel Dave.

"Oh, that is a pity, but you can serve me in another way. Do you recall what came first, the flash or the blast?" he asked.

Angel Dave stiffened; his senses were alert and his body tingled.

"L-Lord?" he stammered.

"*I* was the flash before the blast! I saw you, and I had a sudden thought, a 'flash' of brilliance, you might say. What if I were to save you and set you down here, in a place where I have greater power than all of the angels of the Host combined. I could plant you here and then casually let it be known that you are still alive. Word would travel fast, and then a rescue would be attempted."

Angel Dave went cold because he knew now why he had not died.

"I see that you realise your worth to me now and why you are here," said Lucifer.

The Morningstar beat his mighty wings, and Angel Dave was forced to his knees.

"If you will not serve me willingly, or join me, little one, you will help me to destroy Michael and the Deceiver. Your champions will come for you, and when they do, I shall cast them down and make them suffer. For a very long time."

Lucifer laughed as Angel Dave passed out. When he awakened, the Morningstar was gone and the bridge seemed even darker than before.

Chapter Twenty-Eight

Bulls-Eye and the Bottles

The Tate, or the Tate Modern to give it its proper title, was an amazing building, one of the few restorations that Judas had warmed to over the years. He came here sometimes to sit on one of the many benches outside and watch the people. Occasionally, he would go in and take in some art. It was hard at first because he had known so many of the artists personally. Some he remembered as being brilliant, warm and generous with their time and conversation, a few he had detested; but it was watching them die that troubled Judas the most. It made him more and more aware of his own life and what he had or had not achieved, and when he gazed into the canvas or studied the form of a sculpture, he admired the beauty and the skill of the artist yet cursed them at the same time because he knew his own name and work would never be honoured or loved.

Judas finished the ham and cheese toastie that he had bought from the canteen at Scotland Yard. Mercifully, it had cooled and would not burn his teeth down to stumps. Many a police officer had gone on duty with a mouth full of ice cubes after trying to eat a toastie too quickly, but he had learned his lesson long ago and let his sandwich rest for at least an hour before attempting to eat it. It tasted better cold, anyway.

A young man was trying to make a bit of extra cash using a big bowl of water heavily laced with washing-up liquid, and two short bamboo canes with a piece of string tied to the ends so that it made a circle. He soaked the string and wafted the canes about and with a little help from the wind, his invention created massive bubbles in the air. The passers-by and the little children they were dragging around the tourist spots of the capital loved the spectacle and dropped the odd coin or two into his hat on the ground. They were ignorant, intolerant, and a lot of other things that ended in 'ant', but they were also ingenious and brave, and Judas liked that about the mortals, and he respected them for it.

Judas removed the small glass bottle he had placed in his pocket and looked at it again. Somehow, the essence of a person's life had been trapped inside it and by foul means, a savage poison had been passed back to that person in return. The killer was mobile which made tracking him, her, or it down more difficult; there was normally some sort of pattern to these things. The killer would only kill on certain days or at certain times, they would have a patch, or prefer drowning to decapitation. There was always a link but so far he couldn't see it.

Judas deposited the wrapper from his nuclear toastie in the bin nearby and started walking back to the Yard. His sojourn into the fresh air had worked a little, the change of scenery had done him good. It was when he was nearing the Hallowed Ground that he had felt the guilt come crashing down on him like a Steinway piano being played by a hippopotamus. Angel Dave was gone.

Judas hadn't frequented the Hallowed Ground for his usual pint for some time; he had felt angry, and then sad, and then impotent. Now he was angry again. Back in the office he faced the big map of Greater London on his wall and stared at it for so long that his forehead began to ache. He was just about to put his fist straight through Finsbury Park when it dawned on him. The scenes of the attacks on the tattooed individuals were important, but he had been looking in the wrong places! The house in Tooting was chosen at random, so was the Century Club, and where the tattooed people had lived was a red herring too.

The killer had to pitch his caravan somewhere where it wouldn't stick out like a sore thumb; it had to be a place that attracted lots of different sorts of people. It couldn't be a Fae Fayre because the other magical folk would sniff the danger out and deal with the problem in their own way. So, it had to be a gathering above ground. Judas knew the dates of the attacks, and after a quick trip to the Metaverse via his laptop, he also knew which festivals had happened on the days leading up to the attacks. Instead of focusing on the victims, he just had to find out who was organising the next round of festivals, take a look at the planning documents for each one and attend the festival and catch the killer. Ten minutes ago, he had wanted to make a hole in the map with his fist, and now he was putting shiny new yellow pins into four different locations and feeling rather chipper.

He was smiling when he sat down at his desk, but something was niggling him, and he suddenly realised what it was. If there were a lot of people attending the festival that the killer had targeted and Judas was not there in time or picked the wrong one, then there was a possibility that he would need to get quite a few people away from the festival in such a way that they would cause no harm to each other or anyone else that they came into contact with. Judas removed his silver coin from his trouser pocket to help him think, but he did not need it. The answer was Black Maria! She could help him – he'd seen her stuff twenty drunken fighting football casualties into her pocket without breaking a sweat back in the 80s. Black Maria was one of the Under Folk, too, so she could handle herself. Judas dialled her number on his mobile phone, and when she answered, he told her what was happening and asked for her help.

Chapter Twenty-Nine

Overdosed

Archie was cold and hungry. The nearest shelter wasn't due to open for another few hours, and none of his old acquaintances from the road was out and about, so he found a doorway that hadn't been used as a toilet yet, sat down in it and wrapped his blanket tightly around him. Archie was a drunkard; he'd been on the streets since he was thirteen. An abusive father and a heroin-addict mother had given him the worst start in life a boy could have, and he had been suffering for it ever since. He was not a violent man, though; he was capable of great kindness if left alone and not bothered. A light went on nearby. It must have been triggered by a wandering feline because there was no one around at this time of the morning. Archie rested his head on his knees and was snoring shortly afterwards.

Odhran waited for a short while and then approached the rough sleeper in the doorway. He had a present for him: two two-litre bottles of weapon's-grade cider. The man woke with a start and was suspicious at first, but after some small talk, he took the offerings gladly. Odhran walked away and hid behind a battered yellow skip that had been blessed with not one but two dead mattresses. It was the perfect hiding place, and he was overjoyed when he sneaked a look at the drunk and saw that he had already downed most of the first bottle. By the time Odhran had fetched his caravan, the poor soul was blind drunk and unresponsive. Odhran lifted him easily and placed him inside; it was then but a short ride to the waste ground, and once there, Odhran set about tattooing the man.

He spent most of the night working on him. The images were crude and lacked any style or flair, but there were so many more than usual. He had drawn knives, bloody axes, Gaelic symbols, Greek symbols, flames and poison, devils and dragons until the man's back and his arms resembled a tangled bloody mess. The resulting carnage would fill many of his empty bottles, and he would get back the years that the evil inside him had taken. He dumped the man by the side of the road and went in search of an empty field so that the horse could eat and rest and he could get ready for the festival he had chosen to attend.

Chapter Thirty

Dark Days

The centre of a city, a large city like London, is the scratching of nails down a blackboard to a mariner. Brendan had walked the streets of many of the world's capitals, but he found London to be the worst. It was a heaving grey monster belching from a million orifices and screaming without ever stopping to take a breath. The two soldiers he had rescued before they could wage war on Shooter's Hill and the nearby environs were lucky; they would face some sort of punishment for stealing the weapons and attacking their senior officer, but that sentence was going to be far shorter than the one they would have faced if they had succeeded with their attack.

The tattoos on their bodies were sharper, more detailed and much more potent than the boy's initial clumsy efforts. Something was guiding the lad, pushing him on, teaching him the dark words. That much was clear, and it worried Brendan greatly now. For too long, he had been at sea; he should have searched for the boy long before now.

Brendan entered a small café called Bert's and sat down at a table by the window. An older man waddled over to him wearing a white apron around his waist; this was the proprietor, and he came armed with a small white orders book and a chewed blue Bic biro. Brendan ordered the full English breakfast and a coffee and saw Bert hand his order to the cook, who was an angel. Brendan watched him expertly preparing the orders – frying, chopping and grinding. He was fast and appeared never to panic or get flustered. A handy skill to have in a place like this. The angel seemed more than happy with his lot in life and smiled often.

When the food came, Brendan tucked in; it had been some time since he had eaten properly, and he was glad of his now warm and very full belly. Bert came to clear the empty plate away, and it was while the table was being cleared that it happened. Brendan felt a surge of energy, followed by screaming; the angel heard it, too, and dropped his spatula onto the tiled floor.

But there was no danger here in the café. It was the boy again, and he had been busy. Brendan had been told of a place called the Black Museum by one of the ghost captains that he had traded with off Finisterre. He had learned that the Master of the Black Museum was the defender of the Fae in the city; he was also a mighty warrior and nothing transpired in the metropolis without him knowing about it. Brendan would seek him out and ask for his aid.

Chapter Thirty-One

Blood Red Rust

Simon the Zealot was not a friendly, outgoing sort of chap, unless there was something that he wanted from you, or that could help him get where he wanted to go. He would have been a weasel if he were ever to be reincarnated. He hated the Black Museum, he despised the modern world and its ugliness, and he hated with a passion the man who had sentenced him to hard time inside this awful place. He really hated Judas. But he had a plan, and that plan was very nearly ready to put into motion.

Simon haunted the Key Room like a wraith; he preferred to keep the lights off and he always tried to stay as far away as possible from the door in case his Lord and Master deigned to drop by and persecute him a bit. Luckily, Judas had been busy on a case and Simon had been allowed to roam free. He shuffled along the side of the great table, his eyes searching for the wicked hacksaw that a disturbed Victorian doctor had chosen to commit a string of grisly murders with. Hidden underneath the hacksaw was a small piece of driftwood with a rusty nail that looked like a mast on a very small raft. This key opened the door to a beach – a cold, grey place where a governess paced the shoreline and wept at the sight of the babies she had drowned there. Simon had chosen this key because it was small and easy to hide.

He picked up the driftwood and closed his eyes. When he reopened them, he was there, watching the governess sobbing and ripping great clumps of her hair from her head again. She cried and wailed at the dead babies and the small children, and they cried back, but she could not help them and nor could she make them stop. He passed her by but she did not see him.

Simon walked along the beach, staying as close to the water as possible because as the tide came in, his footprints disappeared. He thought it wise to leave no trace of his visits, just in case. He reached the end of the beach, then turned away from the water and made for the rocks and the cave where he had hidden his things. Inside was a small desk, a couple of iron-bound boxes and two chairs; one for him and one for his new partner.

Simon entered and lit the oil lamp he had stolen from the office. The light instantly transformed the soft grey walls of the cave into hard ragged lines of overlapping darkness. He found the portable heater he had liberated and turned that on too, and then when he was satisfied that the cave was now moderately habitable, he reached into the pocket of his jacket and pulled out the cufflink. He then placed it on the top of the small table; the light reflected off the smooth polished silver and it appeared to glow. Simon waited for his eyes to become accustomed to the light in the cave and then took two very deep breaths.

When he was ready, Simon picked up the cufflink, held

it up to his lips and said, "I summon you, Jack, attend me now."

The light flickered for a second and the motor inside the heater pulsed. Then Simon heard it. Soft at first and hard to pick out, but as the noise grew louder, Simon recognised the sound of a blade being sharpened on a wet stone. It stopped suddenly, and when he heard that laughter again he knew that Jack the Ripper was on his way.

The girl waited. The wind that gusted across the water was strong but it could not move the clouds above; it was as if they were glued to the sky and no matter how hard the wind blew, they would not part. She pulled up the zip of her jacket and raised the collar; it was an instinctive act but she need not have bothered because she could not feel the cold. She was sure that she would be blue by now if she could, but she was dead and felt nothing. She counted to a hundred and then crept as close as she could to the mouth of the small cave that the man she had been told to watch had just entered. Then she closed her eyes and listened to a conversation between two men, and it was not long before she concluded that both must surely be insane.

Inside the cave, Simon the Zealot was holding court, spurred on by Jack the Ripper's occasional witty aside or word of encouragement. They talked of how they would destroy Judas and his Black Museum; how they would empty the gaol of its inhabitants and watch as they escaped back into the real world. The girl listened on.

"But remember, Jack, we must release John the Baptist from his watery grave. Once he is loose, Judas and his infernal angels will have their hands full, and we, my good friend, shall look on and enjoy the chaos and destruction," said Simon.

"We are agreed, Simon. I will uphold my end of the bargain, just make sure that your colossal friend knows that I must see Judas die! It is my only request. Make it happen and we shall get on famously."

Something was puzzling Simon about Jack the Ripper. His voice had changed over the last few weeks. Simon had noticed that it was deeper than before, more rounded, and it was sharper, just like one of the knives he was constantly playing around with. Simon was a quick learner and he had guessed, correctly, that as long as there was something left of the entity – a strand of hair, a button or a cufflink – inside the Black Museum or in these infernal Time Fields, a part of the entity also remained, and it could be restored. That is why he stole the cufflink away from under Judas's nose. For Simon to get out of this prison, he needed someone like Jack. At first, Jack's voice had been thin and reedy, as if he were being grown again, like a plant from a seed. Now, Jack's voice was strong and Simon could sense that Jack's power and confidence had returned. Given half a chance, Simon knew that his partner in crime would run one of those surgeon's blades right through his guts, so Simon had a backup plan for Jack and it involved the cufflink on the table in front of him and a furnace. If Jack tried to play him false, the silver cufflink would go into the fire and not even Jack the Ripper would survive that – he hoped.

The wind outside had grown in intensity, and the girl was finding it hard to hear every word that was said inside the cave so she decided to move closer. It was as she was creeping forward that she accidentally kicked a pebble and it shot straight into the cave.

"There's someone out there!" shouted Jack.

Simon was already on his feet. He snatched the cufflink from the table and quickly bent down to turn the heater and the lamp off. Rocks fell from cliffs, and sand dunes often collapsed, but no stone shot across the ground like that unless it had been disturbed by someone or something. Simon's eyes narrowed and he made his way slowly to the mouth of the cave.

The girl ran back down the beach. She had followed the man to the cave and walked as he had done, at the water's edge so that her footprints would not give her away either but now there was no time for caution. Simon saw the shape of a person disappear around the rocks and head back down the beach. He couldn't make out who or what it was but the fact that it was running away encouraged him to chase after it. He would catch the eavesdropper and make it talk. As he pursued the shape he started to panic. What had it heard? Who was it working for? All of these questions buzzed around inside his head and he saw his grand design failing and falling apart.

The girl reached the governess. She wanted to call out to her, ask her for help, but although the governess was present in body her mind had long ago been destroyed. The girl stopped. The opening she had used to enter this part of the Time Fields was too far away; the person chasing her would catch her before she could step through it. She needed a place to hide but the beach was empty.

Simon saw the footprints in the wet sand leading away from him and shouted as loudly as he could.

"I'm coming for you!"

The girl caught the sound of the man's voice and knew that he would come around the rocks and see her, but she did not panic, and from somewhere, an idea came to her and she acted upon it. Simon vaulted over the rocks at the edge of the beach and he saw the Governess standing at the water's edge just where he expected her to be, but the rest of the beach was empty. There were footprints leading away from the child murderer, but nothing else, not a sign of the other person. He raced along the beach, and then searched behind the dunes but his quarry was gone.

Simon howled, picked up a rock and threw it at some imaginary foe. It would have probably missed its target. Simon was no warrior, but there was no time for anger or inaction, he had to get back to the Key Room now. If someone had followed him here there was the possibility that they had used a key from the Key Room. He reached into his pocket and grasped the piece of driftwood with the rusty nail in it and closed his eyes. Seconds later he was back in the Key Room. Everything was as he had left it; there was no sign of the spy. He replaced the driftwood under the hacksaw, making sure that it was not visible then he moved around the table and dropped the cufflink into a spent shotgun cartridge. It would be safe there. Now all he could do was wait for his accuser to step forward and denounce him.

The girl watched the man disappear right in front of her. He was there one minute and then there was a hole in the air where he had been standing. She was not entirely surprised by these strange phenomena. These Time Fields were still so alien and unpredictable, but she had come to terms with her new existence quickly and understood that she was not in Kansas anymore. Maybe this was why she had decided to use the great big bustle attached to the dress that the Governess was wearing as her hiding place. It must have been the fashion of the day in her time, yards and yards of heavy material fitted over a frame made of ostrich bone or something akin to it. The girl had simply crouched down behind the Governess, lifted the hem of her dress, crawled underneath and allowed it to fall down over her. The girl had been inside smaller tents at festivals she had attended and was able to watch the man search for her, hidden from view and safe from discovery.

She had gambled on the Governess not reacting to her presence or proximity and it had paid off. She had been lucky this time, but there was no time to gloat. She had to get a message to the Master of the Black Museum.

Chapter Thirty-Two

Rough

Little Tom didn't think of himself as a drug dealer. He preferred to be called *The Man.* Tom was a big fat bloke who liked to wear muscle gym sweats and was often seen sporting a thick brown powerlifters' belt. He had never been near a gym or a deadlift in his life but no one would ever dare to mention that in his presence. The belt came in handy sometimes. He used it as a 'starter'. Whenever any of his boys were slow or did not make their collections on time he used the belt to smack them over the head or the face. If the unlucky recipient wasn't watching Little Tom carefully enough, the belt would swish and sometimes the buckle would meet the eye. More than one of Tom's boys had ended up in the A&E department of the local hospital. They entered covered in blood and departed with only one working eye. But them was the breaks when you worked for Tom and pushed heroin for a living.

Tom squeezed into his shiny new black Mercedes sports break. He was a waddling cliché, fuelled by Big Macs and amphetamines, and boy did he know it, but Little Tom was like a pig in poo. He thought it was ironic, and someday the rest of them would catch up with him, but that was the limit of his IQ, and that's why he was more dangerous than any of the other suppliers; he had no morals and no handbrake. But even Little Tom was not ready or prepared for what was about to happen to him.

Archie woke up with the biggest headache he'd ever had; his skull hurt, but there was something else, his body hurt too, and this was unusual. When you had spent as much time as he had on the road and seen life through the thick end of a bottle of vodka, you became immune to hangovers. There was a cure for that: more alcohol. The pain across his chest, back and arms was new, and he was hearing voices now, but he liked what they were proposing.

Little Tom was cruising down Old Kent Road, stopping to check in with his dealers and having the occasional break for a kebab or a burger. Being a drug lord was hard work and he needed his sustenance. He had a big frame, after all. One of his boys worked out of a parked car at the Surrey Linear Canal park. It was a lovely little spot with the Willowbrook Estate on one side and Burgess Park on the other; there was always a steady stream of addicts flowing down the canal or from the cramped streets of the estate.

When he arrived at the car park, he could tell that something was wrong. It was too quiet, and there weren't enough skinny kids in hoodies stumbling along the pavement with their pockets full of Smack and empty of cash. Little Tom parked the Mercedes and eased himself out. He unbuckled his big brown belt and felt the base of his paunch grow cold as the breeze said hello to the sweat that had rolled down his gut and collected under the leather.

Archie had removed his coat, then his outer jumper,

then his sweatshirt. His London gift shop t-shirt was next and then finally, the thermal vest he had acquired at one of the local churches. He was covered in gaudy tattoos. They looked awful and overlapped and stretched whenever he moved. No care had been taken in their placement, but he liked them very much. The voices had told him to like them, and he did. The voices had told him to strip naked and he had obeyed, and then the kind voice had told him to smash the window of the pawn shop and retrieve the samurai sword because he was going to need it to get more money to buy more booze. Archie liked the voices.

Little Tom saw the skinny old man from across the car park; he also saw Rickie, one of his boys, laying on the ground at his feet, coughing up huge gobbets of blood and moaning softly. The old chap was covered in blood, too, but Little Tom knew that none of it was his own. Tom charged at the old man, swinging his belt; he had taken care of more significant threats than this and he was looking forward to smashing the old git into the canal and then standing on his head until his lungs were full of sewage and used condoms.

But Little Tom had got it all wrong and as he drew within striking distance the old man lurched upwards and Tom saw the flash of steel and his own guts fall out onto the gravel. He had been trying to run as fast as a big fat man could and his momentum carried him forward into the bushes nearby. There was some rustling followed by a splash as his body tore a hole through the foliage and then dropped into the water. His brown weightlifters' belt floated away.

Archie listened to the voices as they told him how strong he was and how well-timed the thrust of the blade was, and he revelled in their praise and adulation. Then, the nice voice told him that there would be more money in the fat man's car, so he investigated. The voices were right, as they had been all night.

Stuart and Mike were members of SCO19, the Met's tactical firearms division. They had been watching the events unfold in the car park from the rear of a VW Camper that had been modified for scenarios such as this. There had been a warning that a turf war was about to erupt, and they, and other members of SCO19, had been placed at staging points all around the area so that if violence ensued, they could attend and lend a hand if required. Neither had expected to see what they had just seen, and while Stuart was calling the command centre, Mike made a judgement call and steamed in. It was only an old man with a sword, after all.

The voices told Archie that the man was coming, and that he was armed, so Archie dropped the carrier bag full of rolls of £50 notes back into the boot of the car, turned around and raised his sword. Mike came to a halt two metres from the target and raised his weapon too.

"Armed police, drop your weapon now!" he shouted.

"Run him through with your blade!" said the voices.

Archie did as he was told and moving with surprising speed and grace, he found a small gap just below Mike's protective vest. The blade was very sharp and it slid inside nicely. At precisely the same time as the steel met flesh, Mike's finger squeezed the trigger of his firearm, and the round went through the old man's chest at near enough point-blank range. The force of the bullet lifted Archie off his feet, and he was hurled backwards and ended up with the top half of his body inside the car boot and his legs dangling out to touch the gravel. Miraculously, the sword was still in his hand.

Stuart saw Mike go down; he quickly and concisely related the incident to command and then went to support his fellow police officer in the line of their duty. Mike was on his back and holding his left hand to his stomach to stop the flow of blood; he had dropped his firearm, so Stuart nudged it towards him with the toe of his boot. Mike nodded towards the car and Stuart raised his pistol and advanced.

When the support team arrived on the scene, Mike was dead and Stuart was severely wounded. One drug dealer had been gutted and was laying on the ground next to his car, and the body of another criminal had been found by police dogs in the canal nearby. It had all the hallmarks of a drugs-related battle for territory and power, but there was also something odd about this one. The dead body of an old man had been found at the scene; he was holding a sword and was covered in what later turned out to be temporary tattoos. One police officer suggested that he might be some sort of Japanese samurai-inspired vigilante waging war on the drug trade.

Stuart died on his way to the hospital. Before he passed, he told the paramedic that the old man had shouted that the voices inside his head told him to do it. This was noted down, but it was only after another officer had interviewed the medic that the report was amended. The old man had shouted that the voices inside his head came from the drawings on his body.

Chapter Thirty-Three

Escalation

She was nervous. It was a strange sensation. Witches were not by nature ... nervous. She hoped that he would be pleased to see her again, then a thought barged its way into her mind. What if there was another woman there? He might have another partner; that would be embarrassing, and she almost didn't press the buzzer to Flat 7, but she did. The White Witch had taken a well-earned and long-overdue break from providing security for the Ley Line Express and decided that she would use her time to go and see him. They had only been lovers for a short period of time, and she had worried at first that her feelings would not be reciprocated; she was not young, but she was also not *that old*. They had spoken by mail and over the phone, but neither really enjoyed that sort of contact so it had stopped quickly.

She was about to raise her hand once again and press the buzzer for the second time, but his voice stopped her, and when his face appeared on the small screen above the buttons, her heart began to beat faster. They made love as soon as he had closed the door to his flat behind her. The first time was hasty and rushed; the second time was longer and considered; afterwards, they lay on his bed and held each other tightly; it had been a long time since Judas had watched the crescent-shaped birthmark pass across the skin of her shoulder blades like this. Her skin was very pale, and her hair was the colour of a corridor between two stars in the night sky; she had green eyes that lifted slightly at the corners and freckles across her cheeks and the bridge of her nose. Her eyes were the first thing he had noticed when he had travelled on the Ley Line Express. That moment seemed as though it had happened a lifetime ago.

They rose, showered, and then breakfasted. At first, the words were spare and came in fits and starts, but then they relaxed and slipped into an easy familiarity.

"I'm so glad you came, Esther," said Judas.

"I, also," she said.

Esther had a strange way of talking. It was old-fashioned and short, almost clipped, as though she needed to conserve her words in case they suddenly ran out. Judas loved it because he lived in a world where five words were always better than one to most people.

"You are troubled, Judas. There is a stubborn line across your brow. It was not there before," said Esther.

"It's just something I'm working on, Esther. Nothing to worry about."

Esther was not convinced.

"Tell a tale, leave no word unturned. Learn a new way, part the mist," she said.

"Another one of your old sayings?" said Judas.

"Possibly," she said.

Judas pulled her closer, and when he felt her heart beating against him, he felt something stir. He knew the feeling had a name, but he dared not set it free, not just yet.

"There is a serial killer attacking and murdering on both sides of the domain, killing mortals and Fae alike. He, or it, I'm not sure yet. I think that the victims are tattooed with a particular sort of temporary ink. Once it's on the skin, they lose control of their senses and kill others or incite violence from others, and then they die, and the marks fade. It's a strange one," he said.

"It sounds familiar. I heard long ago that there was some old magic that worked like this. Many sought to find the killer and discover his power, but the killer wandered far and wide and was lost each time the pursuers closed in. There was something concerning a book, but that proved false, and one learned Witch suggested it was the tool rather than the word that did the deed," said Esther.

"The tattooist's needle?" Judas asked.

"Quite so. Back then, at the beginning, it would have been a sharp point, and the ink would have been spat into the holes it created," said Esther.

She moved across the room and sat down on the sofa; Judas followed and joined her there.

"Do you still keep the charm I gave you, Judas?" asked Esther.

"Of course, but I don't wear it all the time," he said.

"Perhaps you should for a while, my love," she said.

"That bad?" he asked.

"It could be, and you never know when you'll need to call out to a friend for aid," said Esther.

Then, she lay her head down on his lap and he stroked her hair. They ate at a restaurant nearby. Esther was no stranger to the mortal world, but even she was not quite ready for the Gurkha's Revenge, a spicy Indian dish from the Imli; it was a world-famous curry house, at least that was what it said on top of the menu. Judas had stopped looking at his mobile phone mere seconds after Esther had arrived. He had turned it to Silent Mode, and there had been a moment, a guilty moment when he thought he should turn it off, but he had so few chances to be really happy, so he forgave himself. The dinner was excellent and when they returned to the flat, he placed his mobile phone on the console table in the hall and forgot all about it in an instant.

He was woken by a hammering on his front door; behind the thumps on the wood, he could hear the squawk of radios and the muffled conversations of young officers trying to work out how violent they could be with the front door of one of their superiors. He jumped out of bed, pulled on some jogging bottoms and put on a t-shirt and quickly unlatched the door. There were some junior officers there, but so was the Chief Superintendent, and he did not look happy.

"There have been five more! Two were serving officers. I suggest you turn your phone on and get to work immediately! I'm going to visit the wives of the two dead officers now. I have no idea what I'm going to say! Their partners were killed in bizarre circumstances, and I'm going to have to lie through my teeth and invent some sort of vague scenario to explain it away. I hate lying because it always comes back like some bloody blame boomerang. DCI Iscariot, I expect a report or a status update from you by the time I return to the Yard!" barked the Chief.

He did not wait for an answer and marched back down the corridor. Judas did not blame him for his temper. He had been a staunch supporter of the Black Museum and Judas had gone silent on him in the middle of a Black Museum operation, and now there were even more casualties, and it made him feel sick. Esther was waiting for him. She had heard what had transpired and knew that their time together was at a close, for now. There was a particular look on her face and it was clear to him that she understood.

"Will you be here when I get back?" he asked.

"Possibly not, my love. Wear the charm. Be safe. I shall see you soon."

Judas showered and dressed, placed the small leather pouch she had given him in his pocket, kissed her goodbye and went to work.

Chapter Thirty-Four

Lace

The Lugger was about a hundred metres away in the middle of the channel. The wind had filled her red sails and she was leaning over and surging through the water. In ten minutes, if Lace could stand to stay there for that long, the ship would disappear around the bend in the mighty Thames, and her lover would be gone. Hornpipe was a captain of the Mudlarks and he had told her that he was going away and she had pretended that he'd forgotten to tell her. It was a low blow and a petty one at that. Their relationship had been heading in the wrong direction for the last couple of months and rather than sort it out, she had tried to force him to do things her way. Something that she deeply regretted standing there on the small wooden wharf with the best thing in her life disappearing from view.

The Mudlarks were the most powerful of the gangs that worked the river, and they had business concerns from the trickle of water that became the Thames far away to the west of the country all the way up and out to the chops of the Channel and beyond. Lace had met him on one of her earlier cases, and since then they had been lovers. She was not sure how much longer he would put up with her stupidity. If the shoe were on the other foot she was not sure that she would take it the way he had. She had come here to say sorry and to tell him how she truly felt but time and tide wait for no woman. Lace turned away from the water with what she felt to be a small dark cloud the size of a top hat hanging over her and occasionally firing animated lightning bolts at her head. She trudged back to her car, and then drove back to her flat.

WPC Claire Evans was waiting for her. Lace had agreed to spend the day with her old friend. They were going to a mini festival nearby. The sun had come out and Lace was committed to two things: having a bloody good time and sorting her mess out with Hornpipe the Mudlark when he returned.

"I've got one of those throw-it-up-in-the-air tents, in case we decide to stay the night, at least 20 packs of wet wipes, you can never have enough of those at a festival, condoms of course, and I've liberated some booze from the Confiscated Goods locker that no one will miss," said Claire.

"I don't think I'll be needing the condoms, Claire," said Lace.

"Still not going well?" Claire asked.

"It's just a bit awkward, to be honest. The feelings are there and the sex is amazing, but I'm scared that either he's not going to stick around or he's going to decide that me being a detective is going to cause difficulties in his world," said Lace.

"And what world is that?" Evans asked.

"Imports and exports, maritime operations really. Quite boring but there's quite a bit of semi-shady stuff that it's better not to know too much about," said Lace.

Evans tapped the sat nav display on the dashboard and Darth Vader's voice told her to take the next left.

"How the hell?" cried Lace.

"Most of the sat navs you can get these days have a few voice options. Some folk don't like taking orders from a woman, some don't like men, but no one argues with Darth Vader!" Evans laughed, and it made Lace smile and then relax.

"Don't underestimate the power of the Highway Code!" said Evans in her best Vader voice.

They drove on for a few minutes and before reaching their destination.

"I never knew there was a beach in Ruislip," said Lace.

"It's a very well-kept secret my friend, and today, tonight and possibly even tomorrow, Ruislip Lido Beach is going to be party central for thee and me, and the first rule of Lido Beach Club is that we don't tell anyone that we're coppers, okay?" said Evans.

"Goes without saying," said Lace.

They pulled into the car park and Evans parked her car in bay seven. She had pre-booked everything in advance and Lace was impressed. They unpacked the car and then walked up to the small wooden office. Inside there was a desk, and two wireless speakers that were already blaring out something that sounded like Hawaiian music that had been rinsed through some hard-core editing software and speeded up. A young lady sat behind the desk. She had her laptop open and at least three mobile phones on the go. The scent of incense hung in the air. It was an old trick to disguise the scent of something less legal but Evans and Lace pretended not to notice. Evans produced her own phone and showed the girl her tickets. The girl nodded, ticked the numbers off and then wrapped a security bracelet on each of their wrists and waved them through the door behind her theatrically.

There were hundreds of people milling about. Some had taken to the water already, and the smell of sausages and burgers with fried onions was everywhere. There were stalls selling artisan cheeses and farm-produced wine, plenty of t-shirt stands, and there were also the big corporations' pop-up tents announcing that you could recharge your phone for nothing so that you could keep sharing those all-important TikToks with your 'people'. Free data, free broadband, free digital stickers, and all for nothing – until you get your monthly bill and you're in deep.

Evans used her mobile to find their camping bay. She had bagged one of the best spots and they were in a fairly quiet position but still close to the water and in stumbling distance of the main stages. Lace released the clips on the tent and then took evasive action as it popped up in her face. They pushed the tent pegs into the ground with the heels of their boots and then dumped their gear inside the tent and locked it with a small combination lock. Then, they went in search of entertainment.

Lace and Evans were half-cut. The tops of their heads were warm, and they had a glow in their cheeks. The music was good, the beer wasn't too warm and they had already consumed a burger and a giant mango smoothie. Lace smiled at Evans.

"Thanks, Claire," she said.

"No problem, sit back and enjoy it. The sun is high and it's warm, the view isn't bad and the night is young," said Evans.

They went in search of a change in music and found it

at one of the Indie stages. A band they'd both heard of was up next and they found a place quite near the front. There were hundreds of picnic rugs laid out around them with groups, families and singles laying back on them. The music started, and all eyes and ears were on the band. All save one.

Trigger Thomas was a small-time dealer. He worked the festival scene and he supplied most things but kept the amount down to a manageable level. He liked the festivals and he didn't want to get banned. He was known to those that needed the extra stimulation and flew low enough that he could continue his business without drawing attention to himself. Life was good, it was sweet, and it was profitable. The only fly in the ointment was WPC Evans and her friend sitting up at the front. She had arrested him last year and she knew him on sight and what he would be doing there, so he decided on a course of preventative action.

Lace was enjoying the verve and the energy of the music and the performers but there was an emergency. Her big glass of Pimm's was nearly empty, and that would never do.

"Claire! Do you want another drink?" she yelled over the music.

"Of course! Same again, please!" replied Evans.

Lace navigated through the maze of picnic blankets and only stepped on three people, which was a miracle in itself. The Pimm's stand was right on the edge of the crowd and Lace was served quickly. It was while she was paying for the drinks that the chap to her left dropped his wallet on the floor next to her. Being a police officer and a servant of the people, not to mention a nice person, Lace reacted instinctively and bent over to pick it up and to return it to its owner. The young man was really grateful and he beamed at her. He tried to say something but the music was still too loud even at the back of the crowd. Lace raised her hands to signal that he was very welcome and then turned to pick up her drinks and head back to her friend.

Trigger put his wallet back in his pocket and made his way back through the crowds too. He had spiked the woman's drinks when she wasn't watching. In about an hour or so, both of them would be too high to recognise him. It was a job well done.

Lace and Evans wandered away from the Indie stage. The sun was dropping towards the top of the trees quickly and they were both ravenously hungry. They found a few stalls selling Jamaican Jerk Chicken, Chinese and Indian, but decided on a big bad-boy steak sandwich each from the Bristol Beef Biz.

Later that evening, Lace and Evans passed a really cool old caravan parked up beneath a tree next to a Tarot card reader and a mobile piercing unit. There was a board outside that read *The Black of Beyond Magical Tattoos*. Neither would have risked a real tattoo, there were plenty of coppers with them already, but they were feeling rather good tonight and after a bit of back and forth, Lace went first, and Evans second.

Chapter Thirty-Five

The Saint From the Sea

Judas stepped out of the lift with his ears still ringing from the dressing down he'd just received from the Chief. The meetings he had attended with the partners of the officers that were killed the day before had not gone well (if ever a meeting of that nature can go well) and the Chief was angry and ashamed. Judas wandered back down the corridor and pushed the door to his office open. When he walked inside, he found an older man sitting on top of one of the filing cabinets against the wall.

"It's strange to see the angels flying past your window all the time," he said.

"It's even stranger that you can get inside my office without anyone knowing," Judas replied.

"Forgive me, Master of the Black Museum. I hope that I'm addressing you with the correct honorific?" said the man.

"Never mind that; who are you, and what do you want? I'm a bit pressed for time at the moment."

"That makes two of us. I have come to you for help; there is a killer at large," said the man.

"What sort of killer?" said Judas, his guard up.

The older man leaned forwards and dropped to the floor. He was tall, at least as tall as Judas, and the skin of his face was weather-beaten. He had a high forehead and blue eyes. He wasn't muscular or wide of shoulder but Judas could see that the man could handle himself if pressed. Judas would hazard a good guess that he was a sailor or had spent some time onboard a ship.

"Introductions are in order first I think. I am Brendan of Clonfert," said the man.

"The *Saint*?" gasped Judas.

"The very same," replied Brendan.

"Well, this might sound a little odd, and certainly unexpected, but my name is Detective Chief Inspector Judas Iscariot of the Black Museum at Scotland Yard."

Brendan of Clonfert did indeed look confused and slightly bewildered but he regained his composure quickly.

"Your parents disliked you, it seems. To christen you in a church, before God, with that name. It's a wonder that any priest would allow it," said Brendan with a chuckle.

Judas took a deep breath.

"No. I am the original Judas Iscariot. Your God wouldn't let me take the easy way out. I tried to hang myself ... actually, that's incorrect, I did in fact hang myself but I was brought back and fixed, as it were. Then I was sent out into the world to make good, if you like, to fight crime and evil," said Judas.

Brendan went as white as a sheet and reached out for the edge of the wooden table at his side to steady himself.

"I have heard on more than one occasion the mortals saying that they believe that Our Lord works in mysterious

An Ink So Dark

ways. The fact that you are standing here in front of me would rather substantiate this, wouldn't you say?" said Brendan.

"It would indeed. I'm on the side of the angels these days. You could always flag one down and ask it if you need confirmation."

Judas gestured towards the window.

Brendan sat down on a chair and rested his hands on the arms.

"Wonders never cease!" he said.

"I wish they'd come around a bit more often to be honest, but no, you're right, they never cease. I must say that you're taking this remarkably well," said Judas.

He removed his jacket and hung it on his coat stand.

"Do saints drink coffee, Brendan of Clonfert?" asked Judas.

"This isn't the dark ages, Inspector," replied Brendan.

He had hesitated just before saying the word 'Inspector'. Judas realised straightaway that he wouldn't be getting called by his first name much in Brendan's presence.

"You're partially right there, Brendan. May I call you 'Brendan'?" he asked.

"Of course, Inspector."

Judas made them both a mug of hot, steaming coffee. The aroma was intense and the tension in the room relaxed slightly. Good coffee can do that.

"My killer was once a young man called Odhran, Inspector. He grew up in Eire long ago. He was a unique child, given to visions and flights of fancy, very bright compared to the rest of the children of his village, and as was the custom of the day, he was introduced to the monks at the nearby Abbey before being handed over to me, for teaching and instruction. But, somewhere along the line, when my gaze was elsewhere, the boy must have been visited by a demon or some other dark force and taken away from me. He was there physically, of course, walking by my side and being very much an excellent servant. It was in the hours of darkness and in the quiet of solitude that Odhran turned away from the light.

"The boy draws images in a book, or at least he used to, and then, once the image is complete, a spell is cast or a curse created; I'm not entirely sure how he does it or where he sources the power from, only that the lines of the images kill or force someone to act in an unusual fashion," said Brendan.

Judas sat bolt upright and placed his mug down on the table.

"Your boy, Odhran, sounds just like the creature I'm looking for. My killer has been tattooing pictures and symbols onto the bodies of complete strangers with some sort of magical ink. I don't think that there could be two, do you?"

Brendan shook his head.

"Can you find him, Brendan?" asked Judas.

"I believe so, Inspector. I am the true Patron Saint of Travellers after all. I seem to have developed – or have been given, I'm not sure which – the ability to follow the journeys of others, to travel alongside them in my mind, in order to keep them safe, as it were. I am drawn to the locations of those in need of my help, and as the boy and I are connected too, there is a convergence," said Brendan.

"If you can find him with your mind, then why not do it and stop the boy from killing anyone else?" asked Judas.

"The child was powerful, Inspector. The man, even more so. The force inside him is warned of my presence and is fighting back." Brendan finished his coffee and placed the empty mug on the table.

Judas stood and walked across the room to the big map of Greater London on the wall. Brendan followed him.

"Ignore the red and the blue pins; the yellow pins indicate a death or deaths caused by our killer. As you can see, they are erratic, and there was no discernible pattern to follow, but after a bit of legwork and some thought, I realised that the places where the deaths occurred weren't important; what was important was where the victims had been shortly before they lost control of their actions. They had all attended a festival in the past day or two, apart from the most recent attack, which leads me to believe that the killer is panicking," said Judas.

"I saved two young men in Greenwich, the day before yesterday. The carnage they were intending to inflict upon the local population would have given the boy and his master a great deal of power. If they needed it and it had been denied to them, that could have made them panic, Inspector," said Brendan.

Judas pointed to the top-left-hand corner of the map.

"The next festival or gathering of large numbers of people is happening right there; it started yesterday and is planned to continue today and close tomorrow evening. After this one, there isn't anything for a few weeks," said Judas.

Brendan raised his hand and placed his palm over the pin, and then closed his eyes.

"Travellers from far and wide are attending. Many cars and tents. There is music there, and there is water. Strange, it feels like a beach with golden sand. And yes, there is evil there, Inspector. I suggest we make our way to it as soon as possible."

Judas turned away from the map and picked up the receiver to his desk phone. He dialled a number and then, after a quick exchange of words, replaced the receiver and put his jacket and coat on.

"Our mode of transport should be arriving shortly, so if you'd care to follow me," said Judas briskly.

Chapter Thirty-Six

Hanging

Evans and Lace woke up to the sounds of the English countryside punctuated with the sounds of retching, vomiting and the out-of-tune voices of die-hard fans who won't accept that the music is over. They used a packet of the wipes that Evans had packed to wash themselves with, brushed their teeth and rinsed from the two-litre bottle of fizzy water they had stashed in the tent, and then got up and made ready to leave the festival and head home. Lace hardly said a word to Evans, and the silence was reciprocated. Neither was in a bad mood or had a hangover; this was something entirely different.

At some point in the evening, Lace had started to feel paranoid. She believed someone was watching her and she told Evans. Her friend felt the same. Both knew that something was very wrong. Their police radar was pinging and Lace had reached for her mobile phone to radio in and confirm her position and ask for assistance. Evans was trying to do the same, but they both stopped just before the calls were answered and switched their devices off.

The voices they were hearing at that moment were very

convincing, and Lace and Evans accepted them without question. They told the police officers to ignore their paranoia. *It wasn't important*, they said. *The chemicals in your body have no power over you; only this voice can help you. Obey it, and the drugs will die inside you.* Lace and Evans had gone back to their tent and slept soundly.

And now they were in Evans's car, pulling out of the Lido's car park and away from its beautiful inland beach and joining the traffic on its way back to wherever it had come from. As they drove, they listened to Lace's music for a while but spent the rest of the short journey chatting about their new temporary tattoos. Lace and Evans had decided to have the same one; it was intricate and delicate. The artist had told them that it was a very ancient symbol of unity and a special marque that would keep them safe from harm. Lace liked hers very much.

"It looks like two pieces of rope intertwined with a little coil at each end," she said.

"From this way up, it could be a hangman's noose, couldn't it?" replied Evans.

When the large grey Norton motorbike with its matching sidecar roared through the gates to Scotland Yard, all of the officers stopped what they were doing immediately. Big fat yellow sponges full of water and washing-up liquid slapped onto the floor as all washing of cars ceased. Metal trays full of greasy spanners clattered to the ground in the repair bays, and wolf-like German Shepherd dogs curled long tails between their legs and squatted to urinate. Black Maria calmly and skilfully negotiated the down ramp without any loss of speed and then came expertly to a halt in front of the two men that had just emerged from the main building. The men jumped into the sidecar with ease; the engine roared once more, and then seconds later, the tall figure, the bike and its whacky racer sidecar were gone.

Judas and Brendan of Clonfert sat in surprising comfort inside the sidecar; its single leather seat had magically become a well-padded leather double seat. Not only did they have leg room, but there was also ample elbow room too. The sidecar was much bigger inside than it appeared from the outside. Black Maria, towering above them, gunned the motorbike down the road at great speed; she weaved through the traffic, and in what felt like minutes, they were out of town and heading for the Ruislip Lido.

In the past, Judas had been transported from one end of the country to the other in a specially constructed leather travel bag, slung over the shoulder of an angel through an ice storm. It had been a challenging experience and very cold, so this was travelling in style.

Lace and Evans were making good time and they smiled as they saw a very large motorcycle and sidecar roar past, heading in the other direction.

"James Bond in Thunderball!" shouted Lace.

"Tintin and Captain Haddock in that animated film!" shouted Evans.

Judas looked at his watch and smiled because they had made the journey in ridiculously quick time. Black Maria could give a Harrier jump jet a run for its money. Brendan sat beside him. He had closed his eyes just before they had set off from Scotland Yard and they were still clamped tightly shut even now. The older man did not appear to enjoy travelling in this way. Judas checked the sat nav on his mobile phone, and he realised that there was only a small stretch of road to go now, and then they were going to take a sharp right turn and arrive at the Lido. He gripped the edge of his seat and hoped that their bird had not yet flown.

They parked the motorbike and sidecar and went in search of the festival office. It was easy to find, and Judas politely yet firmly eased his way through the small crowd of people waiting outside to get their tickets and showed his warrant card to the girl at the front desk. She took one look at it, saw the Metropolitan Police Force crest at the top and turned pale. She then quickly snatched one of the mobile phones from the table in front of her and tapped on its screen; after a couple of rings, the person she was calling answered. Judas heard a man's voice and then what sounded like a belch or a cough; it was hard to distinguish between the two from where he was standing. The girl listened to the man for a second and then rang off.

"You need to go and see Mr. Wilkins, he's the organiser of the festival. His office is the battered old Volvo estate parked under the big oak at the back of the car park," she said.

"Thank you, Miss. Just one more thing, once I've had a chat with your Mr. Wilkins, I'm going to come back here, and if that box of smarties, assorted tabs and pills, the one that you keep trying to nudge under that cabinet with the toe of your boot is still here, my associate is going to put you away somewhere safe and then take you to Scotland Yard for me. That okay?" said Judas.

Judas stood to one side so that she could see Black Maria.

The girl's eyes widened in shock, and her foot stopped moving.

"Y-y-yes, sir," stammered the girl.

"Now, before we go, is there anything that you can tell

me about this Mr. Wilkins before I go and have a chat with him?" said Judas.

After a brief interview, they followed the girl's directions; she had suddenly become very helpful, and they quickly found the old car. It was no longer roadworthy; all four wheels had been removed and its suspension was made from stacks of old red house bricks. All of the seats had been taken out, and the interior had been cunningly converted into a cramped little office. Behind a small wooden table there sat a man separating blue tickets from red ones. He did not look up as they approached and effected not to notice them when they stood in front of the old Volvo.

Wilkins wheezed like an overworked desktop fan, and it was readily apparent to Judas, Brendan and to Black Maria that if the man was fifty years old, a generous estimation, he had been drinking heavily for at least forty-five of them, possibly even longer. He had a ruddy complexion and a nose the size and colour of a healthy beetroot. The girl had described Wilkins as a bit of a soak and a lech. She had also mentioned that he was the owner of the land that the Lido often offered up as its camping area, and from where they all stood, he was obviously drinking the extra money he was receiving for it. They'd learned that it was also his job to show the campers where to pitch their tents and park their motor homes. It was also his responsibility to set out the pitches for the fast-food vans and the music tents.

"He's here, Inspector. He's nearby," whispered Brendan.

"Who's here?" said Wilkins.

"Oh, he's awake, thanks be to the gods for that," said Black Maria.

"And who might you be then, my lovely? Why don't you come on over and sit on Uncle Derek's knee. I could let you have a free pass to the big tent this evening," said Wilkins.

Judas winced and took two steps backwards, making sure to drag Brendan with him. What followed was unpleasant and involved Black Maria ripping the roof off the old motor, lifting the sweating and smelly body of Mr. Wilkins into the air by the scruff of the neck and then casually tossing said person into the large patch of stinging nettles four metres away. Wilkins thrashed and writhed in the sea of stingers as though he was being repeatedly electrocuted, howling all the while.

"Can you do me a favour and retrieve him, please?" said Judas.

Black Maria chuckled and waded into the bushes, located the corpulent form, bent over it, grabbed it by the scruff of the neck and then launched it out like an Olympic shot putter. He landed with a thud on the bonnet of what used to be his office.

"Well, now that I have your attention, I need to see your list of attendees, please," said Judas.

Wilkins had stopped wheezing now and had started whining instead. He looked rather unwell, which was an improvement, and vicious little red dots were starting to appear all over his arms and legs. The rash was taking hold, and from where Judas was standing, Wilkins was going to need a forest of dock leaves to reduce that swelling, but Judas was not overly concerned; he'd come into contact with plenty of men like Wilkins in the past and knew how to deal with him.

"The list, if you please, or if you'd rather not, my friend here will give you a nice facial with those stinging nettles," said Judas.

Wilkins started to stutter and froth at the mouth.

"This is my land! If you don't clear off I'll have the law on you!" he spluttered.

Black Maria sighed and grabbed Wilkins by the ankle, lifting him into the air so that he hung there like a side of well-past-its-sell-by-date beef.

"Shall I strip him, Inspector? Seems a waste to stop at a facial. I could give him the full body experience," said Black Maria.

"Why not? It should speed things up a bit," replied Judas.

Wilkins started to shake. His big fat white belly began to wobble, and his arms flailed around, but he was going nowhere. The only things making a break for it were the contents of his pockets. Black Maria gave him a shake and an assortment of loose change, a couple of chewed tickets, a cartridge for a vape, a tab of ecstasy and four condoms, unused thankfully, rained down on the grass.

"You've got ten seconds and then it's a day at the spa for you," said Judas.

Wilkins shuddered and groaned, then he pointed to a picnic box in the car. Inside, they found a green A4 folder. There was also a half-empty bottle of supermarket brand scotch and a collection of top-shelf magazines that were dog-eared and sticky. Judas used the tip of his biro to move the magazines to one side in order to retrieve the folder. He handed it to Brendan and contemplated keeping the biro for a second until seeing the error of his ways and dropping the pen into the box instead.

Black Maria dropped Wilkins and he bounced off the bonnet, hit his head on the bumper and then rolled away into the long grass. From where she was standing his body could easily have been mistaken for a bag of rubbish, which was more than he deserved, she thought. Judas and Brendan flicked through the pages of the folder until they reached a comprehensive list of everybody that had paid to set up shop for the duration of the festival. They found him in Lot 28.

The caravan looked tiny compared to its much larger metal and fibreglass cousins parked on either side. They were enormous silver beasts with awnings and prickly antennae. Their huge black tyres flattened the ground, leaving long silver serpent tracks in the grass and they were all armed with racks for bicycles and motorbikes like some form of spear point defence. Gone were the days of the humble campervan and the roof rack; here there were giants with flushing toilets in the back, none of your chemical rubbish, and mobile ensuite bathrooms, living areas complete with SKY and Xbox and four-ring hotplates. But for all their size and steel they were mute and unimposing. The caravan, however, was animated and expressive. It wanted you to draw near and make you feel comfortable and joyful, but it was lying; there was sweetness in the air but all it was doing was cloaking the sorrow and the sadness beneath.

A small grey horse was munching the grass next to the caravan. Judas watched it carefully, looking for signs of enchantment or danger but the horse was just a horse. It all looked normal and safe. All that was missing were a couple of dancing girls, a roaring fire and someone playing the violin, but sadly, Judas knew better and as they drew nearer, they felt waves of coldness pulsing from inside as though a giant were breathing. Judas carried on, and when he reached the caravan, he saw a sign that had been placed on the ground in the grass, leaning against the front wheel.

An Ink So Dark

"Black of Beyond Magical Tattoos. This is our boy," Judas murmured.

He placed a foot on the short ladder's first step leading up to the caravan's door. He was about to take the next when Brendan caught him by the arm.

"Inspector. A moment. Would you allow me to try and reason with him first? I suspect that there is more going on here than we realise. He has some power, and he is a survivor, there is no question of that, but he is not the real danger here, I think. I believe that there is something else inside him, controlling him, feeding him and possibly even tormenting him. If we kill him and the evil passes on to another, we may be burying a lot more innocent people before long. He may know a lot more than we give him credit for," he said.

Judas looked at Brendan closely. He had only known the man for the shortest time, and he was reluctant to let him go first. Brendan certainly hadn't earned his trust yet, and the killer could be waiting for them inside, and whoever walked through that door first would feel the full force of whatever it was using as a weapon. Judas decided not to allow Brendan to take his place, but Brendan reached over and placed a hand on Judas's shoulder.

"I am at least partially to blame for his crimes, Detective. He was in my care when all of this started. I must at least try and make amends. Each of us is trying, in our own way to make amends for past crimes. You, of all people, know this to be true."

Judas realised that he'd been outmanoeuvred, smiled and then stepped down.

"Okay, on your own head be it but at the first sign of anything hostile, if that thing in there starts waving an ink-stained quill around or asking you whether you'd prefer a swallow or a Mayan chieftain on your arm, I'm coming in there and arresting him. Don't get in the way; I'd hate to see you hurt in the process," he said.

"You have my word," said Brendan as he climbed the steps.

The inside of the caravan was dark, and the air was musty and fetid. A man was lying on a cot, propped up on an assortment of brightly coloured pillows. His eyes were open, but there was only white in them. Brendan stepped forward and placed his palm down on the man's forehead. His skin was molten to the touch, and he appeared to be in some sort of trance. Brendan studied the figure; the young boy had gone. Here now was the man that he had become. His eyes were still the same shape, and there was the familiar band of small brown freckles over the bridge of his nose; his hairline had receded, and there were small lines across his forehead and at the corners of his mouth. Odhran had been a striking youth, but now, the long years on the road, the constant pressures of feeding his habit and the poison of possession had worked their evil ways with him. Brendan had lost his assistant, and there would be no fairy tale ending to this story. He stepped away from the cot, returned to the door and whispered softly through it to Judas.

"Come up, Inspector, the saints are with us, it seems. The vessel is unaware of our presence, and it appears that the force within him is asleep – I hope."

Judas climbed up the steps and joined Brendan by the side of the cot.

"Look at the glass bottles, Inspector, see how the liquid inside writhes and bubbles. There are tormented souls inside, and that thing lying there is feeding off their pain.

I've heard of something like this in the Far East. The Malay pirates speak of sorcerers that capture the likeness of a person in a picture, and then they burn or bury it and soon after, the person falls ill and dies."

Judas reached across, lifted one of the bottles from the rack, and read the label.

"Red Sword of the Sleeping. That's very poetic, isn't it? This must refer to the rough sleeper that set about those drug dealers and the two police officers with the samurai sword."

Brendan shook his head and reached for another.

"This one is called Blue Fire? Does that mean anything to you?" said Brendan.

"I presume it refers to the policemen that were killed recently; they were firearms specialists."

Brendan sighed.

"So much anger and pain, and all for what?" he muttered.

The man on the cot moved and Judas and Brendan swung round.

"He's returning," said Brendan.

Judas moved between Brendan and the man on the bunk.

"So what are we going to do when this *friend of yours* wakes up?" asked Judas.

Brendan opened his mouth to speak, but all Judas heard was Black Maria shouting instead.

"Inspector! You had better come and see this!" she shrieked.

"You stay here and watch him," said Judas to Brendan.

Then he leaped from the caravan and landed on the grass beside Black Maria. She was swinging a large branch around like a tennis player warming up before a match. In front of her were a number of young people. They all had the same look on their faces, the one that said they were off their individual noggins, high on something or other, and here in body but not in mind or soul.

"Look at their forearms," said Black Maria.

Judas quickly scanned the crowd and saw that each of them was sporting a shiny new tattoo of a medieval shield. It didn't take a genius to work out who had given them the ink and what it meant.

"Someone has recruited a small army to protect him while he sleeps," said Judas.

"They don't look like much, really. Stand aside, Inspector, there's a good lad, this won't take long," said Black Maria.

Judas stepped to one side. Black Maria advanced on them all and casually, but very effectively, knocked them off their feet, scooped them up one by one, and disappeared them into her pockets. A few made a fist of the conflict, and one of them got close enough to smash an empty whiskey bottle over her head, but it was futile and only spurred Black Maria on to greater violence. Soon, only a large figure dressed in black leather was left standing in front of the caravan. Judas could hear the voices of the recently detained coming from inside her jacket, but he was more worried about what was happening back inside the caravan. He scrambled back up the steps and threw the door open.

Fortunately, the scene remained the same; Brendan of Clonfert stood with his back to the man on the cot, reading the rest of the labels on the bottles.

"Everything okay?" he asked.

"It was nothing, Inspector; he remains the same. I did consider joining the fracas, but after taking a quick look and seeing your more than capable friend in action, I decided that my presence might be more of a hindrance than a help. She is formidable, isn't she?" Brendan chuckled.

"Black Maria has served the city of London and the police for a long, long time, and she has never let me down. Her motorcycle riding skills need a little freshening up, but that's something that one of the mounted police officers can try telling her," Judas replied.

There was a polite clearing of the throat from outside the caravan, and then Black Maria's head appeared in the open doorway.

"What's wrong with my riding? Has someone complained?" she asked.

"Nothing at all, just trying to lighten the mood. Thank you for saving us – again," said Judas.

Brendan continued looking at the glass bottles, and Judas noticed that each time he picked one up, a pained expression crossed his face; it was as though he was receiving a shock as he made contact with them.

"Why don't you let me take a look at the rest?" he said.

Brendan smiled, replaced the bottle he was inspecting on the rack, and turned to look at the man on the cot.

"Underneath that tortured face is a young boy called Odhran, Inspector. He was born long ago, across the water, a bright, clever, yet troubled soul. I was supposed to watch him and guide him towards the light, but I failed him because I was looking elsewhere, chasing after an island that may or may not exist."

"Redemption is a feather in the wind. You have to be in the right place at the right time to catch it. The fact that you're standing inside an old caravan talking to the man who sent the Almighty's son up the steps, with a magical motorcycle-riding bodyguard outside and you're putting yourself in harm's way to defeat a demon, or an as yet unspecified monster, must mean that you're doing something right – *right?*" said Judas.

Brendan smiled once again, and his shoulders relaxed slightly, but it was as they were changing places that it happened. Odhran had not been asleep, merely waiting. Brendan moved to one side, and Judas stepped in front of him so that his back was turned, and Odhran leapt from his cot and plunged a short wicked-looking knife firmly into the space between Judas' shoulder blades.

"I will draw such a scene upon your flesh that it will fill a hundred bottles!" snarled Odhran.

Judas crumpled and fell to the floor, taking the entire shelf of bottles with him. Brendan was knocked sideways and fell through the door and down the steps to land at Black Maria's feet. She quickly determined that she would not be able to get inside the caravan; she was far too big, so she lifted him up like a rag doll and carried him away to safety. Then she would return and smash the caravan to pieces.

"The bottles! Forget the man. Get the bottles!" screamed the voice inside Odhran.

He began to snatch the bottles up from the floor of the caravan and put them in his pockets, but there were so few, and the voice inside was getting angry.

"Turn the man over! They are there! Underneath him! I can sense them, retrieve them all or I shall burn you from the inside out, boy!"

Odhran pulled the knife out and rolled Judas over. There were a handful of bottles just where the voice had said they would be, and he quickly collected them all. But there was one small bottle in the man's hand. He must have been holding it when the knife went in. It had smashed, a shard had cut into his palm, and the bright blue screaming ink was mixing with the dull reddish brown of his own blood. Odhran left it. He could not save the precious liquid now; he had to escape the old man, that was all that mattered to him. The voice of the beast would not be happy until his stores were replenished, and it would punish him severely until they were. Odhran parted the thick curtains behind the cot and slid the wooden bolt that secured the side hatch over. The panel fell away, and light streamed in from outside. There was no one in sight, so he vaulted through the hatch and staggered away into the bushes.

Judas felt the intense pain of the knife going in and then again when it was ripped free. He had God to thank for that. He was immortal. That was a good thing; he just wished that he didn't have to deal with the pain – *twice*. His limbs were starting to throb, the tell-tale sign that his body was repairing itself. The big scar that ran from his waist up to the suprasternal notch was on fire, and the thin white scar that ran around his neck was heating up nicely too. These sensations were nothing new. Judas had been killed many times before. But there was another layer of pain that he did not recognise this time. Judas opened his eyes, but instead of seeing the wooden ceiling of the caravan, he saw a noose swinging in the air above him. At first, he thought it was the rope that he had hung over the tree branch in the olive grove in Gethsemane, but the sky was wrong. Judas stood up and looked around. A giant oak tree stood on the brow of a nearby hill. Sheep grazed on green grass, and grey clouds came scudding in from the east. Then he turned and saw her face.

He was about to reach out to her, but the ground started to shake, and there was the sound of thunder all around. Judas blinked and sat up. He was still in the caravan, what was left of it. Black Maria had not been able to get inside to rescue him, so she had started pulling the caravan to pieces, starting with the wheels. The thunder he had imagined was just the roof coming off.

"Steady! I'm still inside this thing!" he shouted.

"Hang on a mo', and I'll have you out in a second," she replied.

Black Maria was true to her word, and seconds later, he found that he was leaning up against a tree, not quite able to stand yet, but on the way. Brendan had regained consciousness after his fall and was sitting on the grass nearby with his head in his hands. He looked bruised but not beaten.

"What now then, Inspector?" asked Black Maria.

"I have to get back to the Black Museum straight away. I think something is about to happen that I need to stop, but this beast or whatever it is, is back on the loose again and I can't allow it to get away," he said.

"I can help there, Inspector. I know how to stop him and the demon he carries with him," said Brendan.

"Can I trust you to see this through?" asked Judas.

"I have a feeling that I know where the wind will take this feather. I can hear the souls of the tormented clearly now. Handling the glass bottles has brought me closer to them, and they will guide me," said Brendan.

Judas didn't have time to press the man any further, and it went against everything he believed in, but he had no choice. What he had seen in the caravan made the hairs on his neck stand up and turned his stomach. He looked down into the palm of his hand and reread the label from the bottle that had smashed in his hand again.

"Send word to me at the Black Museum, and good luck," said Judas.

Brendan nodded and then set off in pursuit.

Chapter Thirty-Seven

The Drop and then the Stop

Lace was feeling out of sorts when Evans pulled up outside Scotland Yard; she had the beginnings of a headache, one of those nasty little blighters that hang around behind the eyes and make your head feel tight. Evans was complaining of the same, so they agreed that it must have been the Pimm's, kissed, and then Lace waved as Evans pulled out into the traffic and sped away. Lace didn't fancy going home to an empty flat, so she decided to go to the Black Museum instead. She could take a shower down on the 3rd floor, change her clothes, get something to eat in the canteen and then head up to the 7th floor and catch up on any paperwork that she had been avoiding. On the way up, she would swing by the shop and get some painkillers; this felt like a bad one.

The first parts of her master plan went swimmingly; she was clean and smelling fresh, had clean clothes on, and had consumed two burgers and drank three cups of tea. She should have felt like a million dollars, but she felt groggy, and her ears had started ringing, which was a new one for her.

Lace entered the Black Museum just as she had done a thousand times, but this time, she could hear the voices of the inmates and the relics more clearly, and there was one voice that sounded louder than the rest, which was odd because after a while they all rolled into one big grumbling mass. Lace sat down and rested her forehead on the desktop, and she decided that the headache had overstayed its welcome and needed killing. Right now. She opened the box of paracetamols, popped two out from the tray, filled a glass with water from the tap in the kitchen and then necked the pills. Lace sat down in her chair, closed her eyes, and waited for the pain relief cavalry charge.

When she opened them again, she was in the Key Room. She didn't remember walking into the Key Room. She hadn't had any need to visit it, so why was she here?

"Why not take a walk down the table?" said a voice she didn't recognise.

Lace closed her eyes again, the headache was making her feel very strange indeed.

"Wake up! Sergeant! Don't listen to HIM!" This voice she did recognise.

"Is that you, Turpin?" she asked.

"Yes, Sergeant, Dick Turpin, friend to the Black Museum. Now listen here, there's something in here that means you harm; you have to wake up!"

"But I'm not asleep, Dick," she said.

"Lace! Lace! You must wake up, *please!*" Turpin begged.

Lace shook her head and pressed her fingertips to her temples like she'd seen countless actors do in television adverts.

"Why not go and see your friend?" said the voice.

Lace squeezed her eyes tightly shut but when she

reopened them again she found that she was standing in front of the table wearing a facemask made from a piece of black leather with two circular holes cut into it for eyes. She knew the mask. She knew the man and his steed and that she would shortly be standing next to his gibbet.

"Dick Turpin," she said.

Black Bess reared up on her hind legs and attacked the air in front of Lace's face with her hooves; they were deadly and had saved her rider, Dick Turpin the Highwayman, many times in the past. Bess was frothing at the mouth, and her eyes were wide; the earth beneath her was being churned into a slippery brown river of mud and the rooks that settled on the gibbet were screeching. They sensed that there was evil nearby. Lace did not see them and did not hear them either; she was listening to a different sound now.

"Stand away now, Bess, my beauty; there's nothing we can do. See, her eyes and ears are closed to us; whatever has her is too strong for her!" cried Turpin.

The Highwayman removed his flintlock pistol, cocked it and discharged it over Lace's head, but there was no indication that she had heard the shot. Turpin dug his heels into Bess's flanks and tried to put himself and his horse between Lace and the gibbet, but she just ducked underneath and ran up the steps to the noose.

"There it is, a noose, just like the one on your arm; see how it swings in the breeze and twists and creaks. Wouldn't it be fine to slip over your neck? I bet that it fits so snugly; why not try it on for size?" The voice was strong now.

"Judas!" screamed Dick.

Lace reached up for the rope and pulled it down over her head.

"See, what did I tell you? Snug as a bug in a rug. It was made for you, my love. Now, take a step, take two perhaps,

and throw yourself from the platform; you'll like what happens next." The voice was excited.

Lace did as she was told. She took two steps backwards, and then, with a little skip, she jumped off the gibbet and into the air. The rope formed a curved grey line against the brightness of the sky for a second, and then, in the blink of an eye, the rope was straight and taught, and the gibbet creaked. Dick Turpin hid his eyes and drove his spurs into Bess's flanks. She did not mind though and paid him no heed because she was in as much pain as he was. They sat together, the Highwayman and his steed; they could not take their eyes off Sergeant Lace of the Black Museum at Scotland Yard as she swung gently on the breeze. Her eyes were wide open now, but she was no longer awake and never would be again.

"Come, Bess, let us be away from here. We must be ready for when the Inspector calls," said Turpin.

Bess snorted and trotted away. When they reached the brow of the hill, they looked back at the gibbet. The crows were circling overhead, but not one of them had dropped out of the sky to scavenge and pick. They were waiting for the body to get cold. Dick shook his head. There was a storm coming, and if Dick knew DCI Judas Iscariot as well as he thought he did, there would be blood aplenty and enough bodies for hungry beaks.

Chapter Thirty-Eight

The Long Walk

The girl had been frightened at first. Hiding under the skirts of the mad woman at the beach had saved her from being discovered by the man that Judas, the Master of the Black Museum, had asked her to follow and observe. Now, she was merely confused and starting to get a bit frustrated. This was not the way back to the path she had used to get here. Nothing looked familiar. Even the sky had changed. The girl got back to her feet.

"No matter. I'm not going to find my way out of here sitting on my bum, am I."

She walked for a while longer, and now and again she saw a tree or a stone that she thought she recognised, but it turned out to be the wrong stone or a tree that looked a little like the one she was searching for but not the tree itself. However, she did not become disheartened and as she walked, the world around her started to sharpen and come into focus. She rubbed her eyes and blinked again and again, and each time she reopened her eyes everything was a bit clearer than before. The mist was lifting. Was it because she was getting further away from the sea, or was it something else?

Her eyesight was not the only thing to improve. She began to hear strange sounds. At first they were just a collection of whistles, high frequency, and then she began to hear words and at one point she thought she heard someone singing. By her reckoning, she had been walking for at least two hours in a straight line. Two hours was a complete guess as she had no watch or phone to check, but it felt like two hours.

"There's got to be a path around here somewhere."

She walked on and shortly after, she was proved right.

Chapter Thirty-Nine

The Fast Maria

"Can't you go any faster!" shouted Judas.

The motorway was busy and Judas was impatient.

"Do you have a portable blue flashing light that I can stick on my crash helmet?" replied Black Maria.

"Of course I don't just happen to have a flashing blue light in my pocket," said Judas.

"Well, sit down and shut up and let me ride my motorbike in peace! The only way I could go any faster would be for the rest of the traffic to pull over, and the only way they'd do that is for me to have a blue light and a siren – okay?" said Black Maria.

"What about the hard shoulder? Why not take that?" he shouted back.

Black Maria opened the throttle so quickly that the motorbike jumped ahead and Judas was caught off-balance and thrown back inside the sidecar. He decided not to question Black Maria's riding skills after that and settled down, but he could not shake the feeling that something was drastically wrong, or about to go wrong. He ran his index finger over the freshly healed scar on the palm of his right hand. The flesh was already knitting together nicely and there was only the slightest hint of pain left. Some of the ink had stained his skin and it tingled. Maybe it was trying to tell him something or get his attention, like a mobile phone on mute?

Whatever it was, it concerned Sergeant Lace, and he was worried for her. Had he really seen *her* face in that noose? He had just had a knife shoved into his back after all and been unconscious. Maybe it was a spell or some form of projection, something to torment him or distract him? If it was the latter it had certainly worked. Judas gripped the rim of the sidecar tightly. Down at this level, much closer to the ground, the cars were just blurs of colour and the noise of the engine much louder. They were navigating the dual channels of cars with ease and London was drawing closer by the second but Judas was uneasy, and his scar had started to ache again.

Chapter Forty

The Drawing Out

Wilkins was feeling sore everywhere. Everything was throbbing, his pride had been giving a right royal kicking, and to add insult to injury, there was a fire burning between his legs where the stinging nettles had caressed his testicles. A dog, one belonging to one of the crusties that attend festivals, had urinated on his head. At least, he hoped that it had been a dog; you never knew with the types that came to these places. His office had gone too, and so had his stash. He felt particularly aggrieved because the magazines were vintage and had taken years to collect. He sat back down in what was left of the Volvo and thumped the dashboard.

"Bloody pikeys!"

Odhran had turned his ankle when he jumped from the caravan. He hadn't noticed it at first, but he was well aware of it now. Each step was agony; as soon as his foot touched the ground, there was a spark right below his heel, and it shot up the back of his leg and set his spine on fire. He wanted to stop, but the voice inside him would not allow it, so he hobbled on with his pockets full of glass bottles and his precious book clamped securely under his arm. He found the old car by accident, perched on some bricks, with a big fat man crying in the back seat. Odhran suddenly realised where he was. The car park was not far from here, and he would be able to steal a car, or better still, a camper van. The horse would find a new master – everyone liked a horse – and the caravan itself? Some fool would take it as a 'project'. But right now he was in too much pain to go around the car, so he decided to brazen it out and take the shortest route.

Wilkins sat up smartly when he heard the rustling in the undergrowth nearby. His first thought was that *they* had come back to finish him off, but instead, he saw a strange little man stumble out of the bushes; he looked like a shifty type and had a limp. Usually, that wouldn't have bothered Wilkins in the slightest. Festivals were full of urban outcasts, and he was a big believer in live and let live, and each to their own. He wouldn't have batted an eyelid if it hadn't been for the package that the man was carrying. From where he was sitting it appeared that the man was trying to hide whatever it was, and suddenly, Wilkins had a lightbulb moment.

"Those magazines belong to me!" he bellowed.

Odhran was mid-hobble when the fat man caught him around the waist and rugby-tackled him to the ground. The sheer force of the unexpected attack drove the air from his lungs. Dazed and confused, he felt the book being pulled from his grasp. Wilkins snatched what he thought to be his beloved skin mags from the man on the ground.

"These belong to—"

His victory cry was cut rather short because either the

magazines had aged dramatically and their pages had been turned brown by the rays of the sun, or he had snatched an old book from a crippled man. Wilkins realised, swiftly, that he had just committed an assault on a perfectly innocent member of the public. His day couldn't have got much worse, but then he hadn't factored his own stupidity into the equation. They would take him to the cleaners. They would have the land off him, for starters. There would be no more backhanders and shady dealings with the festival crews, no more free drugs and drinks, and all because he got upset about some old pornos. Wilkins felt like crying again, but he didn't have any tears left, so he dropped the book and ran for it.

Brendan had been following Odhran's tracks. The boy was clearly injured because he hadn't made it very far. In fact, he had hardly made it any distance at all, and a blind goat could have followed the trail he had left in his wake. For someone trying to escape unnoticed, it was a very poor effort; maybe it was a trap. Brendan pushed on regardless, and soon enough he found his quarry lying flat on his back, groaning and whimpering in a clearing not far from the path back to the festival. He decided to wait a while and observe. Odhran wasn't going anywhere.

The voice inside was angry and full of spite.

"Get up, you pathetic worm, get to your feet, or I shall age you a year for every beat of your heart."

"No," whispered Odhran.

"So be it, maggot," said the voice.

"And where will you go then?" replied Odhran.

His ankle would not take his weight. He was sure of that, and the side of his chest where the stranger had hit him creaked. He licked his own blood from his lips and swallowed. He had heard that it would taste metallic. He only tasted rust.

"Not so long ago, you would have fixed me from within," said Odhran.

The voice formed no words at first, but then, it started to giggle and then it whispered to him.

"I could fix you in a trice, but I have chosen not to, my boy," it said.

"Well then, we shall both die here in this clearing. I will carry you no further," said Odhran defiantly.

"How small you think and what little vision you have. I do not reside inside you alone! The book I gave you and all of its drawings and spells are part of me. The ink in the glass bottles is part of me, the memories inside you are part of me. If you die, I will go on. As I have always done. Farewell, failure," said the voice from within.

Brendan watched as the body twitched and shook; spasms rippled across it, and strange guttural sounds could be heard. Then all movement stopped, and Brendan knew, as all living creatures do when encountering the dead, that the life inside the boy he had known – had gone. He had seen death before, and at the moment of it, the body fought its greatest battle. Striving for one more breath of air, unwilling to close its eyes for fear of never being able to open them again, its heart beating because it has known love. All of these moments, so full of life, so vital ... and then there is silence and peace. After the last battle has been lost, the body is hollow, and the living rejects it. Brendan walked into the clearing and knelt down beside the body.

"Whatever is left of you, speak now," he said.

"There is nothing left of him, Traveller," said the voice.

Odhran's lips had not moved, but Brendan could hear the words.

An Ink So Dark

"Traveller? So you know me then. What do I call you?" said Brendan.

"Call me one of the Fomoire, or one who came from below. Call me what you like, old man," said the voice.

"One of the Fomoire, is it now? A race of giants from under the sea, come to wage war and destruction on the fair folk of Ireland? Giants with the heads of goats and only one arm and one leg? That's the old tale of the Fomoire. Are you one of the dark creatures from the depths, then? Because if you are, you must be one of the stupid ones," said Brendan.

"Stupid, is it? Then how is it that I have walked freely across the land, from the North to the South and the East to the West and grown fat on the torment of others? Isn't it your mission to destroy my kind, Brendan of Clonfert?" The voice was louder now.

Brendan reached across Odhran's body, picked the book up from the grass where it had landed, and laid it down in front of him. Then he started to go through Odhran's pockets. He knew what he was looking for, and suddenly, so did the voice.

"What now then, Clonfert? You'll pack the book off to some secret vault, along with the ink. What will you do then? Study it? Try to understand the old magic?"

"I have no plans to carry you another step, and nor do I want to hear your voice any longer," said Brendan.

"You have not the strength or the guile to send me back under the waves, but you could have if you read the book." The voice had changed; there was fear in it now.

"You would like me to read through these pages, just as Odhran did, and at the turning of the last one, I would be yours, wouldn't I? That is how the spell works is it not?" Brendan started to place the glass bottles on top of the book.

"There is great power inside the book, Brendan. The old

champions of Ireland, the Tuatha Dé Danann, sought it out. They knew its worth. Why not try at least to understand it? Read the book. You won't regret it," said the voice.

Brendan just smiled.

"There is only one other object that I need, will you tell me where it is?" asked Brendan.

"You have everything you need, it seems. All that you require is a flame; burn the book and the inks, and send me away to the dark places," said the voice.

"You'd like me to do that, wouldn't you? Light a fire, toss everything in, watch it burn and crackle, and then rake over the ashes and cast them into the wind. That's what you want, isn't it?" said Brendan.

"It's the only way to kill me!" screeched the voice.

"So you say. But I have another idea, little giant. I think that I will take the special quill from Odhran's pocket, the one you gave him long ago, and I shall write you to death in your own book so that your story dies and you are forgotten, never to return in verse or in a tale. Nothing, this will be your end," said Brendan.

He reached inside Odhran's jacket pocket and found the quill. It had been placed in the pocket over his heart. Then, he started writing, using ink from the first bottle to write the first line, ink from the second to write the second line, and ink from the third to complete his very, very short story. There were twelve bottles remaining. The inks inside them all were behaving erratically, thrashing around and pacing like fierce wild animals in captivity for the first time. Brendan did not know what to do with them, but he had met someone recently that he could ask.

"Little giant? Are you there?" asked Brendan.

"Please, read the book. One page, that's all; grant me one final wish, please?" it said.

"I will do that for you; never fear. Do you have any page in particular that you would like?" asked Brendan politely.

"There is a page marker in the book. It bears a symbol upon it, a flower with a petal dropping from it. Can you see it?"

Brendan located the marker and opened the book.

"Read it! It's a great story. You'll like it," said the voice.

Brendan looked down at the page. He knew exactly which story the Fomorian would want to hear.

"*The Tale of the Great Plague and the Blight*. This is the story of how you overcame the old gods of Ireland not in battle but by destroying their crops and poisoning the streams and the waters of the land, warfare waged by the weak. A tale of cowardice," said Brendan.

"Just read the first couple of lines for me, please?" said the voice.

"I think not. Because if I did, I would never finish, would I," said Brendan.

"It's only a story, Brendan of Clonfert, it cannot harm you." The voice was cold now and calculating.

"How about another story, a new one, very new, in fact. A tale of revenge and of redemption, it features a young boy and an evil giant. Here, let me read it to you," said Brendan.

The voice screamed, shouted and cursed at Brendan, but he continued with the story. It was mercilessly short but incredibly potent.

"The End," said Brendan softly.

The screaming stopped, the cursing stopped, and Brendan thought he heard, right at the end, the sound of sobbing. The small giant, one of the Fomoire, the first race of giants to land on the shores of Ireland, was gone. It would never be spoken of again – for evil that is true death because it can never return.

Brendan opened the book once again and found the page where Odhran had written his own name and a little about where he came from and who he was, about his mother and his dreams. Then he drew a line through every word using the special quill, and when the words disappeared, so did the body. That left only the book and the bottles. Brendan stood up and placed the glass bottles in his pockets and the book under his arm; these he would dispose of at sea.

Brendan of Clonfert, the real Patron Saint of Travellers, navigator, sailor, warrior and searcher, had completed his mission, and now all that remained for him to do was to stick his thumb out and hope that someone, a kind soul and a fellow traveller would stop and offer him a lift to the sea, and then perhaps if he were truly blessed the same driver would turn around and take a letter to Scotland Yard for him.

Chapter Forty-One

The Courtesy of Crows

Judas remembered very little of the remainder of his return journey to Scotland Yard, and Black Maria was true to her word and got him back as soon as she was able, and she was not offended in the slightest when Judas vaulted out of her sidecar and disappeared inside the building without thanking her or saying goodbye. This was a time for action, not for pleasantries.

Judas took the back stairs two at a time to the 7th floor. He could not wait for the lift. The magical wards that had been placed on the only door that opened onto the Black Museum gave way as he approached, as if they too knew that something was wrong. He ran down the corridor and barged into his office, but Sergeant Lace was not there. He called her on her mobile but was sent directly through to her answerphone. This wasn't good. Everything felt wrong. He sat down at her desk and sifted through the pile of paperwork and folders scattered across it. He was hoping to find a note from her, a request for leave that he had already signed, or a Post-it note telling him that she had a dentist's appointment, but there was nothing, just evidence of good old-fashioned solid policework instead.

Judas picked up the desk phone and dialled the number for the front desk.

"Hello, it's DCI Iscariot on the 7th. Has Sergeant Lace left any messages for me?"

"Checking for you, Sir," came the reply.

He could hear the duty sergeant chewing gum, or maybe it was a nicotine substitute, while he consulted the roster.

"Here we are, Sir. Sergeant Lace is back on duty. She has had a couple of days off and returned this morning. I have her booking in at 10.30, and she hasn't left the building as far as I am aware. That okay, Sir?"

Judas nearly dropped the handset.

"So, she's here, in the building?"

"Yes, Sir, would you like me to call her?" asked the duty sergeant.

"No, that's all right, Sergeant. One last thing though, when she booked the time off, did she give you any details of where she could be contacted in an emergency."

"One moment, Sir. Yes, here it is; she was attending a festival, it says here, with WPC Evans."

Judas replaced the handset and then placed his forehead on the desktop. It felt cool, and on any other day, it might have been relaxing – but not today. Lace was in the building, but she was not here and was not answering her phone either. A thought struck him like one of the Archangel Michael's right-handers and he redialled the front desk.

"It's DCI Iscariot again. Can you check the CCTV for me, please?"

The Duty Sergeant was one of the older hands at the Yard and had already anticipated this request.

"I have, Sir. I've got her entering the shower block, and then eating in the canteen, and then she takes the lift up to the 7th, and then I lose her because we don't have any cameras on your floor, Sir."

"Thank you very much, Sergeant," said Judas.

"Pleasure, Sir," he replied.

Judas hung up and then walked into the Black Museum. The exhibits were chuntering away, as usual; it was only a mild hum of conversation, but it irritated him, and he lost his temper and did something that he hadn't done for over a hundred years.

"Shut up! All of you! You useless dead things, be quiet! Or I'll brick this place up, and then I'll burn you all out and you can rot! It should have happened to this place long ago!"

Instead of the silence he needed so badly, he received angry, venomous comments, threats and whispers of rebellion in return. The Black Museum was not used to being treated in this fashion, and Judas knew it, but he couldn't help himself and hated himself for being weak. The noise followed him as he made his way to the Key Room. He had insulted the inmates and they would make life difficult for him now, and all because he was upset and afraid.

He closed the Key Room door behind him, approached the table, and stood at its head. He was alone now. Judas had worked out that the only way Lace could disappear from Scotland Yard without being seen or having to sign out and leave a signature behind was through this room, the Key Room. There simply wasn't any other explanation. He sat down on one of the cheap plastic chairs that gathered dust but never occupants and put his head in his hands. In that ink-fuelled vision, back in the caravan, he'd seen her head in a noose with a grey sky above and heard the creaking of old timbers.

"Not much to go on," he whispered to himself.

Judas took out his silver coin, more in hope than anything else, and closed his eyes and listened to the darkness. It was in the stillness that his chance to locate Lace would be found. He never, ever prayed, so he hoped as hard as he could instead.

The crows were agitated. The big, black horse patrolled nearby, and it could bite and stamp and was not to be trifled with. And then there was the man in the mask. He had taken to discharging his thunder stick at them, and his aim was good. The grass was already littered with beaks and wings and feathers. Dick reloaded his flintlock pistol and placed it on the wooden rail at his elbow so that he could snatch it up and blow another crow out of the sky if it came too close. He and Bess had decided to remain with the body and watch over it for a while. They wanted to cut Sergeant Lace down and lay a coat or a blanket over her, but they did not have the power. The Time Fields had rules. So they stood guard and on the hour, every hour, Dick would climb the steps, careful not to touch Lace, and then reach up and grasp the rope the hangman had tied and call out for help.

Dick Turpin was beginning to lose hope, but Bess would not be denied, and she stamped and snorted and would not turn away.

"Okay, my lovely, once more," said Dick.

He reached up again, closed his fingers tightly around the rope, and shouted.

"Inspector! Can you hear me?"

An Ink So Dark

Judas was sitting quietly, tracing small circles on his silver coin with his thumb, and getting desperate and nowhere nearer to working out where his sergeant could be. Then something occurred to him, and he sat up quickly. The charm that Esther the White Witch had given him was a location charm; he could use it to find Lace. The charm was contained within a small pouch that he wore around his neck on a leather thong. He took it out and held it in the palm of his hand.

"Where is Sergeant Lace?" said Judas.

At first, nothing happened, and then he heard a voice.

"Inspector! Can you hear me?"

Judas stood up and walked down the table with the charm held tightly in his hand.

"Inspector! Can you hear me?"

The voice was getting louder now, and Judas was starting to feel that all was not in fact lost.

"Inspector! Can you hear me?"

Judas stopped walking and stared down at the keys on the table. There were cudgels used by footpads, custom-made coshes, and even an old iron that a murderer had used to kill all of his victims, but Judas was staring intently at one key, and one key only.

"Inspector! Can you hear me?"

Judas reached out, grabbed the old leather mask with the two eyes cut out, and held it tightly.

Black Bess reared up on her hind legs suddenly and whinnied so loudly that the crows took to the air squawking. Dick felt it too and holstered his pistol. The air around the gibbet crackled, and then the Master of the Black Museum appeared.

"Inspector!" Dick cried.

Judas heard Turpin call out to him and saw Black Bess,

but he had no words for them. He had found his sergeant, but not in the way that he had hoped.

Judas lowered her body to the ground and removed the noose from around her neck. She had been dead for hours, and her skin was cold to the touch. Judas looked into her eyes and saw her, and then Williams, and then all of the other men and women that had stood by his side in the most dangerous situations and with no thought for their own safety, and it made him feel sick to his stomach. Again.

Judas thanked Turpin but could not stay in the Time Fields any longer. He carried Lace up the steps of the gibbet and reached out for the rope that had taken her life, gripped it tightly and then closed his eyes.

Chapter Forty-Two

Threads

The Chief Superintendent's reply to his email was as expected. It was terse and formal, and he was less than happy that yet another of his officers had been killed in the line of duty. Gone was the pleasant tone of his previous communications. He understood the nature of the work that the Black Museum did and had the greatest respect for DCI Iscariot but didn't think that it would be wise at this time to suggest a replacement from within the rank and file of the Met. Had Judas explored the possibility of a specialist in the occult magic field being recruited from outside the police force? Were there better-suited individuals in other areas of the city?

There were the usual and expected pleasantries at the end of the message, of course, and then there were the horrible parts pertaining to the next of kin and to the arrangements regarding the funeral. Judas accepted the Superintendent's suggestion that he and not the Black Museum handle this. In better news, WPC Evans had been saved from doing herself any serious harm. A rapid-response team had been sent to her location and found her teetering on a stool underneath a light fitting on the ceiling with a rope around her neck.

She was receiving treatment at an undisclosed location and reporting to Bloody Nora for debriefing, which was ongoing and proving difficult, in Bloody Nora's words. Black Maria released the festival goers that Odhran had tattooed and turned into his own personal troop of bodyguards; they were now in the Priory, recovering from suspected drug poisoning. That was what they were being told – officially.

Judas received Brendan's letter; it described how and when Odhran had died, who the demon inside him had been, and what was left of the caravan, the ink, and the book. There was also a note attached to the envelope with a request from a member of the public who had driven the old man all the way around the M25 and then onto the Isle of Sheppey. Once there, the good-spirited chap had dropped him off at a small inlet. It was strange, he said, because the older man kept remarking on how well his ship looked, although there was nothing on the water. Then he turned around and took the man's letter all the way to Scotland Yard, and as such, he was asking for the remuneration of the large sum he had spent on the three tanks of fuel he had paid for – out of his own pocket. Judas smiled at that.

"The Patron Saint of Travellers travels for free, apparently," he said to himself.

Judas made sure that the exact sum was sent to the good Samaritan.

Chapter Forty-Three

She Wanders

Simon the Zealot had not slept well; the last two nights had been torture. On his arrival at the Black Museum, Judas had made him clear out one of the unused rooms on the 7th floor and supplied him with some furniture from the lost and found to make it *homely*. He could not wander far or leave the building; that was the price he had to pay for his rescue from the gangs of Marseille. It was little more than a bedsit in size. The bed and mattress were old IKEA models, unloved but sadly not unused, and the sheets and the pillowcases had come from the old police accommodation block; he shuddered to think what they had witnessed. He had lain awake each night, and each time the lino in the corridor contracted with the heat, or a door slammed, he imagined his gaoler striding down the corridor, on his way to wring Simon's neck for getting into bed with Jack the Ripper.

But Judas had not come. Well, not yet anyway.

Simon got up and performed his customary bird bath in the sink and put on some clean clothes. Then he ambled down the corridor and tried to look normal. He'd never been any good at hiding his guilt, and quickly entered the Black Museum before Judas saw him. It was alive and in turmoil. He had never experienced it like this before; there were raised voices and hisses from the exhibits. Simon immediately thought the worst, that they were all cursing him for planning to bring the Museum down, but when he listened, it wasn't him, Simon the Zealot they were angry with, it was Judas, and it brought joy to his tiny, shrivelled heart.

Simon entered the Key Room and hurried into the darkness at the far end. When he felt comfortable and safe, he reached over to a large brown teapot, the sort you'd find in a factory canteen and capable of rehydrating twenty thirsty labourers with one pour, and reached inside it. The teapot had been used to poison many innocent people and was the Key to another prisoner. Simon wanted the cufflink inside it. He removed it from the pot and held it tightly. He had become used to the sensation of travelling from the here and now to the Time Fields, and he didn't flinch or react as he had once done upon opening his eyes and finding himself in some murderer's boudoir or watching a deranged nurse administering her own form of justice to the innocent patients of a medical ward in a hospital.

He found Jack the Ripper reclining on a chaise longue in front of a fire. The monster had completely regenerated and was no longer a spectre with a gravelly voice. Simon had not decided which one he preferred, but if the creature could help him release John the Baptist from his watery prison, he would work with him. Afterwards, he'd see what happened.

"He doesn't know about the plan to free John the Baptist. We'd have known by now if he did," said Simon the Zealot.

"The eavesdropper?" said Jack the Ripper.

"I haven't heard a thing, and Judas hasn't mentioned it either. I think that whomever it was is lost out there, in the Time Fields," said Simon.

"Well, hadn't we better get going then, Simon? We need to find them and shut them up before the Master of the Museum comes a calling!" said Jack the Ripper.

"Let's go to the beach; we can start looking from there," said Simon.

Chapter Forty-Four

The Bridge

Judas stood by the window at the back of his office and watched the angels flying past. He had always felt that the city was more awake at night, paradoxically. London always made him feel more alive, and its energy had a knack of lifting him whenever he felt down, but right at this moment in time, he was numb to it, and if he were being truly honest with himself, he was out of love with the place and would have taken a one-way ticket to anywhere. He had lost another partner. He had liked Lace. She was strong and capable, and she had made him smile. But now she was gone, and he was unlikely to get any more help for a while.

Maybe that is for the best? he thought.

Judas didn't need another cup of coffee, but he made one, all the same. He needed to be doing something right now. It didn't matter what, just as long as he was not thinking about tattoos, death and demons. He was making his way back to his desk when he realised that he was not alone; he placed the mug down on the table and turned around slowly.

An Ink So Dark

"A little warning would be nice," said Judas.

'It would, wouldn't it!" said God's enforcer, the Archangel Michael.

"Look, Micky, now isn't the best time. A lot has happened recently, and not much of it was good. In fact, it's been bloody awful," said Judas.

"Oh, how terrible for you. How long will you be in mourning?" asked the Archangel.

"As long as I want and need. Was there anything else?" said Judas.

The Archangel produced what looked like a roll of carpet from a pouch he wore on his belt. It turned out to be a roll of parchment, and he threw it onto the desk. It was at least two metres long and knocked the computer terminal from the table onto the floor. The crash and the shattering of glass that followed did not seem to bother him in the slightest.

"You do know that I have to pay for that?" said Judas.

"Oh, how terrible for you. Hang on, have I said that already?"

"It's an age thing, Micky; it happens to the best of us when we're getting on a bit but don't worry, I'll get you an ear trumpet," said Judas.

The Archangel said nothing and instead just pointed at the parchment. Judas took the hint and untied the leather strap that secured it. It opened and proved to be a map, but a map unlike anything that Judas had ever seen before. On one side of the map were hundreds of small overlapping circles, like chain mail armour. Each one had either a symbol or some form of script inside. He recognised some of the symbols, but not all. And on the other side of the map was a large smudge. It had hardly any detail at all, and looked like an angry thunder cloud. Connecting the two sides of the map was a thin silver line, and in the middle of the line there was a star.

"That is the place I told you about," said Michael.

"The nasty bridge," said Judas.

"Your friend is there. The line in silver is the Winghurn Bridge. It has other names, the Chinvat Bridge, the river Vaitarani, some of your older scholars called it Jacob's Ladder; the name matters not. Your friend is trapped there. The souls of the dead arrive in the centre and then are drawn either to the City of the Heavens or to its dark mirror, Hell."

"Why hasn't he walked into Heaven yet? Why is he trapped?" asked Judas.

Michael made no reply, he just stared at the silver line on the map, and it made Judas feel very awkward.

"I love our awkward silences, but this one isn't helping," said Judas.

"Because it is a trap, Judas. Undoubtedly a trap – for you. The small angel is the bait. Your love for him and his for you is the honey on the speartip. I can take you to the bridge, but I cannot stand upon it nor aid you once you set foot upon it. If you don't go, he will stay in that dark place forever," said the Archangel.

"Who would want to punish me this badly and orchestrate a meeting in a place where no angel can come and save him if things get rough?" Said Judas.

"The list is not a long one, Judas." Said Michael.

END

Afterword

If you've enjoyed this book please do consider leaving a brief review of it on the Amazon website. Even a few positive words make a huge difference to independent authors like me, so I'd be both delighted and grateful if you were to share your appreciation.

Many thanks, Martin

Also by Martin Davey

Judas the Hero

The Children of the Lightning

Oliver Twisted

The Curious Case of Cat Tabby

The Blind Beak of Bow Street

The Death of the Black Museum

The Murder of the Mudlarks

About the Author

Martin Davey is the author of the Black Museum series of novels featuring the world's most unlikely and misunderstood hero – DCI Judas Iscariot. An Ink so Dark is the 8th story in the series.

Martin studied at the prestigious Central St. Martins School of Art in London. After graduating, he worked in advertising agencies in London, New York, Barcelona, and Amsterdam. He has also worked on a speedboat on the Costa Del Crime. These days he can be found in Tunbridge Wells with his wife and two children. He is a proud member of the James Bond Fan Club with his own 'oo' number and is a serial collector of unusual experiences.

Printed in Great Britain
by Amazon